"I'm not a hero.

"The heroes were the men who were more alert than I was and saw the danger," Randon said. "They managed to get the rest of us out."

"A hero is someone who shows courage in the face of danger or adversity," Millie replied. "It's not someone who never makes a mistake."

He chuckled. "Who told you that?"

"It was part of the speech my dad gave you and Brian before you got on the plane to leave for basic training." Her voice was thick with emotion.

"I forgot about that."

He'd forgotten about a lot of things. Like how much he loved the White Mountains in the fall. Like how much he missed talking to Brian. Most of all, he'd forgotten how Millie's smile could make him feel like he was floating.

Millie touched his cheek. "You're a good man. Don't forget that again."

Dear Reader,

I have been looking forward to Millie and Randon's story ever since catching a glimpse of them in *His Hometown Redemption*. When I decided to write their story, I knew that Randon's character would be hard. I had no idea just how hard it would be.

Thankfully, my good friend and fellow Harlequin Heartwarming author Patricia Forsythe put me in touch with her nephew, retired SFC Matthew Statler. After four tours of duty in Iraq, Matt's insight and experience was an invaluable resource. I couldn't have written this book without his help.

I love connecting with readers. You can find me at leannebristow.com, Facebook.com/authorleannebristow and Instagram.com/authorleannebristow or email me at leanne@leannebristow.com.

Blessings,

LeAnne

HER HOMETOWN
SOLDIER'S RETURN

LᴇANNE BRISTOW

Harlequin

HEARTWARMING

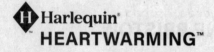

Harlequin®
HEARTWARMING™

Recycling programs
for this product may
not exist in your area.

ISBN-13: 978-1-335-05123-3

Her Hometown Soldier's Return

Copyright © 2024 by LeAnne Bristow

 Harlequin Enterprises ULC
22 Adelaide St. West, 41st Floor
Toronto, Ontario M5H 4E3, Canada
www.Harlequin.com

Printed in Lithuania

MIX
Paper | Supporting
responsible forestry
FSC® C021394

LeAnne Bristow writes sweet and inspirational romance set in small towns. When she isn't arguing with characters in her head, she enjoys hunting, camping and fishing with her family. Her day job is reading specialist, but her most important job is teaching her grandkids how to catch lizards and love the Arizona desert as much as she does.

Books by LeAnne Bristow

Harlequin Heartwarming

Coronado, Arizona

His Hometown Redemption
Her Hometown Cowboy
Her Hometown Secret

Her Texas Rebel

Visit the Author Profile page
at Harlequin.com for more titles.

This book is dedicated to
the men and women of the armed forces.

CHAPTER ONE

RANDON FARR THREW the duffel bag over his shoulder and looked around his childhood hometown, Coronado, Arizona, filled with people who had known him his entire life. People who delighted in watching his father fail. People who expected him to do the same thing.

His chest tightened. He once swore not to set foot in this town until he'd made something of himself. Yet, here he was. Lower than when he left.

The whoosh of the bus door shutting behind him prodded him to take a few steps toward the sidewalk. He sighed as he watched the bus pull away. The building that loomed in front of him was too familiar. A mural depicting the White Mountains covered the side of the building, complete with Big Lake, Black River and a variety of wildlife. The words *Coronado Market* arched above the scene. Pride rippled through him. He'd painted that sign. It was his only contribution to the small town.

He didn't have to go inside the market to know the smell of coffee would be thick in the air and fishermen, eager to get an early start at the lake, would be stocking up on bait and snacks. As badly as he wanted coffee, he would not go inside. He didn't want anyone to know he was in town. Walking inside would be as effective as waving a flag and the entire town would know within hours, if not minutes, that he was back.

Most of all, he couldn't risk running into Millie. He doubted that Millie still worked there now that she'd graduated nursing school. Even if she did, she probably wouldn't be there this early. Stacy, the owner, always opened the store. Had that changed now that she was married with children? Two little girls, adopted from the country of Georgia, according to the letter Millie sent him before he left for Kuwait.

Millie. Just thinking her name sent waves of pain through his body. He had joined the military to prove to himself that he wasn't like his dad. To prove he was someone who could be counted on. And to prove he could be worthy of someone like Millie. He'd messed that up and now even the Army couldn't use him anymore. The only promise he'd managed to keep was his promise to keep her brother safe. And he'd barely managed to do that.

He sucked in a heavy breath and started walking away from town. The streets were mostly empty this early in the morning. He pulled at the collar of his shirt. Time to go home.

Two miles later, Randon found himself standing in front of the two-bedroom hewn log cabin that had been both his home and his prison. The yard was so overgrown with weeds that the stone pathway leading to the porch was obscured. Shingles were missing from the roof. Most of the shutters were either missing or only hanging by a hinge.

The cabin appeared as if it might collapse with the next strong wind. Randon's heart ached. His great-grandfather had built the cabin. His grandfather had upgraded it, adding electricity and running water. When he was a little boy, he'd followed his grandfather around while he made repairs and improvements, learning everything he could about how to take care of the home that would one day be his.

His hands shook as he climbed the rickety steps to the front porch. The door swung open with a loud squeak and stuck about halfway. Randon shoved. The door opened another couple of inches. He shoved again.

The smell of cigarettes, dirt and trash assaulted his senses all at once. Gagging, he pulled his T-shirt up to cover his nose. Was this the condition it was in when his father died? Or had squatters taken up residence?

He made his way across the great room to the

kitchen. On the window sill above the sink, dozens of medication bottles stood in line. He picked one up, reading his father's name on the prescription. Had cancer changed the man's ways at all? Dreading what he might see under the sink, he opened the cabinet door, anyway. Dozens of empty liquor bottles. Even cancer hadn't stopped his dad from drinking. It wasn't surprising that in the end, he'd died from drinking and not lung cancer.

He turned the handle to the faucet, but nothing happened. Was the electricity off, too? He walked over to the light switch and flipped it on. No electricity, either. His gaze strayed to the refrigerator. Had anything been left in it? He took a deep breath and held it before opening the door. There wasn't much in there. Some beer cans. Something that looked like it had once been hot dogs and a few other things he wasn't brave enough to examine were on the shelves. He left them there and closed the door.

Randon picked his way through the debris on the floor, down the hall, to where his room had been. Like the front door, it was warped and swollen and required a couple of shoves to get inside. His mouth dropped open. Nothing had been touched. Everything was just like he left it.

A plume of dust rose in the air as he dropped his duffel bag on the bed. He sat on the edge of the bed and buried his face in his hands. He should have come home last winter. If he'd come home when his father had been hospitalized, he wouldn't have been on patrol that night.

What did it say about him that his regret wasn't due to any obligation he felt toward his father? The man's death hadn't bothered him. At least not much. But because he ignored it, he put his best friend in danger, as well as the other members of his squad.

His heart began to race and he could feel the walls closing in around him. A shooting pain shot through his head and he squeezed his temples with his hands, trying to stop the pain. He gasped for air and pushed away from the waves of nausea as black waves threatened to engulf him.

Inhale. Count to five. Exhale. Repeat. Over and over, he sucked in air like his life depended on it. He lost track of time as he tried to regain his grip on the world around him. When the crashing of the waves finally stopped, he was left sweaty and cold.

His lip twitched. Dr. Harlow was wrong. Getting off the military base, away from the constant reminders of where he'd been, didn't help. Randon couldn't wait to tell him. No. He wouldn't give the doctor anything to report to his new employer.

Bravos, a military contracting company, had hired him despite the fact that his shoulder would never be the same. They even knew he was dealing with some post-traumatic stress syndrome episodes. It was to be expected, the recruiter told him, when a soldier returns to civilian life after going through the things he'd gone through.

They had given him thirty days to get his father's estate in order and return for a full medical workup. He had thirty days to learn how to control the PTSD episodes. His career depended on it. Maybe his life.

He stood up. Might as well get busy if he had any hope of making this sardine can inhabitable again. As soon as he did, he would put it on the market and sell it. It was the only way to cut his ties to Coronado and never have to return.

Without electricity and water, there wasn't much he could do except clean out the trash. He glanced at his wristwatch. The utility office opened at nine o'clock. How much cleaning could he do in two hours? He gingerly walked down the narrow hallway and across the living room to the kitchen. Cleaning supplies and trash bags had always been kept under the sink. He pushed the empty vodka bottles around, but he didn't see anything. No trash bags. No cleaning supplies. Nothing. Looked like he had no choice except to go to the market, after all. The thought sent chills down his arms and a weight settled in his chest.

He stepped outside and forced the door to close. An orange paper that he hadn't seen when he came in flapped in the breeze next to the door.

He pulled the paper free and read it.

Condemned. This structure has been deemed unsafe and is set to be demolished. Please contact the Apache County Sheriff's Department for questions.

Condemned. Just like him. He wadded the paper in his hand and shoved it in his pocket. He better go see Sheriff Frank Tedford before he did anything.

He glanced at the large barn standing on the edge of the property. He was certain his father's pickup truck was parked inside, but he'd rather walk across the entire country before he used anything that was his father's.

Fifteen minutes later, Randon approached the entrance to the Sheriff's Department. Standing outside the double doors, he clenched his fists and waited for his heart to stop trying to leap into his throat. As soon as he walked through those doors, people would know he was here. Not that he really thought he could stay in Coronado for an entire month and no one would know. Taking a deep breath, he pushed through the doors.

The entrance was smaller than he remembered. An end table in the corner, littered with magazines, sat next to a row of three chairs. A sliding glass window separated the receptionist from people in the lobby.

The woman behind the glass glanced up. She raised her eyebrows and smiled. A few moments later, a buzz signaled the opening of the door and a tall burly man stepped toward him.

"Randon Farr!" The man reached out to shake his hand.

"Good morning, Sheriff Tedford."

"You're all grown up now! Call me Frank." The sheriff pumped Randon's hand enthusiastically. "I didn't know you were coming home. How long is your leave?"

Randon frowned. No one in this town ever greeted him with this much enthusiasm before. He couldn't bring himself to admit he was on permanent leave.

"I report back mid-November." It wasn't a complete lie. He would be reporting to Bravos, not the Army. He had to make it through one more medical evaluation before starting his new job.

"How're you doing?" Frank gave him a sympathetic glance. "I heard you had to stay in the hospital a while after an ambush. You're recovering okay?"

He stiffened. Of course, everyone in town knew about the incident. He doubted anyone knew the truth. He swallowed. "Yes, sir."

"Glad to hear it." Frank slapped the top of Randon's arm and grinned. "I didn't think you could get much bigger, but look at you. What brings you by here?"

Randon glanced down. He'd lost almost twenty pounds in the last eight months. Of course, he'd gained over fifty pounds since leaving Coronado. It was amazing what three square meals a day could do. It was more than he ever got at home.

He pulled the condemned notice from his pocket. "I wondered what we could do about this."

"I see that you went by your cabin."

Randon nodded. How could he be sad about a place he was so eager to be rid of? Still, it was the only home he'd ever known. "When is it supposed to happen?"

"Let's go back to my office." Frank turned and walked down the hallway. He opened the door to his office.

As soon as he closed the door, Frank leaned against his desk. "I put that sign up to keep vagrants out. It hasn't been condemned."

Relief flooded through him. "So it's okay for me to stay there?"

The sheriff arched one eyebrow. "Have you been inside? It's falling apart. It's only a matter of time before it's really condemned. Why don't you let me put you up in a cabin at Whispering Pines?"

"No, thank you." Randon shook his head. "I'll repair it while I'm here, but the electricity and water have been shut off."

"I can get that taken care of. What else do you need?" Frank moved around the desk to sit in his chair. "I don't think I'll have any trouble rounding up volunteers to help you."

"No!" Randon's heart threatened to jump out of his chest.

Frank looked at him in confusion. "Why not?"

Randon's stomach twisted into a knot. "I just… I don't want anyone to know I'm here, yet."

"Why?" Frank's voice was low and his eyes held a note of sympathy.

He glanced at the wall behind the sheriff's head. Medals from Frank's service during Desert Storm decorated the wall, along with a few pictures of Frank, surrounded by other soldiers, all dressed in fatigues.

Randon swallowed. If anyone in Coronado could understand how he felt, maybe Frank could. "I needed time away from the military base. The last thing I want to do is talk to people about…"

"About what happened," Frank said softly.

"Yes."

Frank nodded, his eyes full of understanding. "It's a small town. Word is bound to get out sooner or later."

"I know," Randon said. "I just need some time alone."

"What about the Gibsons?" Frank asked. "I'm sure they'll be thrilled to see you."

"No." He shook his head. "Not even them."

MILLIE GIBSON FLIPPED through the mail before closing the mailbox. She hadn't received any responses to the letters she'd sent Randon over the past six months. If it had been her brother who saved his squad from an ambush eight months ago, she would say he was too busy enjoying his newfound fame to bother writing her back. But this was Randon, her brother's best friend. He hated being the center of attention. She supposed that writing her back was probably at the bottom of his to-do list. He had a long recovery ahead of him. At least, that's what his last letter said.

She closed the mailbox and kicked a rock from the edge of the graveled driveway that led to the two-story home she'd grown up in. Green vines climbed up the lattices in front of the wraparound porch and although most of the delicate white buds had disappeared with the chilly October nights, the occasional aroma of honeysuckle still hung in the air.

Tucking the mail under her arm, she entered as quietly as she could. Her father often took a nap around this time and she didn't want to disturb him. She glanced in the living room and, sure enough, her father was asleep in his recliner. Her heart ached a little at the sight of him.

She tiptoed into the room and watched him for a moment. His face was smooth and peaceful, not marred with the confusion or worry that normally plagued him. At least while he slept, she could remember the father she'd grown up with.

Rattles from the kitchen told her where her mother was. Millie followed the sound and dropped the mail on the counter. Her gaze scanned the room, but she didn't see her mother. "Mom?"

"Down here," a voice answered.

Millie walked around the island in the middle of the room to see her mother, Laura, sitting on the floor, scrubbing the front of a cabinet with an old toothbrush.

Alarm bells went off in her head. Her mother only cleaned like that when she was upset or stressed. Millie sighed. "Didn't you do that a couple of weeks ago?"

"No," Mom said. "It's been at least a month."

These intense cleaning sprees were usually brought on by something outside of her mother's control.

Millie knelt down next to her and touched her hand. "What happened?"

Mom dropped the toothbrush. Tears welled up in her eyes. "He couldn't remember my name."

Millie wrapped her arms around her mother and hugged her tight. "We knew this would happen eventually."

Her father had been diagnosed with Alzheimer's six years ago. So far, they'd managed pretty well. Her mother put sticky notes all over the house to help him remember where things were or to remind him to do simple things like brush his teeth. But forgetting Mom's name was a sign that her father's illness had progressed to stage six.

She knew what was going through her mother's

mind. The countdown to the end had begun. At best, her father had six or seven years left. More than likely, it would be less. And the time left would be difficult. Her mother knew that, too.

"Thank you." Mom wiped a tear from the corner of her eye. "I don't know what I'd do without you."

Her four older brothers had left Coronado almost as soon as they graduated high school. Millie would never leave. Even before her father's diagnosis, she'd planned to stay. Now she was glad she had.

"I can call Stacy and tell her I can't work today," Millie said. "Why don't you call Summer's Spa and get an appointment for this afternoon? I'll stay with Dad."

"No." Mom shook her head and picked the toothbrush off the floor. "Things are probably going to get tough around here, so you better help Stacy while you can."

Her mother wasn't wrong. Millie might be the nurse in the family, but her mother knew as much about Alzheimer's as she did. After his diagnosis, Mom read every book, blog and article she could get her hands on. Millie only hoped it was going to prepare her for what was coming.

"I better shower if I'm going to the market." Millie looked down at the scrubs she was wearing. "I smell like Mrs. Jennings's house."

"How is Mrs. Jennings doing?"

Millie shrugged. "She's fine."

She wasn't fine, but she didn't tell her mother that. Partly because it was a HIPAA violation to discuss sensitive information about patients. And partly because her mother had enough to worry about and she didn't want to add to that burden.

Mrs. Jennings had been her mother's third grade teacher. She couldn't tell her mother that the woman's neuropathy was getting worse and she'd be lucky if she didn't lose her right foot by the end of the month.

Mom shook her head. "Her daughter told me she keeps finding cookies under her bed."

Millie sighed. "That explains why she can't keep her diabetes in check."

"It's hard to teach an old dog new tricks." Mom dipped the toothbrush into a bowl of soapy water and resumed scrubbing the crevices on the front of the cabinets.

Millie left her mother to her cleaning and went upstairs to shower. She knew her mother thought it was foolish for Millie to work at the market in addition to working as a home-health nurse, but she enjoyed it. And it wasn't very often. Stacy Tedford Murphy, the owner, only scheduled her when things were really busy or if no one else could work.

She'd been working at the Coronado Market since she was sixteen years old. It had been her first part-time job. Stacy had adjusted her hours so she could participate in high school activities and then college. When she finished nursing school, Stacy had been in the front row, cheering for her like she was family. And in a way, she was. Stacy was the closest thing to a sister she had.

There might come a time when she had to quit working at the market, but for now, it was almost her stress reliever. She didn't mind working whenever Stacy needed her.

It didn't take long to shower and pull her curly hair into a messy bun on top of her head. She slipped on a pair of sneakers and went downstairs.

She plucked her jacket off the coat tree in the hallway. "Do you need anything at the market?"

There was no answer.

Millie walked into the kitchen to see her mother hanging up the wall-mounted phone. Although cell service was good in town, her parents refused to give up their landline. Worry lines were etched deep into her face.

"What is it?" Millie asked.

"That was Brian," her mother answered. "He wants to know if we've heard from Randon."

Millie's breath hitched. Eight months ago, her brother and Randon had been on patrol on the outskirts of a small town in Kuwait when they were ambushed. Brian escaped relatively unharmed, thanks to Randon. Brian had been released to return to duty after a couple of days, but Randon was transferred from the military hospital overseas to a larger hospital in the States.

After several surgeries to repair damage done to Randon's shoulder, he was finally moved to a rehabilitation clinic to begin physical therapy.

She could only assume Randon was still there. The letters they had exchanged regularly when he joined the Army stopped after their argument just before he left for Kuwait. But after he was injured, she wrote him several letters a week. Obviously, he couldn't write while he was recovering from his injuries, but she expected the letters to resume once he was at the rehab center. They hadn't. Except for one letter she'd received right after he got out of the hospital. That had been six months ago.

Her heart leaped to her throat. "What about Randon? Is he okay?"

Mom waved her hand. "He wants to know how Randon is doing. Says he won't answer the phone."

"How would we know? Randon hasn't called or written in months."

Randon's last letter had been short and impersonal. Not at all like the letters she'd become accustomed to over the past six years.

When Brian returned from Kuwait a couple of months ago, he went to see Randon before he came home to see his parents. More than once Brian said that Randon was having a hard time. Ice water flooded through her veins.

"No." Mom shook her head. "Randon was released from the Army last week."

"Released?" Her heart lurched.

Mom bit her bottom lip. "I guess his injuries were worse than we knew."

Millie's breath caught in her lungs. She'd read enough medical journals and seen enough statistics to know that Brian had good reason to be worried for his friend. "He thinks Randon is in Coronado?"

"Where else would he go?" Mom clasped her hands together. "If he was here, why wouldn't he tell us?"

Randon had spent more time at the Gibson house growing up than he had his own. Her mother often joked that she considered Randon one of her kids. The only one who didn't see him as just another Gibson boy was Millie. She didn't consider him a brother. Not at all. For one thing, she would never dream of sneaking a kiss with one of her brothers in the tree house. The memory sent heat rushing through her.

"Does Brian know when he left?"

Mom frowned. "No. He stopped by the hospital on Saturday and Randon was gone."

Millie pressed her lips together. This was Tuesday. Unless Randon was walking, he'd had plenty of time to get to Coronado.

"If he's in town, sooner or later he'll have to come to the market," she said. It was the only store around. "I'll ask Stacy if she's seen him. If he hasn't shown up by the end of my shift, I'm going to his house."

"Let me know as soon as you hear something."

"I will." She hugged her mother and walked out of the house.

She draped her jacket over her arm and started walking down the street toward the market. Soon, it would be too cold for her to walk. Already, winter was leaving its icy fingerprints on the windows each night, but for now, the fall sunshine was enough to keep the cold at bay. It was almost noon and the temperature was pleasant enough that she didn't need her jacket for the half-mile trek to the Coronado Market.

As she walked, memories of Randon danced through her mind. She was only five years old the first time Brian brought him home after school. He was a dirty little thing, with pants three inches too short and hair that hadn't seen a comb for days. A few years later, when Brian yelled at her for following them to their secret clubhouse, Randon waved her in and convinced Brian to let her be their lookout. From that moment on, Millie had been in love with him.

Where are you, Randon?

CHAPTER TWO

"Hᵢ, Kʏʟɪᴇ." Millie greeted the teenage girl behind the counter. "Has it been busy today?"

"No." The teenage girl sitting behind the counter didn't look up from her phone.

"Where's Stacy?"

Kylie glanced up. "Fixing the girls a snack."

Millie scanned the empty trays sitting on the back shelf of the deli section of the store. "Did you stock the deli?"

No. Of course, she didn't. The girl probably hadn't been off her phone since Stacy walked through the door that joined the store to her apartment.

Kylie looked up. "Oh. Sorry. I forgot."

"Did you check the soda machine?"

This time she didn't bother looking up from her phone. Millie sucked in her breath. She knew Stacy liked to give local teens a chance to get some job experience, but this one needed to go. Thankfully, the only time the girl was alone in the store was when Stacy's girls needed her. Then it was only for a few minutes.

Millie pasted a bright smile on her face. "I've got things now. You can go."

As soon as the teenager moseyed out of the store, Millie did a quick check of the register tape. Two sales for the whole afternoon. Kylie was right; the store hadn't been busy. Had anyone walked out in disgust because Kylie was too busy with her phone to wait on them?

The empty trays weren't going to fill themselves. She snagged the apron hanging on the hook behind the deli counter and tied it on. She checked to make sure no hair had escaped from her ponytail before washing her hands and stocking the deli.

Country music blared from the ancient radio on the wall. No one was allowed to change the station, just in case Matt Spencer's latest song came on. Coronado was the proud home of Luke Sterling, the man who wrote it.

Singing along with the music, she started slicing tomatoes. She was just sliding the filled container into the refrigerator when she heard the bells hanging on the front entrance chime. "Be right with you," she called over her shoulder while trying to shuffle things around to make more room.

She straightened up and turned to greet the customer, but no one was there. Scanning the store, she couldn't see anyone, but heard the door on the upright refrigerator at the far end of the market sliding shut.

The deli section was on one side of the entrance and the cash register was on a counter on the opposite side of the door, so Millie stepped around the deli counter and crossed the aisle to the checkout counter. Whoever was at the back of the store took their time getting to the front.

Just before rounding the corner that would put the customer within her sight, the footsteps stopped. She waited, ready to greet whomever it was. And waited.

She was about to meet them in the aisle to see if they were looking for something when a tall figure stepped around the corner. Her breath caught in her throat as light hazel eyes locked onto hers.

His once long shaggy hair was short, almost shaved in the back, but the blond locks on top were just as wild as she remembered. Almost as if he'd just gotten out of bed. Massive biceps stretched the sleeves of an olive-green T-shirt, hugging groceries to his broad chest. The size of him alone warned most people to stay away, but Millie had never been intimidated.

Her chest swelled with joy and she fought the urge to rush over to him. "You're home!"

"Hi, Millie." His gaze avoided hers.

She crossed her arms to keep her heart from leaping out of her chest. He looked different. He'd gained weight since he left the first time, although his face had the sunken look of someone who had recently lost a lot of weight. His hazel eyes had lost their twinkle. Even his dark blond hair looked duller than she remembered.

"When did you get here?"

Randon lifted his arms a bit, balancing the items he was holding. "I just got here this morning."

"Come to dinner tonight. Mom and Dad would love to see you." Her heart raced like a jackrabbit and she squeezed her fingers into the palms of her hands to keep from throwing her arms around him.

He frowned. "I can't. I have a lot of work to do at the cabin."

"Okay." She followed him to the counter and stepped behind the cash register.

One by one, he laid items on the counter. Her hands shook as she rang up each item and placed it in a paper sack. She was happy to see him. No, not just happy. Ecstatic. But he stood there like he didn't even know her. How many times had she lain awake at night trying to think of the perfect thing to say to him the next time she saw him?

He used his debit card to pay for the purchase and then reached for the paper sack. She pulled it back and kept her hand on top of it until he looked her in the face.

"I wrote you dozens of letters in the last six months. Why didn't you write me back?"

His eyes locked with hers. Millie held her breath. No matter how good he was at covering up his emotions, his eyes always betrayed him. She could tell when he had fought with his dad, even though he pretended everything was okay. She knew when he'd been hurt by the offhanded remarks of teachers who never expected him to be anything more than a troublemaker. She even knew when he was covering up for Brian. His eyes gave him away every time. Until now.

Either he'd gotten very good at masking his feelings, or he was even more removed from his emotions than Brian had been able to tell.

He lifted his chin. "I didn't have anything to say."

Her gaze pierced his, looking for some sign of emotion. Nothing. The once warm laughing eyes were now cold and hard. "That's it?"

"It has to be." Picking up the grocery bags, he walked out the door without looking back.

His words dug into her like daggers in her heart. She pulled her phone from her back pocket and sent a text to her brother. I just saw Randon.

Almost immediately, her phone rang.

"Hey," she said, her throat thick with emotion.

"Where?" Brian asked.

"He came into the market."

"What did he buy?" Her brother's voice was full of concern.

"Typical stuff. Milk, eggs, bread, peanut butter, sandwich meat. He also got some cleaning supplies. Why?"

"I'm really worried about him," Brian said. "He's cut himself off from everyone. I know he has PTSD, but there's more to it. Something he won't tell me."

She sighed. Brian knew him better than any-one else, although she liked to think she knew him almost as well. But the Randon who just left the store wasn't the Randon she grew up with. "What do I do?"

"Keep an eye on him. And, whatever you do, don't lose your temper."

She let out a huff. Everyone accused her of having a temper just because she had red hair. She didn't have a temper. She just had a low tol-erance for people who didn't do what they said they would do and didn't mind telling them. "I don't have a temper. And if I did, I know better than to go off on someone struggling with PTSD. I *am* a nurse, you know."

Brian chuckled. "I know. But you always had a soft spot for him. He's going to push you away. He may even say some things to try to make you mad enough to back off, but don't fall for it."

That should be easy. She had years of practice at ignoring the verbal jabs of her brothers. Still, it hurt to imagine Randon doing that. He'd never been one to lash out at anyone, even when he had good reason to.

Millie bit the inside of her cheek. Did her brother have any idea *why* Randon affected her the way he did? She doubted it. "So what do you want me to do?"

"Check on him as often as you can. If he's acting really off, don't leave him alone," Brian said.

"You don't think he'll try to hurt himself, do you?"

"I hope not." Brian's voice shook. "We're the only family he has left now. I'm trying to get leave approved and I'll be there as soon as I can."

"I will. You're not the only one who loves him," she said.

"I know."

He disconnected the call before she could find out if Mom said anything to him about Dad. Probably not. While Mom was willing to let her guard down around Millie, she wasn't that way with her brothers. Maybe it was because Millie was the only girl. Or maybe it was because she was a nurse…or maybe it was because she was the only one who stayed to help.

Her mother would never admit it, but Millie knew she was disappointed that not one of her four boys wanted to make a home in the Coronado area. As soon as they graduated high school, they left the tiny town and only returned for the holidays…sometimes not even then.

Michael, the oldest Gibson brother, lived in Seattle. He was a doctor and only came home to visit every other Christmas. The rest of the holidays were spent with his wife's family. Collin was a lawyer in Houston and was too busy with his career to come home. At least he remembered to call every Sunday. Jarrod was a commercial airline pilot based out of Phoenix. He came home as often as he could, which was only every couple of months. And then there was Brian, the youngest of the boys. Sometimes Millie wondered if he chose to enter the military because he wanted to escape the shadow of his older successful siblings.

Despite how proud her parents were of the things the Gibson children accomplished or how successful they were in the world, Millie knew each absence left a gaping hole in her mother's heart. She refused to be the final blow.

Besides, she loved Coronado. This is where she wanted to be for the rest of her life. When she was younger, she always imagined raising her own family in the same house she'd grown up in. But before she could have a family of her own, she needed someone to build a family with. For most of her life, the person she'd dreamed of doing that with was Randon. Just before he left for Kuwait, though, he made it clear that was never going to happen. At twenty-four years old, she was starting to wonder if she'd ever have a family of her own.

RANDON STRETCHED HIS arms over his head. It had taken all afternoon, but at least the trash was bagged up and he could see the floor again. It felt good to see his progress.

Working all afternoon seemed to have helped. It kept his mind occupied and he hadn't had an anxiety attack all day. He glanced at his watch. It was almost five o'clock. He wasn't sure what time Millie got off work, but he didn't want to be home when she did. He wouldn't put it past her to show up and expect him to come to dinner. Or worse, bring her parents to drag him to their house.

Laura Gibson was the closest thing to a mother he'd ever known. She took care of him when he was sick, gave him haircuts and always made sure he had food. Darrel Gibson, Brian's dad, took him fishing, taught him how to work on a car and made sure he kept his grades up so he could graduate high school. The last thing Randon ever wanted to do was disappoint them, which was why he couldn't take a chance that Millie might show up.

He picked up his jacket and walked outside. From where he stood on the porch, he could see all the way to the main road. A trailer park now stood between the highway and his driveway on what had once been land that belonged to his family.

When his grandfather died, his father came up with a plan to get rich quick. He did some wheeling and dealing with private investors and promised everyone in town he was going to put Coronado on the map. When the deals fell through, the bank auctioned off most of the land and instead of getting a fancy country club and gated community, Coronado got a trailer park.

Randon had nothing against trailer parks, but his father hated them. At least he hated the one in front of their home. The Coronado Corral was a constant reminder of his failure. His father had tried to make the people living in the trailer park as miserable as he was. As a result, Randon was isolated from everyone. The more prominent members of the community would have nothing to do with Gregory Farr and the people in the trailer park learned to steer clear of anyone named Farr.

The gravel crunched under Randon's feet as he walked down the driveway from his cabin to where it joined the road going through the Coronado Corral. The road made a giant loop around the trailer park and was the only way to get to the cabin.

Just before he reached the trailer park road, a worn footpath led away from the road and toward a grove of trees that marked the boundary between the town and the forest. Spruce and fir trees jutted up like soldiers, which was fitting because they had always been Randon's best protection.

He took the trail and didn't slow down until the trees closed in around him. Except for the crunching of leaves under his feet, no sound stirred the air as the path curved around trees and up a ridge.

His lungs burned by the time he got to the top. He leaned over with his hands on his knees and waited to catch his breath. From this vantage point, he could look down over Coronado. Homes dotted the landscape. He stared hard, his heart still pounding from the exertion of the hike. Millie was right. From here, a person couldn't tell the fancy homes from the poor homes.

The paved highway went through the heart of the town and met another highway, forming a T-intersection. Beyond that highway, lush green meadows stretched in several directions until the valley that sheltered Coronado from the surrounding mountains ended.

He walked until the trail entered a meadow. A large tree stood in the middle of the meadow and was exactly halfway between his cabin and the Gibson home. The tall pine tree was different than most of the trees in the area. Instead of one main trunk growing toward the heavens, the trunk was split.

Brian always said a lightning strike must have caused the split when the tree was young. Millie thought it was two trees that had grown so close together they'd joined.

Randon laid his hand on the trunk and looked up. The tree house he and Brian had built was still there. Were the boards still solid? He scaled the tree until he reached the platform that was the floor of the structure.

The tree house had a roof and three sides. He'd always planned to add a fourth wall so that it was completely enclosed and offered a little more protection from the elements. He pulled his knees close to him and rested his elbows on them, allowing his back to lean against one wall.

This place had been his sanctuary. Whenever his dad went on a bender, this was where he escaped to. It was the first place Brian looked for him. Randon scrubbed his face with his hands. He never understood why Brian had befriended him. They were as different as night and day. Two kids from opposite sides of town. One had everything. One had nothing.

He closed his eyes and thought about all the sleepovers he and Brian had had here. All the conversations. All the plans they made.

His chest tightened. His plans almost got Brian killed. All he'd wanted to do was prove he was a good soldier, a good man, a good person. Not like the man who'd sired him. But in his eagerness to do that, he got reckless and failed to see what was right in front of him.

He cast his eyes toward Heaven. "Now what? Where do I go from here?"

"Who you talking to, mister?" a small voice interrupted.

Randon looked over to see a boy's head poking

up over the edge. Wide blue eyes observed him with caution.

"Myself, I guess." Randon searched the area for any sign of the child's parents.

"Why?" The boy's face scrunched up. "Don't you have anyone else to talk to?"

Randon shrugged. "Not anymore."

The boy tossed a sleeping bag into the corner and climbed the rest of the way onto the platform. "Why are you in my tree house?"

"Your tree house?" Randon admired the boy's tenacity.

He lifted his chin and gave Randon a defiant stare. "Yeah. I found it."

"I built it."

"You did not." The boy's brow furrowed.

Randon nodded and pointed to the corner post. "See these initials carved into the wood? GRF. That's me. Gregory Randon Farr." He held out his hand to the boy. "But everyone calls me Randon."

"Edward Michael Sheldon." The boy shook his hand. "People just call me Eddie."

"It's nice to meet you, Eddie."

The boy moved to get a closer look at the post. "Who's BDG?"

"My best friend. We built this together."

"Then how come I ain't seen you here before?"

Randon moved over to give Eddie room. "I don't live in Coronado anymore."

"Where do you live?" Eddie pulled a package

of jerky out of his back pocket and offered Randon a piece.

"That's a good question," he said. "I'm trying to figure that out."

"Are you homeless?"

"No," Randon chuckled. "I was in the Army, so I lived wherever they sent me."

Eddie nodded. "How old were you when you built this?"

"About ten, I think." He couldn't remember for sure.

"Same age as me." Eddie cocked his head.

Randon took a bite of the jerky. "This is really good."

"It's elk." Eddie leaned against the wall and took another bite. "I helped my dad make it."

It made him feel better that Eddie mentioned his father. When he was a kid, he never talked about his dad to anyone. "Your dad's a hunter?"

"Yep." Eddie's face brightened. "He's taking me on my first elk hunt next month. Do you hunt?"

"Not anymore." Unless hunting terrorists for the Army counted.

"My friend Toby wants to go hunting real bad." A wistful tone filled Eddie's voice. "But if you don't take the hunter safety course you can't hunt until you're fourteen."

"Toby hasn't taken the course yet?"

"No." Eddie took another bite of his jerky. "His dad said it cost too much."

Darkness had been creeping in as they talked, as well as a chill in the air. Randon nodded toward the sleeping bag. "Are you planning on staying the night?"

Eddie shook his head. "No. I have to be home in time for dinner."

"Who's the sleeping bag for?"

Eddie's face scrunched. "Can you keep a secret?"

Alarm bells rang in his head. He couldn't make that promise without knowing what it was. He swallowed. "That depends."

The boy's eyes narrowed and he studied Randon for a moment. His voice was almost a whisper. "It's for Toby. I leave it here when his parents fight."

Randon stiffened. "And they were fighting today?"

He nodded. "I could hear them fighting all the way from my house." Eddie's face pinched. "Sometimes he needs a place to stay."

"Can't he stay with you?"

The boy shook his head. "Last time we had a sleepover, his dad showed up in the middle of the night. He was hollering and being loud, so my dad wouldn't let Toby go with him and they almost got in a fight. So now Toby won't come over 'cause he doesn't want it to happen again."

Randon's heart ached. He'd been in Toby's shoes. The blood rushed to his head as he watched the concern on the boy's face. It was the same look Brian had had when he found him hiding out here.

"Did you bring food for Toby?"

Eddie shook his head. "Just jerky."

"I used to come here when things got bad at home, too." Randon moved to the edge of the platform to make his way down. "Do you think it would be okay if I left some food here? I'll bring enough to share with you and Toby."

Eddie smiled. "I think Toby would like that."

"Good. I'll see you later." He put one hand on a board by the entrance to steady him as he turned to climb down. It looked different than the rest. He ran one hand over it.

"I replaced that one." Eddie saw what he was looking at. "It was warped, so I took it off and put another one up. Put a new roof on, too."

Randon looked up at the tin roof covering their heads. His throat tightened. "I'm glad you're taking care of it."

"I'm glad you built it."

"I better get going." He moved to the edge. "Don't stay up here too long. It gets cold fast."

"I won't. Toby should be here soon."

"See you around." He slipped over the edge and dropped to the ground.

As he walked down the ridge, he realized that was the first normal conversation he'd had with someone in over six months. He rolled his shoulders. No tension. His insides weren't shaking and he didn't have to struggle to figure out what to say. It felt good not to be walking on eggshells for once.

CHAPTER THREE

As soon as Randon got back to the cabin, he opened the pantry and took out the jar of peanut butter. He made four peanut butter and jelly sandwiches and wrapped them in aluminum foil. He put the sandwiches, some chips and several bottles of water into a plastic shopping bag.

He inspected the small care package, trying to think of anything else Toby would need. Eddie left a sleeping bag for Toby, so he would have something to keep him warm while he slept. Randon walked across the cabin and paused outside his father's bedroom door. It was the only room he hadn't touched. Sooner or later, he would have to, but he wasn't ready yet.

With a shaky hand, he pushed the door open. The room still smelled of cigarette smoke. Except for the layer of dust covering everything, it was surprisingly clean. He walked over to the bed and picked up a pillow, thumping it against his hand a few times. Dust particles filled the air and he sneezed.

He carried the pillow into the living room and stripped the pillowcase off it. After shaking the pillow out a few more times, he took a sniff and almost choked. It still reeked of smoke. He tossed the pillow on the floor next to the garbage can and went to get the pillow from his own bed.

Just before he walked out the door, he stopped and grabbed a flashlight, too.

It was dark enough that Randon could barely make out the trail ahead of him, but when he stepped into the open meadow close to the tree house, the moon gave off enough light to see clearly. The flickering light from a lantern could be seen inside the tree house and he heard voices inside. He didn't want to startle the boys, so he put his fingers to his lips and whistled softly.

Two heads popped over the edge to look down at him.

Eddie grinned. "You're back."

Randon held up the bag. "I brought some food. Anyone hungry?"

The two boys looked at each other for a moment, then Eddie waved him up.

"Hi," he said, when he'd climbed high enough to poke his head inside.

"Hey," Eddie said.

The other boy watched him with wary eyes. His face was tight and, even in the dim glow of the lantern, Randon could see that his eyes were red and puffy.

"You must be Toby."

Toby nodded, but didn't say anything.

Randon recognized the fearful expression on his face and changed his mind about going the rest of the way inside. Toby had likely been betrayed by most of the adults in his life and he wasn't going to welcome Randon with open arms.

And that was okay. Toby should be wary of strangers. Randon's heart ached. He'd been in Toby's shoes and he wanted to protect the boy.

His gaze darted to Eddie. Would Eddie's family keep an eye on Toby the way the Gibsons had done for him?

He lifted the bag and placed it on the floor between the boys. He removed the pillow and tossed it next to the sleeping bag. "Are you both staying the night?"

"Why?" It was the first word Toby said.

Randon didn't blame him for being suspicious. He nodded toward the sleeping bag. "There's only one sleeping bag. If you need another one, you're welcome to borrow one of mine."

When neither boy said anything, Randon pointed toward the trail. "I live in the cabin at the end of Farr Lane. Do you know where that is?"

Toby nodded his head, but Eddie lifted his chin. "I thought you didn't live in Coronado?"

"I don't. But that's the house I grew up in and I'm staying there until I can fix it up and sell it."

"Thanks, but we're fine," Eddie said.

Randon gave the boys a pointed look. "I'm going now, but my door is always open if you need anything. And I do mean anything. Food. Water. A place to stay. Whatever."

They nodded and Randon started back down to the ground. As soon as his head was out of sight, he heard the rustle of the shopping bag.

"I told you he was all right," Eddie whispered. "He brought food."

"Yeah, until we eat it and die," Toby argued. "Or wake up in a cage somewhere."

Toby was right to be cautious, but it made Randon sad that the boys needed to be. When his feet touched the ground, he whistled again.

Eddie's face appeared in the opening of the floor.

"Could you toss me one of those sandwiches to eat on my way back? I'm getting hungry."

A second later, he caught the falling sandwich. "Thanks."

He unwrapped the sandwich and took the biggest bite he could. Hopefully, it would put their minds at ease. He made sure to swallow it while both boys still watched him. "I'm sorry. I didn't even think to ask if either of you are allergic to peanuts. If you are, I can bring you something else."

"No," Toby said. His face had lost a little bit of its hardness. "We're not. Thanks."

"Good night." He took another bite and waved to them before heading back toward his cabin.

The tree house had been his safe haven. He was glad that it was now Toby's, but it angered him that Toby needed one. There were so many questions he wanted to ask. Eddie said Toby didn't like it when his parents fought. Did he leave his home so he didn't have to hear yelling and screaming? Or was he escaping from something worse?

His fists clenched as he approached the main road. If there was more going on, why hadn't anyone done anything about it? Eddie's dad had stood up to Toby's dad at least once. Surely, he wouldn't stand by and let his son's friend be abused.

Maybe he doesn't know. Randon had done a good job of hiding things from people, and his father didn't hit him often. He wasn't sure if it was because his dad showed some measure of self-control, even at his drunkest, or if Randon was really good at reading the signs and left before the hateful words escalated into violence.

When he grew taller than his father, the hitting stopped entirely. Greg traded his fists for a more damaging form of punishment: words. He never missed an opportunity to tell Randon what a burden he was, or to remind him that no one wanted him...not his mother, not her parents and not him.

He stopped at the edge of the property and took a deep breath. Did he have one good memory from this place after his grandfather died? He should put it on the market as is, cut his losses and never look back.

The tall grass brushed his thighs as he made his way through the yard. The grass and weeds ended just a few feet from the porch. Randon stared down at the cement slab that the porch was built on. The cement extended a few feet from the structure and had once had a flower bed in front of it. The flowers were gone, exposing long forgotten etchings in the cement.

Randon knelt down for a better look. Two hand-prints were pressed into the cement, one large and one small. He ran his fingers over the smaller one. Underneath the handprint, his name was written in crooked letters. His throat tightened as he placed his hand over the larger one. His hand was bigger than his grandfather's had been. He smiled. Once, he'd asked his grandpa if he would ever be as big as him. Grandpa laughed and said that Randon would be bigger. At the time, Randon couldn't imagine being bigger than the man he admired so much.

He stood up and looked at the cabin again. Slowly, he turned and looked around the property, seeing it as if for the first time. The tree where his grandfather hung the tire swing stood close to the cabin and Randon's heart swelled a little when he saw it. Before the barn at the edge of the property housed his father's pickup, it had been Grandpa's workshop. His grandfather had taught him how to build things in that shop. First, a birdhouse, then the deck at the back of the house.

The more he looked around, the more memories flooded through him. He walked around the cabin and down the slope to the backyard. He and his grandfather had walked around the backyard multiple times while he sketched the cabin. His grandfather had patiently listened to his ideas on how to build a deck off the back of the cabin without having to haul in tons of fill dirt to level the backyard.

The result had been a large deck supported by beams. Lattice panels were placed in between the beams to create storage space beneath. His grandfather had been so impressed with Randon's sketches that he bought Randon a sketchbook to keep all his drawings in.

Randon took the stairs up to the deck. His hands shook as he gripped the doorknob. Had his grandfather's memory chased away his father's ghost? He wasn't sure, but he knew he couldn't walk away from the cabin until he'd restored it in a way that would make his grandfather proud. The cabin deserved a future, even if it wasn't with him.

He lifted his chin and pushed the door open, ready to tackle what he could. When he stepped inside, he was taken aback. He hadn't realized how much he'd done. All day, he'd swept and cleaned and hauled out trash. The cushions on the sofa had absorbed cigarette smoke for decades, so Randon hauled it outside. Most of the other living room furniture followed.

The only thing that remained was the wooden dining table and chairs. No wonder his body ached. Of course, gathering trash and hauling out furniture was the easy part. The hard part would be getting the repairs done.

He walked over to the kitchen counter and picked up the list he'd made. Shingles. Chimney. Rotten floorboards. Leaky roof. Window shutters. Kitchen cabinets. Hot water heater.

He leaned against the counter and let his gaze sweep over the space. He pictured the cabin the way it should be.

It was small, with only two bedrooms and a loft, but the open floorplan made it feel much bigger. The great room was large enough to have a family gathering and not feel cramped. He could almost picture people gathered around the large table, passing plates of food around at Thanksgiving. There would still be enough room for a big-screen television and a couple of large sofas to sit on and watch the football game.

But first, the Macy's Day parade. He could hear Millie's voice arguing with her brothers on Thanksgiving morning.

His gaze lingered on the fireplace. It could keep the cabin warm through the coldest winter. He walked over to the mantel and ran his hand over the wood. It was perfect to hang stockings on. He closed his eyes and pictured a large tree in the corner, stacked with presents.

Millie would insist on letting the kids open one present on Christmas Eve.

What was he doing? He'd stopped dreaming of a life with Millie when he asked her to leave Coronado and she said no. Now he was too broken and damaged for someone like her.

MILLIE TIPTOED DOWNSTAIRS after her shower and paused at her parents' bedroom door to peek in on her dad. He was snoring softly. She smiled. It was when he was asleep that she could pretend nothing had changed.

She walked into the kitchen to see if her mom needed help with anything, but Mom was nowhere to be seen. She noticed there was food in the oven, being kept warm. Sighing, she walked to the living room and peered through the window.

Mom was sitting on the porch swing, staring into the night. She was wearing only a light jacket, so Millie picked up a quilt from her dad's reclining chair and walked outside. Her footsteps barely made a sound as she padded across the front porch in her socks.

"Want some company?"

Her mother smiled and moved over. Millie sat next to her and arranged the quilt over them. Several minutes passed with only the creaking of the swing's chain.

"He said he wasn't coming," Millie reminded her.

Mom's eyes never left the line of trees across the street. "He's coming."

Millie wanted her mother to be right. She would give anything for Randon to emerge from the trail, apologize for being late and ask if there was any dinner left.

"He probably just got busy with something and lost track of time." Mom tucked the quilt tighter around them. "He tends to lose track of time when he's involved in a project."

Her gaze strayed across the street again.

Millie had seen that look on her mother before. It was the same look she had when one of her children was late for curfew. A mixture of worry and anger. Her chest tightened. Her mother had enough to worry about without adding Randon to it.

Millie cast a sideways glance at her mother. *It's because of me.* For most of her childhood, she followed Randon around like a lovesick puppy. He tolerated her, but never encouraged her. Six years ago, before he left for basic training, she tried to tell him how she felt. When the words wouldn't come out right, she kissed him. Instead of laughing at her or pushing her away, he kissed her back. And, oh, what a kiss it was.

The memory of it still took her breath away. Her hand covered her lips. It was the first time he'd revealed that he saw her as anything other than his best friend's little sister. She was only eighteen at the time, but when he asked her to wait for him, she said yes.

For the next three years, they exchanged emails and phone calls, but they never discussed their future. Twice a year, Randon and Brian came home on leave, but other than a few stolen kisses when no one was looking, their relationship seemed more or less platonic. When he came home on leave before shipping out for Kuwait, she gathered up her courage and asked him if he still felt the same about her. He kissed her again and for the first time they discussed their future. That's when he told her he'd decided to make the Army a career. He'd been taking some college classes and when he returned from overseas, he would take more until he could apply to go to Officer Commissioning School. He wanted her to go with him.

Millie was happy that he found something he was so excited about, but by that time her father was already showing signs of Alzheimer's and she knew she couldn't leave. Her parents needed her. When she told him she wouldn't leave Coronado, she expected him to change his mind and say he'd stay in Coronado with her. But he hadn't. When forced to choose between her and the Army, he hadn't choose her.

How much could he really love her if he'd been able to walk away from her so easily? She was hurt, but she wished him good luck and told him they were still friends. He'd written her a couple of letters after he got to Kuwait, but she hadn't written him back.

Then he was injured and she was scared she would lose him forever. She realized she needed him in her life, even if it was only as a friend. For the next six months, she wrote him every week. This time, he was the one that never wrote back.

"How did he look?"

"Huh?" Millie was jolted out of her thoughts. "What did you say?"

"I asked how he looked. Physically, I mean. Did you see any scars? Was he using his arm okay?"

"He looked fine, physically," Millie said. "He's probably gained twenty pounds."

Mom chuckled softly. "You said he didn't say much. Did he seem preoccupied?"

"He seemed..." Millie paused, searching for the right words. "Absent."

"Absent?" her mother repeated.

She nodded. "I've always been able to read him, even when he was trying to push everyone else away. But today, he looked me right in the eye and acted like he didn't even know me."

Mom gave her a sad smile. "He's been through a lot in the last eight months. Give him time."

Her chest constricted and she fought the lump building in her throat. "How much time?"

"As much as he needs," Mom said. "He lost his dad, his career and he almost lost his life. Give him time to adjust. He's out of the Army now, so he's not going anywhere."

Millie bit her lip as hope fluttered in her belly. When he decided to make a career out of the Army, she'd had to accept the fact that there was no future for them. She could never leave Coronado. But he wasn't in the Army anymore. He was back in town. And she wasn't a little kid anymore. Could they have a future?

Her mother nudged her. "What are you thinking about?"

"Nothing." Her cheeks flamed, despite the chill of the air. "I'm just glad he's home."

"I know you are." Mom stared at her for a moment. "Be careful."

She squirmed in her seat. "What are you talking about?"

Mom raised one eyebrow. "You've been in love with Randon since the day he threatened to beat up Aaron Walker if he pulled your hair again."

"I have not," she grumbled. Actually, it was much earlier than that. She was ten years old when Aaron started tormenting her on the playground.

"Earlier, then?" Mom shook her head and laughed.

Millie snuggled closer to her mother. "How did you know?"

"There's not much that goes on around here that I don't know about." Her hand squeezed Millie's. "He loves you, too. I'm not saying it's the same as what you feel for him. Maybe he loves you like a little sister. I do know you're as important to him as anyone in this world."

She swallowed. It wasn't sisterly love that he felt when he kissed her and asked her to wait for him. Her breath hitched. Had he confused sisterly love with the kind of love she felt? Was that why it was so easy for him to pick his career over her?

"I've got enough big brothers," she mumbled under her breath.

"I know." Mom stroked her hair. "But be careful."

"What are you talking about?"

Mom sighed. "When you want something, you go after it with everything you've got. Randon's not like that. Everyone he's ever loved has abandoned him, so he's scared. The more you push him, the faster he'll run."

Millie shifted on the swing. "Don't worry. He barely looked at me today, so I don't think it matters."

"If what Brian says is true, he has more to recover from than an injured shoulder. The mind sometimes takes longer than the body." Mom's gaze strayed to the trail leading to his house. "He'll come around."

Millie swallowed. "It really bothers you that he didn't come over, doesn't it?"

"Of course, it does. I love that boy like he was my own. But I also know there's a reason he didn't let us know he was home. And when he's ready, he'll tell us."

Millie pressed her lips together. Was she the reason he hadn't come over? He was the one who picked the Army over her, so she should be the one avoiding him. Not the other way around.

Mom stood up. "I guess he's not coming. I might as well go to bed."

"Good night." She folded her legs under her.

"Are you coming in?"

Millie glanced toward the forest. "Not yet. I think I'll sit out here a bit longer."

Mom nodded and went back inside the house.

If Randon didn't come see her mother tomorrow, she was going to confront him. She wasn't sure if her refusal to leave Coronado had angered him or relieved him. Either way, he needed to know that she wouldn't make things awkward for him. She'd moved on. At least that's what she would tell him.

CHAPTER FOUR

THE SUN SANK low in the sky and Millie wiped the deli counter for the last time. Ten more minutes until she could close the store. All afternoon, she'd waited for a text from her mother telling her that Randon had stopped by. He never showed up. She kept hoping Randon would come to the store again today. But he didn't.

She could understand why he didn't want to come over on his first day home. But going to see her parents should have been the first thing he did today.

The longer she watched the clock, the more angry she became. Who did he think he was? Didn't he realize her mom spent as much time worrying about him as she did about Brian? If he didn't want to see her, fine, but she would not let him avoid her parents.

She glanced at the clock. Five minutes until she closed.

The door that separated the store from the apartment where Stacy lived with her family opened and Millie heard the patter of bare feet running down the aisle.

"Millie! Millie!" Stacy's daughter Khatia raced toward her.

Millie scooped her up. "What's wrong?"

"Look." The little girl opened her hand.

Millie ran her finger over the bright red bump on the end of Khatia's index finger. "How did you get that splinter?"

"I was helping Mama—" She paused, her face scrunched as she thought. "I mean Dad. I was helping Dad carry wood in."

Stacy came to stand behind her daughter. She glanced at Millie. "The Georgian language is a little backward. *Mama* means dad and *deda* means mom."

"Interesting," Millie said. "I had no idea."

Up until a year ago, she didn't know her boss and friend was originally from Georgia. When Stacy and her husband visited the country on their honeymoon, they returned with two beautiful little girls they had adopted.

Stacy nodded toward Khatia's finger. "Can you get it? She refuses to let either me or Caden touch it."

Khatia gave her mother a serious look. "She's a nurse."

Millie laughed and carried the five-year-old to the counter so she could wash her hands. Stacy handed her a cotton ball, rubbing alcohol, tweezers and a small sewing needle. She sterilized the needle and swabbed Khatia's hand with an alcohol-soaked cotton ball.

"How's kindergarten?" She gently pushed on the tip of Khatia's finger with her thumb.

"Fine." Khatia's gaze was focused on the needle in Millie's hand.

Millie set the needle on the counter as she continued to poke the skin around the splinter. The entire time, she asked the little girl questions. It wasn't long before Khatia was so caught up in telling a story that she didn't notice when Millie picked up the needle.

While Millie worked on the little girl's hand, Stacy turned the sign in the window from Open to Closed.

Using the point of the needle, Millie coaxed the splinter out far enough that she was able to grab it with tweezers.

"There."

Khatia's brown eyes widened and she stared at her finger. "I didn't even feel it."

She turned to her mother. "I told you she was the best nurse in the world."

Stacy laughed. "I believe you. Now go brush your teeth."

The girl ran back to their apartment, slamming the door behind her.

"Thanks for doing that." Stacy pushed a couple of buttons on the cash register and pulled the cash drawer out.

"Anytime." Millie took off her apron and hung it up. "I'll see you tomorrow."

Millie normally walked from her home to the store, but not today. She got into the car and glanced at the box in the back seat.

Her mother had packed a box full of things she thought Randon might need. Sheets, pillows, canned food, cleaning supplies and toiletries. And on top was a large plate of homemade oatmeal raisin cookies. His favorite.

Her nostrils flared when she looked at the box. She promised her mother she would take it to him, but that didn't mean she couldn't give him a piece of her mind with it.

To get to Randon's cabin, she had to drive through what her parents described as the *wrong side of the tracks*. Coronado didn't have railroad tracks, but this part of town was the polar opposite of hers.

She passed one home with two vehicles sitting on blocks. One had no tires, the other had no doors. Both were rusted and hadn't been moved in years. Music blared from one home, the deep bass shaking the windows in her car.

It had been a while since she'd been here. Her friend Emily used to live on this street and Millie had babysat for her every Thursday night. Last

April, Emily had married her son's father, Luke Sterling, and they moved to a larger house.

The road made a loop and at the backside of the loop, a gravel road turned off and disappeared into the forest. According to her mother, the Farrs had once owned all the land in the area. Randon's dad took out a mortgage against the property with dreams of building a fancy subdivision. He hadn't been a very good manager and the bank foreclosed on it. The new owner put in a trailer park. At least Gregory had managed to keep the cabin and the few acres it sat on.

After Brian and Randon left for basic training, Millie often drove by the house. When she started working as a home-health nurse, Gregory had been one of the first patients assigned to her. She suspected it was because no one else would put up with the man's belligerent attitude.

Most of the time, Gregory was too drunk to carry on much of a conversation but Millie would stop by even when she wasn't on duty to see how he was. Did Randon know that she had been with his father when he died? Probably not.

She pulled in front of the house and gasped. The place had really fallen into disrepair since Gregory passed. Not that Gregory was very good at keeping the place up. She turned the engine off and got out of the car. She held the box with both hands and made her way through the weeds that had overtaken the yard.

She knocked. There was a light on, but she didn't hear a sound from inside the house. She pushed the door open. "Randon?"

The strong scent of bleach hung in the air and the house was empty except for the dining room table and chairs. Where had the rest of the furniture gone? She walked into the kitchen and set the box on the counter.

"Randon?" She walked down the narrow hall to where his bedroom was.

The room was exactly as she remembered, but the walls were bare. Dark spots on the wood paneling showed where pictures had once been. She frowned at the largest spot. A corkboard that had been on the wall above his dresser was gone. It had been covered with pictures of Brian and Randon's exploits, ticket stubs of movies they had all gone to and other small items. Several pictures of her had been there as well. They were all gone.

A noise behind her made her jump. She whirled around to see Randon standing in the doorway.

His eyes weren't angry. Just empty. "What are you doing here?"

Heat flooded her neck at being caught in his bedroom. "I wasn't snooping. I was looking for you. You weren't in the living room so I thought you might be back here."

"I didn't mean in my bedroom. I meant here. Why are you at my house?"

Once again, she felt like he was absent. The

anger she felt toward him earlier subsided. Physically, Randon was one of the largest people she knew. At six foot three, his massive frame filled the door, yet somehow he looked small. She could still picture the scrawny little boy Brian had dragged into the house that first time after school years ago.

"Oh," she breathed. "When you didn't come to the house, Mom got worried, so she put some things together for you. I left the box on the kitchen counter."

His right eye twitched. "She shouldn't have done that."

"It wasn't any trouble. Most of it was part of the care package she was putting together to send to you, anyway." Millie tried to keep her tone light.

"I mean, she shouldn't worry about me."

"Too bad. She does, anyway. Because that's what families do."

"You're not my family." His voice was flat.

"Do you really believe that?" she asked. "Because I don't. Mom and Dad don't. My brothers don't. Like it or not, you're part of our family."

His face tightened. "You're better off without me."

The words were spoken so softly she barely heard them. Was he talking about his family? Or her?

She took a deep breath. "Am I the reason you haven't come over?"

"No."

The look of surprise on his face made her feel marginally better. "Good. Because I didn't hold it against you. Breaking up with me, I mean."

"I didn't break up with you," he said. He lifted his gaze to meet hers. "I asked you to come with me and you said no to that. And technically, there was nothing to break up from."

Her cheeks grew warm as he stared at her. "Not you." She shook her head. "I never said no to you."

He pressed his lips together. "Same thing. You said no to the career I chose. You said no to the life I could build for us."

She lifted her chin. "Why couldn't we build it in Coronado?"

"I tried." Randon shook his head. "Why do you think it took me so long to join the Army? I spent two years after high school trying to make a life here. I could barely make enough to scrape by, much less support a family."

Millie's chest squeezed. She remembered being surprised that Randon didn't leave town as soon as he graduated. "You stayed for me?"

He shrugged. "Why else would I have stayed?"

Hope fluttered in her stomach. She stepped closer to him. "You're home now. That's what matters. We can—"

"I'm not staying." He caught the hand she was lifting to touch his face.

"Why not?" Her words came out in a rush. "Where are you going?"

"I'm going to work for a military contractor. It's not the same as being in the military, but it'll be close."

She took a step back. "What does that mean? What does a military contractor do?"

"Anything the Army does." His gaze held hers. "I've asked to be assigned to the unit that will provide security for government personnel in Kuwait."

The hope that had fluttered to life died. "Then why are you even here?"

"They gave me thirty days to get my affairs in order."

Her mind raced, looking for a way to convince him to stay. "I don't mean to sound insensitive, but how can you go to work for a military contractor if you were medically discharged from the Army?"

"They have different requirements than the Army does," he said quietly.

Pain pierced her heart. "You never even considered giving us a chance, did you?"

"No." He walked into the living room and opened the door. "Go home, Millie."

"I would love to," she told him, "but not until you promise to go see Mom. She's not going to stop worrying until you do."

Randon's face paled. "I'm trying to give her one less person to worry about."

Millie shook her head. "It's not working. Just stop by and see her. If for no other reason than to let her thank you for saving Brian's life."

Pain flickered in his hazel eyes and he shook his head. "That's the last thing I should be thanked for."

Her brow furrowed. That was an odd thing to think. "Why?"

"Please," he said, his voice so low she could barely hear him. "Just take the box and go."

She shook her head. "If you don't want it, take it back to her yourself. And tomorrow would be good. I have patients all day so there's no chance of us running into each other."

RANDON WAS STILL staring at the ceiling when dawn started to peek into his bedroom window. He was accustomed to not getting a lot of sleep but normally it was because nightmares plagued him. Now it was a pair of blue eyes looking at him with disappointment that had him tossing and turning all night.

Millie's words replayed in his mind. *Not you. I never said no to you.* He had never thought about her rejection like that. She hadn't said no to him, only to leaving Coronado. At the time, the only thing that mattered to him was that she'd said no. It hadn't mattered why.

I never said no to you. For a brief moment, her words sparked a bit of hope. Did she still care about him? He wasn't in the Army anymore. If he stayed in Coronado, would things be different?

He threw back the covers and shivered when his bare foot touched the wooden floor. The only heat source the cabin had was the large fireplace in the living room. It wouldn't keep the entire house the same temperature the way central heating did, but it was enough to ward off the chill. But until he inspected the chimney and the flue, he wasn't about to build a fire, no matter how cold it was.

Millie thought he hadn't gone to see her parents because he was avoiding her. That was a small part of it, but mostly he was too ashamed to show his face at the Gibson house.

For years, he'd allowed himself to pretend he could be part of their family. He knew that Laura worried about him almost as much as she worried about Brian. He received as many letters from her as Brian did. Sometimes Brian joked that his mother loved Randon more than him.

His chest tingled as shame overwhelmed him. He had no right to Laura's compassion. He had no right to Laura's love. Today, he would return her care package and apologize for intruding on their lives.

His gaze drifted to the window, where it was barely light enough to see. It was too early to go to the Gibson home yet and it wasn't bright enough to get much work done outside.

He rolled his shoulder back, trying to loosen up the stiffness he often felt in the morning. After three surgeries to repair tendons and six months of physical therapy, the range of motion in his shoulder was still limited.

Fortunately, his injury didn't prevent him from getting a job with Bravos. However, he still had to pass a basic physical fitness test so, unless he got back into shape, he wouldn't be going anywhere.

Since he couldn't do much around the cabin yet, he might as well start on getting in shape. He hadn't enjoyed a morning run since he was in Kuwait. He and Brian often ran together just as the sun was coming up in the desert. While he was in rehab, the physical therapist encouraged him to use the gym twice a day, but it hadn't given him the same satisfaction as running in the great outdoors.

He dressed in a pair of sweats and tied his sneakers before stepping outside. After a few stretches to loosen up his dormant muscles, he headed down the road.

As he approached the end of his driveway, he could see the mobile homes in the Coronado Corral trailer park. He thought about Eddie and his friend. Both boys must live close by for them to have stumbled on the tree house while out playing. Did they live in the trailer park?

By the time he'd gone around the loop once, his lungs burned and he was struggling to catch his breath. Running before he'd had time to adjust to the higher elevation might not have been the best idea. When he got back around to Farr Lane, he stopped running and walked the rest of the way.

He took a quick shower and made himself a bowl of cereal. As he ate, he glanced at the box on the counter where Millie had left it. Even if Millie hadn't told him there were oatmeal raisin cookies in it, he would've known. Those had always been his favorite and his stomach growled thinking about them.

Curiosity got the best of him and he picked up the foil-covered plate and set it aside to peek at the contents. Towels, sheets, soap and toothpaste. He placed the cookies back into the box and picked the box up.

The shortcut to the Gibsons' home took him right past the tree house, but he doubted the boys would be there this early. Surely, Toby hadn't stayed there two nights in a row. Still, when he entered the meadow, he whistled and waited. Nothing. He continued on.

When the trail emerged from the forest, the scene was much different than where he began. The houses on this street were painted in soft colors and lined the road like dollhouses. The yards were perfectly manicured and none of the shutters were missing.

Randon walked to the last house on the end and stopped to gather his nerves. He walked up the steps to the front porch and shifted the box so he could knock on the door.

A moment later, Laura opened the door. A huge grin broke out over her face and one hand covered her heart. "Randon. I'm so happy to see you."

A lump swelled in his throat. He hadn't expected to feel such a rush of joy to see her. He cleared his throat. "I wanted to return these things. I don't need them."

Laura's brow furrowed and she took the box. "I don't understand."

"I—" Butterflies filled his stomach. He took a shaky breath. "I should go. I just wanted to return your things."

"Nonsense," she said. "Let's go sit in the kitchen."

His brow furrowed. This was going to be a lot harder than he thought. One look at the concern on her face and his intention to hand her the box and leave disappeared. This woman had done more for him than any other person on the planet and the last thing he wanted to do was hurt her feelings. She'd already wasted too much time and energy on him.

She turned and walked through the foyer toward the kitchen. "Come on."

He shouldn't follow her, but he did. He closed his eyes and inhaled. Vanilla and butterscotch.

This place smelled like home. Much better than cigarettes and stale beer.

He glanced into the living room as he walked past the entry. In the corner, Darrel sat in his recliner, his eyes on the television. Randon started to walk over to him, but Laura cleared her throat and shook her head.

She set the box on the kitchen table. "He wouldn't recognize you today."

"I'm sorry," he said. "Brian told me, but I didn't realize…"

"Some days are better than others." She gave him a sad smile. "Now, what's this about?" She motioned to the box.

Steeling his nerves, he lifted his chin. "I already picked up what I needed, so you don't have to take care of me anymore."

She raised one eyebrow. "I don't mind going out of my way for the ones I love. And if you think I'm going to stop trying to take care of you just because you're a full-grown man, then you don't know me very well."

"I don't deserve it." His words came out in a rush. "I tried to be…" Words failed him and his throat tightened.

The longer he stood in front of her, the more ashamed he felt. His temples throbbed and he struggled to breathe. Heat rushed through his body. He had to leave.

"I'm sorry." The back door was the nearest escape route and he headed for it. He turned the knob but it didn't budge. His hands shook as he tried to unlock the door.

"Gregory Randon Farr, you stop this minute." Laura's sharp voice penetrated the haze.

His fingers paused over the lock but he couldn't turn around. He couldn't face her.

"Sit down." The authority in her voice matched that of any of his commanding officers.

Slowly, he turned to look at her. Her eyes were narrowed and her face was tight. She pointed at the nearest chair. "I said, sit down."

The band across his chest tightened and he struggled to breathe. "You don't know what I did."

She put her hands on her hips. "I know more than you think. Now sit."

He was tired. His bones ached. His limbs were heavy. For eight months, he'd carried around the guilt of what he'd done. If he told her the truth, would it rid him from the dark cloud he'd been living in? Would trading his guilt for her disdain be worth it?

She waited for him to sit down at the kitchen table before she sat next to him. "Now tell me what you think you did."

"Brian…" His voice came out in a whisper. "I almost got him killed."

Instead of arguing with him, she nodded. "Yes. Then you saved him. If it wasn't for you, he'd be dead."

He sat in the chair next to her and fought the waves of panic rising in his chest. Brian's face flashed in his mind. Then the faces of the other men in his squad. If he hadn't been so full of himself, he would've seen the danger in front of him.

Randon inhaled through his nose and exhaled through his mouth, willing his heart rate to slow down. "It was my fault. I—"

"You were so eager to impress your superiors and prove yourself that you tried to capture the bad guy on your own and accidentally led your unit into an ambush."

His mouth fell open. "How did you know?"

"Because I know my boy." She lifted one hand to touch his cheek, leaving no doubt that she was referring to him. "You've been trying to get out from under your father's shadow since you were ten years old. Of course, you took a chance."

The warmth of her hand burned his cheek. How could she stand to look at him? "People got hurt because of me. *Brian* got hurt because of me."

Laura shook her head. "Oh, honey. Do you think Brian would've done anything different that night? If he'd been team leader, he would've done the same thing. So would any one of those men."

He shook his head. "But it wasn't them. It was me. I have to live with it."

"That's true," she said. "Only it seems the only one blaming you is you. Your commanding officers don't. Your unit doesn't. Brian doesn't."

She leaned forward to look him straight in his eyes. "I don't."

Randon buried his face in his hands. He'd heard that before. His captain told him before he was medevaced to Landstuhl Regional Medical Center in Germany. The counselors at Landstuhl told him. His psychologist at Walter Reed Hospital told him. Brian told him when he stopped by the rehab center. He couldn't believe them.

Laura's hand stroked the back of his head. Her voice was barely more than a whisper. "We forgive you. It's time to forgive yourself."

Randon kept his elbows on the table and covered his face with his hands. His entire body trembled. "I don't deserve it."

"Deserves got nothing to do with it." Laura put her thumb under his chin and lifted his face to look at her. She nodded toward the living room. "Does Darrel deserve what he's going through?"

"Of course not." He sat up. His pulse had slowed and he could take in a full breath of air.

"Sometimes we have to play the cards we're dealt, whether we deserve it or not. The difference is how you deal with it." She took both of his hands in hers and squeezed. "I expect you to hold your head up and face things like the man I know you are."

He swallowed. "That's what I'm trying to do. Confess my mistake and accept the consequences."

She arched one eyebrow. "By cutting yourself off from the people who love you?"

His gaze dropped to the floor. "I didn't think you would want me around after you found out what I did."

"And you thought pushing us away first would make it less painful?"

Randon's brow furrowed. Is that what he was doing?

Laura swore under her breath. "If Greg wasn't already gone, I'd make him wish he was." She leaned over him and enveloped him in her arms. "No child should grow up thinking that he'll be abandoned for his mistakes."

Randon's throat was thick and he couldn't breathe. He stopped fighting his emotions and hugged her back. He couldn't remember his own mother and from what little he knew about her, she wasn't much better than his father. How he got lucky enough for the Gibsons to love him, he didn't know, but he would do his best not to let them down again.

"Thank you," he choked.

Laura gave him a sad smile. "I'm glad that's settled. Now, what are you doing to deal with your PTSD?"

He flinched. "You know?"

"It's hard to miss," she said. "What are you doing? Are you taking medication for it?"

"No." The last thing he wanted to do was become dependent on any type of drug. His father got addicted to painkillers and then graduated to whiskey. "I'm trying to figure out how to deal with it on my own."

"Hmm." Laura looked him in the eyes. "You spend too much time alone. You need to be around people."

The thought of being in a crowd caused his heart to race. "I don't think that's a good idea."

She stood up and walked over to a small crate on the end of the kitchen counter. She pulled a flyer from the stack of papers and handed it to him. "I think this is just what you need."

CHAPTER FIVE

MILLIE PUT THE dishes from lunch in the dishwasher and dried her hands before going to the living room to check on her father.

Every Friday, she stayed home with her dad so her mom could drive to Springerville, the closest town large enough to have more than just a convenience store. Millie didn't mind staying with her father during these weekly shopping trips. She suspected her mother needed time out of the house even more than she needed to stock up on groceries.

Darrel was sitting in his recliner, watching a game show on television. "Hi, Millie Bug."

Her heart did a happy leap. He remembered her! "I'm going to get some decorations from the attic. Want to help me?"

Darrel turned the television off and stood up. "That depends. What holiday is it?"

He didn't remember everything, it seemed. Oh, well. She would take what she could get. "It's almost Halloween."

"Don't forget the skeleton," he said.

She smiled. The eight-foot-tall self-inflating skeleton had always been his favorite. "I won't." She just hoped it still worked.

Halloween had always been her dad's favorite holiday, but it had been several years since they had celebrated it. Without children around, it seemed pointless, her mother had said. The truth was it was too painful to try to enjoy the holiday when her father didn't understand what was going on.

But now that Stacy had two girls who were the perfect age for trick-or-treating, her mother insisted on decorating both the inside and the outside of the house. Mom promised to stock up on candy while in Springerville, but Millie suspected she would return with a trunk full of new decorations as well.

How happy would her mother be to see Darrel enjoying the holiday again? As quickly as the thought lifted her spirits, they fell. How long would it last? By the time Mom got home, he might forget again.

Her father cheered when she emerged from the attic with the box of Halloween decorations. Taking the box from her, he carried it to the kitchen and placed it on the table. Together, they went through the items.

"I can't believe your mother kept this mask," he said, holding up a hockey mask. "What movie was this from?"

"Friday the 13th." She was only eight when her three oldest brothers convinced her to sneak into their room and watch the horror film with them.

Brian had declined to watch the movie. He and Randon went outside to try out Brian's home-made telescope instead. It wasn't until years later that Millie learned Randon was terrified of horror movies.

Darrel laughed. "Your mother was so mad that the boys let you watch that movie. She was sure you'd have nightmares for weeks."

Millie smiled. "Mom wanted to ground them for it."

"As I recall—" he nodded "—you were the one who ended up getting grounded."

She lifted her chin. "Which wasn't fair. It wasn't my fault Collin ended up with ten stitches in his head."

"Not your fault?" He waved the mask in the air. "You jumped out at them wearing this and scared them half to death. Collin was so scared he ran into the door and busted his head open."

She took the mask from him and wiped the dust way.

Darrel leaned closer to her. "I was so proud of you."

"For scarring my brother?"

"No." He shook his head. "For standing up for yourself and letting those boys know not to mess with you."

Every year after that, they tried to get even with her, but Darrel always warned her what they were planning and Millie managed to turn the tables on them. "We made a good team, didn't we?"

"We sure did, Millie Bug." He yawned. "I wonder what they're planning this year? I hope they don't have a football game on Halloween."

Her heart sank a little. Even when he remembered, he still forgot little things. Like the fact that her oldest brother had been out of high school for seventeen years.

He yawned again.

"Why don't you go watch TV for a little while?" She knew he would be asleep within five minutes of sitting in his recliner. He rarely missed an afternoon nap.

"That sounds like a good idea." He started to walk toward the living room. "Holler at me when you're ready for me to hang the lights outside."

She waited a few minutes and then peeked into the living room. Sure enough, he was sound asleep with the remote in his hand. She glanced at the clock. Her mother would be back from her weekly shopping trip soon and she wanted to surprise her by making a jack-o'-lantern for her.

She moved the decorations to the dining room table and spread newspaper over the kitchen table. She hummed to herself as she sank her knife deep into the flesh of the pumpkin on the table in front of her. After removing the top, she used a large spoon to remove the pumpkin seeds and guts.

After the third try, she gave up and used her hands. Slime squished between her fingers as she scooped out the pumpkin guts.

Millie flicked the last few icky bits of pumpkin onto the newspaper that covered the table. She washed her hands and went to check on her dad.

He was still sound asleep. She leaned against the doorway and watched him for a moment. Her heart swelled. Overall, the day had been...perfect. Perfectly normal. She returned to the kitchen.

She picked up her phone and searched for pumpkin design ideas. Wow. When she was little, giving a jack-o'-lantern fangs inside his smile was considered artistic. She scrolled until she found one she thought she could do.

It didn't take long to draw the design on the pumpkin. The tricky part was carving it. One slip and the entire design would be ruined. She was deep in concentration when she heard the doorbell.

She stepped into the foyer and saw Randon standing on the opposite side of the screen door. He was wearing the dark green sweater she'd given him for Christmas the last time he was home on leave. Although she couldn't remember it fitting him as snug then as it did now. It brought out the green flecks in his hazel eyes.

"Hi." She leaned against the door frame.

He shoved his hands in the front pocket of his jeans. "Hi."

What was he doing here? Whatever he'd discussed with her mother yesterday seemed to have helped. He didn't seem as sullen.

He glanced over her shoulder. "Laura told me to be here at four."

Millie frowned. Why would her mother do that? She was rarely home from shopping before four o'clock. "Mom went to Springerville. You want to come in and wait?"

He shook his head. "No. I'll stop by later."

"Okay." She closed the screen door and walked away without looking back to see what he was doing.

A bubble of pride rose in her chest as she walked back to the kitchen. She hadn't asked him what he wanted. She hadn't begged him to come in. She hadn't done any of the things she would normally do.

She picked up the carving knife to go back to work on the pumpkin. Guilt tugged at her and she pulled her cell phone from the back pocket of her jeans. Her mother had to have a reason to have told Randon to be at the house so early.

Hopefully, Mom was still in Springerville, or at least close enough to the town to get service. She pressed the call button and waited.

"Hello? Is everything all right?" Mom's voice held a hint of worry.

"Dad is fine," Millie said. "Randon knocked on the door a few minutes ago and—"

"He remembered!" Mom seemed delighted. "He's going with you to help set up the community center for the Harvest Festival."

"What? Why?" Helping to set up for the annual festival was a Gibson family tradition. At least it had been until a few years ago and Darrel was no longer able to help. When Brian was in high school, they always invited Randon to come along. Every year he said no.

"Because Tricia needs the extra help and since your father and I can't do it anymore, Randon is filling in."

Millie frowned. That still didn't explain why he had shown up so early. "Setup doesn't start until five. Why did you tell him to be here so early?"

"Did I?" Mom's voice rose an octave. "I must have got my times mixed up. I'll be home soon, so offer him some food and keep him company until I get home."

Millie shook her head. Her mother was the most organized person she knew. Getting times wrong was out of the question. "He already left. He said he'd come back later."

"Why didn't you tell him to come in and wait?" The disappointment in her tone was evident.

"I did, Mom," Millie said. "He didn't want to."

Mom sighed. "I'm on my way home now. We'll get it sorted out when I get there."

Millie disconnected the call. Was this her mother's latest plan? Pushing the two of them together to allow them to determine what their true feelings were? She already knew. He cared about her...just not enough to stay for her.

A movement outside the screen door caught her eye. Randon was sitting on the steps of the front porch.

"I thought you were going to come back later," she said through the screen door.

"I was." He shrugged. "But your mom texted that she was almost here and told me to wait."

She shook her head. She was going to have to have a long chat with her mother. "Am I so hard to be around that you would rather sit outside?"

"No." He stood up and turned to face her, shoving his hands in the front pockets of his jeans. "I didn't want to bother you."

"You're going to bother me whether you're in the house or on the porch. You might as well come in." She pushed the door open.

Randon hesitated.

Millie let out a huff. "What's your problem? Are you afraid I'm going to throw myself at you?"

"No." He lifted his gaze to look at her. "That's not what I'm worried about."

"Then what's the pro—"

"Elizabeth! When did you get here?" Millie's father stood in the archway between the foyer and the living room. He smiled at her and shuffled across the entryway to hug her.

All the joy from the day disappeared as he hugged her. When he stepped back, she took his hand. "I'm not Elizabeth. I'm Millie."

Darrel cocked his head slightly and looked at Millie. "Where is Elizabeth?"

"Your sister died ten years ago." Millie guided him back to the living room.

Her mother insisted on always telling him the truth, even when he was confused, but Millie knew it would only help for a little while.

She picked up a photo album from the coffee table. She sat on the sofa and motioned for him to sit next to her. "Here, Dad. Let's look at some pictures to help you."

Darrel opened the album that his wife had made especially for him. Next to pictures, there was a note about each person explaining who they were. His fingers touched the page with Millie's picture on it. "Millie," he said with a sigh.

"Yes, Dad." She glanced up to see Randon looking at them with an alarmed expression. "I'm going to be a little busy for a few minutes. How good are you at carving pumpkins?"

He shrugged. "Don't know. I never tried."

She nodded toward the kitchen. "I wanted to have it done before Mom got home. It's on the kitchen table. Could you finish it for me?"

He didn't say a word. He just nodded and disappeared.

For the next half hour, Millie sat with her father as he looked at the pictures. Sometimes he asked questions. Other times he just stared at the photographs. The hardest ones were the pictures of family members that had passed on. Tears welled in his eyes and he experienced the grief of losing them all over again.

"I'm back!" Mom called from the porch.

Before Millie could get up, Randon was at the door, holding it open for her.

Mom's eyes widened when she noticed what Millie and Darrel were doing. She gave Millie a questioning look. Millie frowned and shook her head slightly.

Randon took the grocery bags from her mother. "I'll put these away and get the rest of the things from your car."

"Thank you," she whispered and hurried to sit next to her husband on the sofa.

As soon as Mom took over the photo album, Millie went to help Randon with the shopping bags.

"Are you okay?" Randon handed her a shopping back from the trunk of the car.

"Not really." Millie's throat was thick. "We've known this was coming for years, but it doesn't make it any easier."

He nodded and picked up the last bag of groceries and followed her into the house.

Millie set a shopping bag on the table. The pumpkin on the table grinned at her. It wasn't the simple design she'd chosen. "You did a great job with the pumpkin. Better than I could have done."

"I doubt that." Randon put a gallon of milk into the refrigerator. "You were always more artistic than you admitted."

"We better get to the community center," she said when the last of the groceries had been put away.

"What about all these?" He pointed to the stack of decorations her mother had bought.

"We'll deal with it later." Millie grabbed her purse and opened the back door.

When Randon got in the car and fastened his seat belt, she cast him a sideways glance. "How did my mom rope you into doing this?"

"She thinks being around people will help me." His voice was hardly more than a mumble.

"Help you with what?" She tried to keep the bitterness from her voice. "I mean, it's not like you need to adjust to being a civilian. You're going right back to a military-style life, so why bother?"

"It's not that simple." He stared out the window. "My application was accepted, but I have to go through a medical evaluation before Bravos will assign me to a unit."

Millie sensed the trepidation in his voice and

she sighed. "Are you worried that you won't pass? How bad is your shoulder?"

"It's not my shoulder." His voice quivered. "It's my head."

Alarm bells rang in her ears. His shoulder wasn't the only injury he'd received when he was in Kuwait. Her nursing instincts kicked into high gear. "I thought your concussion was considered minor. Are you having headaches? Nausea?"

He shook his head. "My brain is fine. My mind... not so much."

She started the car and backed out of the driveway. Focusing on the road would give her time to sort through all the questions she wanted to ask him.

"Go ahead," Randon said.

"What?" She glanced around, looking to see if something was outside of the vehicle.

"Say whatever it is you're wanting to say."

She lifted her chin. "I wasn't going to say anything."

He laughed softly. "The wheels in your head are spinning so fast even I can hear them. Besides, you always bite your bottom lip when you're trying to hold your tongue."

She pulled in front of the community center, put her car in Park and turned to face him. "I have some questions."

One corner of his mouth turned up in a faint smile. "What do you want to know?"

Her brow wrinkled as she tried to figure out how to ask without upsetting him. From the cryptic things he had said, he was aware that he had PTSD. The question was, would he admit it to her? Or even to himself? Admitting the problem was the first step in dealing with it.

She took a deep breath. "When you said that it's your mind you're worried about, exactly what do you mean?"

"Laura didn't tell you?"

Her mother knew? Millie frowned. "No."

"I have PTSD." His voice didn't falter. "The only part of the evaluation I'm worried about is where they check to see how well I'm handling it."

The tension in her shoulders dissipated. At least he admitted that he had issues. That was more than some soldiers could do. "That's not uncommon for people who've experienced what you have. Does it interrupt your day-to-day life?"

He shrugged, his gaze avoiding hers. "Yes and no. I'm fine for a while. Then something happens…"

Millie didn't push him to finish the sentence. She waited a moment, but he didn't seem to want to say anything more. "What triggers it?"

"I don't know," he said. "Dr. Harlow didn't notice any kind of pattern. He thought getting away from the base for a while might help."

"Has it?"

He shook his head.

She furrowed her brow. "Why would you want to go back? If being in the military is what caused your PTSD, why put yourself in a position to make it even worse?"

"I have some unfinished business over there." Randon's face tightened. "Besides, what else can I do? It's the only thing I'm good at."

She hated that he always put himself down. "You're good at lots of things," she said. "You can do anything you want."

"Right now, I want to learn how to get my PTSD under control so I can go back to Kuwait."

There was an urgency in his voice she didn't understand. Whatever was fueling his desire to go back overseas was bigger than concern for his own safety or well-being.

She took a deep breath and exhaled it slowly. "And you think helping to set up for the festival will help?"

"I hope." His face tightened. "I need to see if I can handle being around a crowd."

"And if you can't?"

"Then I'll find a way to do it. I have to. This is my last chance to make things right."

Her stomach twisted into knots. The thought of him putting himself in harm's way again terrified her. But there was something in his voice that scared her even more. He was determined to go back. What would happen if he wasn't able to?

She swallowed hard. "I've done a lot of research

on PTSD. Do you want this job bad enough to let me help you?"

"You would do that?"

"Yes." She would do anything to make him happy. Even if it meant losing him.

CHAPTER SIX

RANDON SAT IN the car for a few seconds after Millie exited the vehicle. Would she really help him? *Could* she really help him? She'd only been a nurse for a couple of years and how much experience could she get with PTSD in Coronado?

Randon had been surprised that Laura suggested he come to the festival setup with Millie. He knew Millie and her mother were very close and he assumed Millie told her that their conversation at the cabin the other night had ended badly.

The hurt in Millie's eyes when he said he wasn't staying in Coronado bothered him. After all, six years ago he'd practically confessed his love for her (not in those exact words) and they planned a future together. Three short years later, all his hopes were dashed when she told him she wouldn't leave Coronado.

It was better this way. He had nothing to offer her, especially now.

Millie was halfway up the sidewalk to the community center before she must have realized he wasn't following her. She turned to look at him. He got out of the car and walked toward her. She turned and resumed walking toward the large metal building in the center of the property.

Inside, people milled around setting up tables and hanging decorations on the walls.

"Millie!" A woman rushed over to them. "I was just looking for you."

She paused in front of them. "You must be Randon."

"Yes, ma'am." The woman looked vaguely familiar, but he couldn't place her.

"What do you need us to do?" Millie asked her.

"Can you start bringing in the chairs?"

"Yes, ma'am." Randon nodded. "Where are they?"

"Yes, ma'am?" The woman grinned at him. "I like you. They're in the storage shed out back."

"You heard the woman," Millie said. "Let's go."

He followed Millie out the back door and across the yard to the storage shed. "Who was that?"

"Tricia Johnson. She retired from teaching last year and moved back to Coronado this summer. But she can't seem to slow down and runs everything from church yard sales to the PTO."

"Moved back?" Randon couldn't place her. She must have left a long time ago.

Millie propped the door to the shed open. "Do

you remember Denny Morgan? He owns the hardware store."

"Yes."

"That's his oldest daughter."

Randon frowned. "Is she Emily's mother?"

Denny's granddaughter, Emily, moved to Coronado while he was still in middle school and rumor had it that Emily's mother sent her away. The woman he just met didn't seem like the type to abandon a child.

"No. That's Denny's youngest daughter." Millie pointed to the chairs, folded up and leaning against each other on the far wall. "How many do you think she wants? She forgot to tell us."

Randon scanned the area, purely out of habit. This was Coronado. There weren't snipers hiding in the trees, but no matter how hard he tried, he couldn't force his body out of a state of constant alert.

She picked up a couple of chairs and moved to the side, letting him get his own. They carried them inside where Tricia was waiting to tell them where to place them before going back to the shed for more.

"You get those, I'll get these." Millie pointed to the ones closest to the door.

Randon slipped his hands under the back of the chairs to move them when a loud crash shook the inside of the shed. He dropped his chairs, automatically reaching for his weapon as he plastered himself to the wall. His breath came in ragged gasps as he inched toward the door to scan the perimeter.

"Randon." Millie touched his arm. "It was the chairs. The chairs fell."

His heart was in his throat and his pulse raced so fast a haze distorted his vision. He squeezed his eyes shut to clear his eyes.

It took a minute for Millie's words to penetrate the haze. He looked past her to the pile of chairs that had slid from where they were leaning against the wall.

He sank to the floor and buried his head in his hands. He moved away from her and leaned against the shed. His whole body shook and sweat clung to his forehead.

Her hand touched his chest. "Are you okay?"

He nodded, unable to speak. He closed his eyes and forced himself to inhale and exhale slowly.

When he opened his eyes, her hand was still on his chest, her face inches from his. Her expression was one of concern, but not fear. He lifted her hand and pushed it away. "Don't you know better than to touch someone when they're having a PTSD episode?"

She arched one eyebrow at him. "Depends on who's having it."

He'd been worried about having a PTSD episode while in the middle of a crowd. It might have been understandable. But the scrape of a chair hitting a metal wall was all it took to send him into a panic and have a meltdown.

Randon stood up. "I never should've come. I'm sorry."

His chest was still so tight he could barely breathe. All he wanted to do was get away.

Before he could take a step, she moved in front of him. "Don't even think about it."

He looked down at her. "This was a dumb idea."

"Go ahead. Run away." She glared at him and stepped back.

The expression on Millie's face when he opened his eyes was frozen in his mind. Concern, mixed with sympathy. He hated that look. He could've handled it if she'd laughed at him and teased him for being jumpy. But that's not what she did. She wanted to know if he was okay. She felt *sorry* for him. The one person who was never supposed to look at him like that.

"I'm sorry." He stepped around her, searching the grounds for the quickest escape.

"No." There was an edge to her voice. "Don't be sorry. You're just doing what everyone expects you to do."

He froze and whirled around. "What's that supposed to mean?"

"Since you're giving up, I can only assume you won't pass your medical exam. But that's no problem. You can lie around and wait for your disability check to come in every month."

"I'm not giving up," he snapped. "I just need to be more prepared. I need…"

"What are you really scared of?"

Of having you look at me with pity again. Of having PTSD turn me into someone else. Of losing myself. He swallowed. "Nothing."

Millie shook her head. "You're not a very good liar, Randon. You don't have to be scared of PTSD. You're already coping with it better than I expected you to be."

Coping with it? She thought he was coping? He almost laughed. "How could you think that?"

Her face softened. "Because as soon as you realized what was happening, you were able to calm yourself down. You couldn't do that if you weren't aware of what was happening."

His stomach clenched. "For now. What if it's worse next time? What if I hurt you or someone else?"

Her eyes widened. "Is that what you're worried about?"

Randon nodded. "I've seen men fly into a rage and lash out at everyone around them. Other soldiers. Doctors. Even their own wives. It's like they turned into a different person."

His chest felt heavy. Bravos wouldn't keep him on if he had a reaction every time he was in public. The future he'd carefully mapped out was evaporating. "It's better if I stay away from people until I know I can control myself."

"Yeah. You're probably right. You'd be better off home alone." She pulled her car keys out of her pocket. "On the way home, want me to drive you to the liquor store to stock up on whiskey and vodka? You can hide the bottles under the sink like your dad did."

"I'm not my dad," Randon said through gritted teeth. He wouldn't even take the pain medication his doctor prescribed for him because he was scared he would become addicted.

"Then stop acting like him."

His face flushed with anger. "I've never acted like him."

Millie snorted. "He didn't know how to deal with his PTSD, so he self-medicated with a bottle. If you go back to that empty cabin and shut yourself off from the world, sooner or later, you'll do the same thing."

"I'm not like him." Randon clenched his fists. "I'm trying to protect people, not hide from them."

"If you believe that, then you're lying to yourself." Millie gave him an odd smile. "Huh. He was a liar, too."

"I don't need this." Randon turned to walk away. His whole body shook. All he wanted to do was run out to the middle of the forest and scream. Maybe even punch a tree.

Millie was right behind him. "Running away won't change anything." She grabbed his arm and turned him to face her.

"What do you want from me?" he snapped. "Why are you deliberately trying to push my buttons?"

Millie got in his face. "Are you mad yet?"

His breath came in ragged gasps. "Yes, I'm mad."

She lifted her chin. "Do you want to hit me?"

He froze. Was he scaring her? There wasn't a hint of fear in her blue eyes. "Of course not." Randon stepped away from her.

She crossed her arms and grinned. "You're welcome."

"What are you talking about?"

"You can control yourself. You're not dangerous," she said. Her voice returned to a normal level. "What you can't control are things that might trigger you, but we can find ways to help you deal with it."

He wasn't imagining it. She had been trying to make him mad. She'd done it to prove a point and it worked. He'd controlled his actions, even when he couldn't control his emotions. The tension rushed out of him and his muscles trembled.

Millie tucked one strand of bright red hair behind her ear. "Having an episode doesn't mean you're getting worse. It's not unusual for loud noises to trigger a reaction like that."

He bowed his head. "I don't want to turn into someone like my dad," he whispered.

She took his hands in hers, her blue eyes full of trust. "You're not going to. I won't let you."

"How?" His stomach was a hard knot.

Millie let out a deep sigh. "There are lots of different kinds of therapy, so give me some time to look into them."

Time? He didn't have much time. "I only have four weeks."

She nodded her understanding. "I know. Now let's get these chairs inside before someone comes looking for us."

MILLIE HELD HER breath until Randon walked back to the shed to pick up the fallen chairs. She could understand his fear. While in nursing school, she did her clinicals at a large hospital in Phoenix.

Her pulse raced as she remembered trying to comfort a family whose son had committed suicide not long after returning from deployment. Another patient was in the ICU after her husband went into a PTSD-induced rage and beat her almost to death.

Seeing what could happen after soldiers didn't get the help they needed scared her. Randon and her brother had already been deployed twice since joining the military, so she was determined to learn as much about it as she could. She only hoped it was enough.

She walked back into the shed and Randon handed a few chairs to her. His face was pinched, but the tension in his shoulders was gone. With two chairs on either side of her, she hooked her hands under the backs and followed Randon, who carried four on each arm, back inside the community center.

It was busier than when they'd left the building. People were moving tables around while Tricia checked their placement on her map. She looked up and saw Millie and Randon. She waved and headed toward them.

"You can lean the chairs against the wall, right there. People can set up their own chairs after their booth is ready."

Millie nodded. "What else do you need?"

Tricia looked Randon over. "Luke and Noah Sterling are bringing in a load of hay. Can you help them unload it?"

"Yes, ma'am." Randon nodded.

Tricia pointed in the same direction they had just come in from. "Good. They should be pulling up in the back any minute."

Randon turned to walk back outside, but Tricia put her hand on Millie's arm to stop her. "I have another job for you."

"I really need to stay with him," she said.

Tricia smiled. "Your boyfriend will be just fine without you for a few minutes, I promise."

She opened her mouth to argue, but closed it again. Her gaze followed Randon out the door. He was fine. He would be fine.

Tricia led her to the front of the building and outside where even more activity was going on. While the area in front of the building wasn't as expansive as out back, there was room for several booths to be set up by the front entrance. Each booth had a tall propane patio heater next to it.

A pickup truck had backed up to the sidewalk and a man was unloading pumpkins from the bed of the truck. Some of the women from the Ladies' Auxiliary were moving the pumpkins from the truck to the booths.

Millie glanced at the man with the pumpkins. "Excuse me, Tricia," she said. "I'll be right back."

She hurried over to the truck and tapped the man's shoulder.

The man jerked around. His face lit up when he saw her. "Millie!" He lifted her off her feet and swung her around.

"Hey, Coy!" She hugged him back. "Since you haven't called me to bandage you up, this must not be a forced visit. How long have you been home?"

Coy Tedford was Sheriff Tedford's son and Stacy's cousin. He was a bull rider, so he traveled a lot. The only time she usually saw him was when he came home to recover from an injury.

"I just got here," he said. "I stopped and picked up pumpkins in Duncan, so I'm dropping them off before heading to Dad's."

"How long are you staying?"

Coy shrugged and pushed his cowboy hat back a little. "I'm not sure. A couple of weeks."

Millie raised one eyebrow. She couldn't remember the last time Coy had stayed in town for more than a few days.

She glanced at the welcome booth were Tricia was studying her clipboard. "I better get going. I'm sure I'll see you around."

His brows furrowed for a moment. "Hey, Millie." He paused for a moment. "Are you going to the dance after the festival?"

His question caught her off guard. And why was he looking at her like he was nervous? Alarm bells rang in her head. Was he trying to ask her out? As far as she knew, Coy had never dated anyone except Becky. She'd heard they broke up last winter, but she didn't believe it.

"Um…" She swallowed. "I'm not sure."

"Luke's playing some of his new songs that night, so a bunch of us were going to go. You're welcome to join us."

Relief rushed through her. "Oh. Yeah. Sure. I'll ask him." She wondered if Randon would want to come.

Her cheeks were hot with embarrassment as she hurried over to Tricia. She couldn't believe she thought Coy was about to ask her on a date.

"You're back." Tricia handed her the clipboard. "Here's a list of all the booths. There are boxes of prizes in the office. Can you make sure every booth has a box?"

Millie took the clipboard from her. "Sure."

Once inside the office area, she spotted a collapsible wagon next to the door. She filled the wagon with boxes and started with the booths at the back of the community center. Only because there were more there, she reasoned. It had nothing to do with the fact that she could see Randon if she was behind the building.

In the back corner of the large lot, Randon was helping the Sterling brothers unload hay from a flatbed truck. The brothers weren't small men, but Randon towered over them. Well, he towered over most people. He picked up and moved the large hay bales like they weighed next to nothing instead of close to one hundred pounds.

She was about to head back inside to get another stack of boxes when, out of the corner of her eye, she saw Randon stiffen and drop the bale of hay he was moving. His shoulder! Why had he agreed to help move heavy things with his shoulder? Her heart skipped a beat and she started to walk toward him. Before she got halfway across the yard, he cupped his shoulder with his hand and rolled the joint around before picking the bale back up.

Luke saw her walking toward them and shook his head slightly. Millie stopped and turned around before Randon saw her. He wouldn't appreciate her running to him like he was a hurt child. She had to trust that Luke and Noah would keep an eye out for him.

The next time she came outside, the men had finished unloading the hay. They were standing next to Noah's truck. Coy had joined them and the four men were laughing. She relaxed and focused on the job Tricia had given her.

A half hour later, the outside yard was lit up with lights and most of the work had moved to decorating inside the building and out of the cold.

"Are you done?" Randon appeared behind her.

"Almost." She reached as high as she could, trying to tape a paper pumpkin to the wall.

He took the decoration from her and held it up. "Say when."

She eyed the pumpkin and motioned for him to move it up and to the left. "Right there."

"Shrimp," he teased, and taped the pumpkin in place.

Her heart swelled hearing his nickname for her. "You're in a good mood."

He frowned for a moment before a smile slowly crossed his face. "I am. I actually had a good time."

"Of course, you did." She shook her head. "You got to set up outside with the other guys, while I was stuck in here listening to gossip and getting advice."

Randon chuckled. "And you loved every minute."

She sighed. "I did."

She loved Coronado. She loved everything about it. Even the little old women who asked personal questions about her private life and offered unsolicited advice.

"Speaking of gossips—" his eyes scanned the room "—I haven't seen the Reed sisters. Aren't they always involved in things like this?"

"They don't like to drive at night," Millie said. "Tricia offered to give them a ride, but Edith has a cold, apparently, so Margaret said they would stay home tonight and help out tomorrow, if Edith is feeling better."

"How old are they now?"

"They just turned seventy-eight." Millie checked in on them often, especially in the winter. "They're both still sharp as a tack and just as busy as ever."

"That's good." His voice was soft as he followed her to her car.

When they got to the car, she tilted her head back and looked up. "Look at the sky. Have you ever seen so many stars?"

"Yes." Randon opened the door and got into the passenger seat.

She frowned and got into the cab of the car. "When? Where?"

He laughed. "Coronado's not the only place you can see stars, you know. The sky above Kuwait is dark and so broad you see millions of them."

"Hmm." She started the car. "This sky is still better."

He laughed again. "You need to get out of Coronado more often."

She pressed her lips together. Her brothers told her that all the time. They couldn't understand that she didn't want to be anywhere else.

"Are you going to the dance after the festival tomorrow night?"

She stared at him. "I haven't decided. Why?"

He shrugged. "The guys were talking about it. Luke's trying out a few of his new songs."

"I heard that," she said.

"Did you know Coy and Becky broke up?"

His mood was completely different from what it had been on the car ride to the festival. She stifled a grin. "Yes. Last winter. Hard to believe, isn't it?"

"When Coy told Luke he had a date for the dance, I couldn't believe it." Randon shook his head. "I asked where Becky was and they all got real quiet. Then Coy told me they broke up and tried to act like he didn't care. But you can tell he does."

Coy had a date? That made her feel better, knowing Coy hadn't been asking her out. "Who's he dating?"

"Don't know." Randon shrugged. "We all asked him, but he wouldn't say. He said he'd have to see if she shows up tomorrow."

Millie frowned. "I can't imagine Coy with anyone besides Becky."

"Me, either. It would almost be worth going to the dance to find out who the mystery woman is."

She took a deep breath. "There'll be a lot of people there. And the Watering Hole is a much smaller space than the community center."

"I know." He frowned. "Let's go to the festival first. If it goes okay, we could try."

"Sounds like a good plan," she said.

CHAPTER SEVEN

RANDON OPENED HIS EYES. The room was flooded with light. That couldn't be right. He rubbed his eyes and looked again. He sat straight up in bed. It was morning. Had he really slept most of the night?

He hopped out of bed and stretched. His body hummed with excitement. After talking to Laura the other day, the weight on his chest had lifted. But after spending the day with Millie yesterday, he'd felt a flutter of hope that he hadn't felt for a long time.

This evening, they were going to the Harvest Festival. He still wasn't sure he should go, but Millie had promised to find some techniques for him to try if he felt the walls closing in. The only way to know which technique worked best was to subject himself to a large crowd. Millie promised they wouldn't go into the building until he was ready. Until then, they would walk around the outside activities. If he started to feel overwhelmed, it would be easy for them to disappear for a while.

Opening the drawer of his nightstand, he pulled out the packet from Bravos and scanned the list of requirements again. As a military contracting company, they gave preference to ex-military applicants. While they were willing to overlook the shoulder injury that got him discharged from the military, they would not overlook psychological issues that might impede performance, such as PTSD. That's why they gave him an additional thirty days before reporting for the medical evaluation.

Could Millie help? It was a chance he was willing to take, although spending any time with Millie was dangerous. She was bright, funny, had a great sense of humor and was fiercely loyal. It wouldn't take much for him to completely lose his heart to her.

Most people thought he joined the Army because Brian did. After all, they'd been inseparable since second grade, so no one was surprised when they enlisted together. But he hadn't done it for Brian. He'd done it for Millie. If he could find a place in the Army, if he could stand out and climb the ranks, he could finally prove that he was worthy of someone like her. Now, the Army didn't want him and he was right back where he started.

He dressed quickly and tied the laces of his sneakers. He opened the back door and stepped onto the deck. The forest behind the cabin exploded with color. Orange, yellow and red leaves decorated the aspen trees growing in between the dark green of the pines. It was too bad he didn't have any art supplies anymore. He would love to capture the scene on canvas.

That was odd. He hadn't missed painting since he entered the Army. Now his fingers longed for a brush. There wasn't a store in Coronado that sold art supplies, but Springerville did. Maybe he would ask Millie to drive him. Maybe they could have lunch at the Mexican restaurant she loved so much.

No. That would be a bad idea. If he spent too much time around her, he might forget that he had business in Kuwait to take care of. Most of all, he might forget her brother was his best friend. She was off-limits. How many times had Brian told him that?

Not that it mattered to Millie. She was ten years old the first time she told him she loved him. She came home from school crying because a boy had been picking on her. The next morning, he walked her to the playground and found out who the boy was. He very nicely told Aaron Walker to leave Millie alone. Okay. Maybe it wasn't nicely, but Aaron got the point and didn't bother Millie again. Millie was so grateful to him she declared she loved him and was going to marry him.

For several months after that, she followed him around everywhere until Brian finally put a stop to it. Randon wasn't sure what Brian said to her, but she stopped trying to hang out with them, except at the Gibson home.

By the time Millie started high school, she had a very strong sense of fairness and seemed to make it her mission to ensure everyone was treated equally. She couldn't resist a project, especially one that involved the underdog. And Randon fit that description to a tee. Once she got something in her head, it was impossible for her to think about something else. When she overheard one of the high school teachers telling him he'd never amount to anything, she jumped in to defend him.

After that, she was constantly suggesting things he could do to improve his image. She checked to see if he'd turned in his homework, encouraged him to volunteer for school activities. There was no end to the things she wanted him to do. It didn't end until he graduated from high school.

It wasn't completely one-sided, though. He looked out for her, too. The difference was she didn't know he was doing it. When she was a freshman, Dane Kirby took an interest in her; he got offended when she turned him down. When Randon found out Dane had been harassing her, he made it clear that bothering Millie would bother him. By the end of the school year, most of the boys were afraid to ask Millie out.

When Millie was a sophomore, she moped around the house because no one would ask her to go to the high school prom, so Randon asked Brian for permission to take her. He hoped Brian would give him his blessing, since it was their senior year. But no. Brian told him that Millie was off-limits. He said it was because if things didn't work out, he'd have to take his sister's side and he'd be out a best friend. Part of him always wondered if Brian really thought Randon wasn't good enough for her.

He thought he'd kept his feelings for her a secret and—ten-year-old Millie's declaration of love aside—he had no reason to believe she thought of him as anything more than a big brother. Just before he left for basic training, she stopped by the cabin to talk to him. While trying to tell him something, she got embarrassed and flustered. Then she kissed him. Maybe it was because he was leaving. Maybe because he was tired of fighting how he felt. Maybe he was just acting a fool. Whatever the reason, when she kissed him, he kissed her back.

When he left for basic training, he was so scared she'd fall in love with someone else while he was gone that he asked her to wait for him. She laughed and told him she'd been waiting for him since she was ten years old, so a few more years wouldn't matter.

But they did.

In the Army, he found something he'd been missing his entire life. Structure. Brotherhood.

For the first time, he felt like he was part of something bigger than himself. He belonged. He knew Millie wanted to stay in Coronado, especially after her father was diagnosed with Alzheimer's, but if she really loved him, she'd come with him.

While home on leave before deployment to Kuwait, he told her he wanted to make a career of the Army. That's when she told him she wouldn't leave Coronado. He'd been hurt, but he thought he could change her mind. He even told Brian of his plans. Only Brian wasn't on board with it. They'd been fighting about it the night the ambush happened. After that, none of it mattered anymore.

No, it would be better if he didn't spend much more time with Millie. He did one last stretch to loosen his muscles and went down the steps to the trail that disappeared into the forest.

His footsteps didn't make a sound on the trail. Fallen leaves lay so thick that the path was invisible but he knew the trail was there. As he went deeper into the woods, the trail grew rocky and uneven and he had to watch his footing. A feeling of calm enveloped him as he concentrated on his steps and breathing.

The path leveled out and Randon was able to enjoy the scenic trail. He'd never appreciated the beauty of the Arizona White Mountains until he moved away. He caught a glimpse of a young pine tree with a large spot of bark that had been rubbed off and he smiled. When a bull elk's antlers were finished growing, the velvet that protected them needed to be scraped off. They accomplished it by scraping their antlers against small flexible trees. While it rarely killed the tree, it did leave a scar on the trunk.

A couple of miles into the trail, he came to a stream crossing. He stopped to catch his breath, still disappointed that he needed to.

The snapping of a twig caused him to freeze. His hands reached for a weapon before he realized he didn't have one. His heart pounded in his ears and he slowly scanned the area. When a strong, musky odor assaulted his nose, he relaxed. It took him a few moments, but he finally located a bull elk on top of a nearby ridge. The animal stood still, staring at him, his massive antlers showing the scars of recent fights. The smell alone was enough to tell him the bull was still in the rut, but the swollen neck confirmed it. He moved backward slowly, knowing when bulls were looking to mate, they were unpredictable.

The elk lowered his head and bugled. The sound echoed through the forest. It was a sound like no other on earth. The large male was calling to his harem, making sure that Randon's presence wouldn't go unnoticed. Randon searched the trail in front of him to make sure there were no cow elk in his path. On the other side of the ridge, he could hear the answering calls and his shoulders relaxed. They were moving away from him and not worried about him.

When he was a safe distance away, he resumed his jog back to the cabin. The stairs to the back deck groaned as he stepped on them. A sharp crack sounded as one of the boards started to give way. Luckily, he was moving too fast to fall through. One more thing to repair. His list was getting longer every day.

He fixed himself a bowl of cereal and looked at the list of things he needed to do. He was rinsing his bowl in the sink when a knock sounded on the door. The knock got louder.

Three older women smiled at him, each one holding a dish of some kind. The woman in front was married to the pastor of Coronado Community Church.

"Mrs. Jones." Randon opened the door.

"Hello, dear." Mrs. Jones reached out with one chubby hand and patted his cheek as she walked by.

The other women followed, nodding to him as they made their way to the kitchen.

The first woman, a thin woman with silver hair and glasses perched on the end of a hawklike nose, set a large casserole dish on the counter. "Hello, Randon. I'm Alissa Brandenburg."

"Nice to meet you," he said, still wondering why the three women were at his house.

"I'm Kelly Franks," the last woman smiled and

nodded at him before bustling past the others. She opened the refrigerator and placed her tray inside. Frowning, she began rearranged the contents on the shelves to make room for the other dishes as well.

"You've been busy," Mrs. Jones said. "The last time I was here, you couldn't even see the floor for all the filth."

When he was in grade school, Mrs. Jones would pick him up and take him to Sunday school, but as far as he could remember, she never came inside the house. The one and only time she tried, his father had made it clear she wasn't welcome.

She must have noticed the look of confusion on his face. "We brought food to your father several times after he got sick."

"And he let you?" Randon's eyebrows raised.

Mrs. Brandenburg looked at the other women. "I don't think Millie gave him much choice."

"Millie?" What did she have to do with his father?

"Yes," Mrs. Jones said. "She was his home-health nurse and she set up a meal train for him. I think she's the only person who could go toe to toe with him and win."

He frowned. Why hadn't Millie said anything about taking care of his father? "Not to be rude or anything, but why are you here?"

"To welcome you home, of course," Mrs. Jones said.

"Yes," Mrs. Brandenburg added. "And as members of the VFW Ladies' Auxiliary, it's our job to welcome our heroes home and make sure they're taken care of."

Heroes. Randon's heart began to race. He tried to swallow, but he couldn't. He was no hero. "Thanks for dropping by." He walked to the front door, hoping they got the hint.

"I left my number on the counter," Mrs. Jones said. "I'll pick up the dishes when you're done."

He nodded as they walked out the door. As soon as they were gone, he leaned against the wall. Inhale. Exhale. Inhale. Exhale. He closed his eyes and waited for his hands to stop shaking.

He knew he'd overreacted. The women didn't know about what had happened in Kuwait. They did the same thing for all the returning service members, whether they deserved it or not.

MILLIE GOT OUT of the car and tightened her ponytail. It had been a long day and all she wanted to do was sink into her oversized bathtub and relax before picking up Randon and going to the festival.

"Mom, I'm home." She frowned and closed the front door.

During the day, her mother left it open to allow fresh air to come through the screen door and cool the inside of the house. But the chilly October air was much too cold in the evenings, especially for her father.

"In here," Mom called from the kitchen.

The faint smell of smoke hung in the air and her mother was scrubbing a blackened pan in the sink. No wonder she had opened the door. "What happened?"

Mom's smile was strained. "Your father decided to make himself a grilled cheese sandwich."

"I see." Millie didn't dare ask any questions for fear her mother would break down in tears.

"He spilled shampoo all over the bathroom." Mom put her hands on her hips. "I was in there cleaning it up—it wasn't that I wasn't paying attention."

Her voice rose an octave as she talked and Millie wrapped an arm around her. "It's okay, Mom."

"No, it's not. He could've burned himself. Or burned the house down."

"But he didn't." Millie took a deep breath. "Between the two of us, we'll take care of him."

"What would I do without you?" Mom hugged her.

"I don't know." Millie shrugged. "I *am* the perfect daughter, after all."

"Of course, you are." She patted Millie's cheek. "How was your day?"

"Fine."

Mom returned to the sink and picked up the scrubbing brush again. "I left dinner in the oven for you."

"Thanks." Millie opened the oven and her eyes

widened at the amount of food. "Were you expecting company?"

"No," Mom said. "I was going to take some to Randon. Then the smoke alarm went off and your father got upset and..."

She scooped some food onto a paper plate. "It's okay. I'll take it to him when I pick him up."

"Do you two have plans tonight?"

Millie took a bite of mashed potatoes. "We're going to the Harvest Festival."

"Oh." A smile tickled the corners of Mom's mouth.

"And don't think I don't know what you were up to yesterday," she said between bites.

"I don't know what you're talking about." Mom continued to scrub the pan in the sink.

Millie shook her head. "You made sure Randon got here before you did so we would be forced to talk."

"That's silly." Mom placed the pan in the drying rack on the counter. "Do you think going to the festival is a good idea?"

"You're the one who told him he needed to be around people," Millie reminded her.

"In small settings. He's not ready for something with that many people and that loud."

"We won't know until we try," Millie said. "We're going to take it slow and go to the outside activities first."

"And this is supposed to help him with his PTSD?" Her voice was skeptical.

"Yes. We know that sudden, loud noises trigger his PTSD. Now we need to see how well he can deal with crowded places. It's the only way we can determine the best strategies for him to cope with it." She glanced at the small backpack sitting on the table. She had spent hours researching different techniques to help him and had a bagful of tricks. Literally.

Mom dried her hands off with a towel. "Don't try to turn him into one of your projects."

Millie stared at her mother. "What are you talking about?"

"Remember back in high school when you heard a teacher say something mean about him, so you spent weeks following him around, telling him how to act and what to do to make teachers like him?" She stepped into the small laundry room right off the kitchen and returned holding a laundry basket full of towels.

"Mrs. Porter was a horrible woman. I don't know why they let her teach," Millie said.

"Regardless, Brian told me how much Randon hated you always trying to tell him what to do." Mom gave her a sad look.

Millie frowned. "He wasn't a project. I was just trying to help."

"I know. But, he thought you were trying to change him." Mom started folding the towels.

"No one wants to think the person they love will only love them back if they have to change."

Millie's mouth opened. "You think he loved me? Back then, I mean?"

"Yes. Maybe not the way you loved him, but he loved you." She placed the folded towels into the basket. "That's why it upset him so much when you came home from school crying because everyone but you had a date to the prom."

"I was sixteen. What sixteen-year-old doesn't want to go to the prom?" She frowned at the memory. "Brian offered to take me, but I was too embarrassed to go with my brother."

Mom picked up the laundry basket. "Brian offered because he was afraid Randon was going to."

Millie's eyes widened. "Why wouldn't Brian let him take me?"

"Would you want to risk letting your very best friend go out with your brother? If things worked out and you two fell in love and lived happily-ever-after, Brian would lose his best friend. If things didn't work out and you got hurt, Brian would lose his best friend."

"That's silly." Millie shook her head. "I could never come between Brian and Randon."

Millie's father stood in the door frame. "Laura, I can't find the *TV Guide*. Where did you put it?"

Mom set the basket back on the table. "We haven't gotten that magazine in fifteen years.

The television has a guide. What do you want to watch?"

Millie watched her parents walk away and fought back the tears. For now, he was able to respond when her mother corrected him, but how long would that last? Would he get angry and combative when he didn't recognize people around him? Would he shut down?

She threw her paper plate in the trash and picked up the laundry basket. She carried it to their bathroom to put away. The walls of the bathroom were covered with pictures. It was her mother's way of trying to keep her father's memory active. She scanned the walls. Her parents' wedding. School pictures of all their children. Family pictures. Thanksgivings. Christmases. Summer fishing trips. Fall hunting trips. Winter ski trips. A lifetime of memories in pictures. Would it be enough?

She reached up and touched a picture of Randon and Brian standing in front of Randon's old car. Her father had helped them work on it all winter. The whole family celebrated when they got it running.

Randon didn't think he was part of the family, but he was wrong. He thought he needed the military lifestyle to feel like he was part of a family. Or in his case, military contractor. He belonged here. She knew it. He knew it. She just needed to get him to admit it.

She placed the towels in the cabinet and glanced

at her watch. So much for relaxing in the bathtub for a half hour. She'd have to settle for a quick shower instead.

Fifteen minutes later, she grabbed a jacket and headed downstairs.

"Are you leaving now?" Mom called from the living room.

"Yes. I'm not sure how long I'll be gone." If things went well, would he still want to go to the dance?

She picked up the backpack from the table in the entryway. Randon might want to leave as soon as they got there. Or maybe some of the things she had in her bag could help him.

"Have fun." Mom crossed the room to her. "You were right. Randon needs to do this. I'm glad you're helping him."

CHAPTER EIGHT

THE DRIVE TO Randon's cabin didn't take long. The door opened before she got to the porch. "Hi."

"Hi," he replied.

"You look nice." She let her gaze sweep over him. He looked nothing like the lanky teenager he'd once been. His long-sleeve shirt emphasized how much he'd filled out since he joined the Army. She bit her bottom lip. Every single woman in town was going to ask her about him.

He gave her a crooked smile. "Thanks. So do you."

"I was afraid you might change your mind." She averted her gaze away from him so he couldn't tell how much he unnerved her.

"I almost did." He shrugged.

She frowned at him. "If you don't want to go, I understand."

"No. I think it's a good idea. I'm just a little nervous. I'll be fine as long as I have you for protection." He flashed her a teasing smile.

"What am I supposed to protect you from?" She turned to walk to the car.

"People."

"Well, rats," she said. "I left my scary Halloween costume at home."

"You don't need a costume to scare people away." He opened her car door for her.

"I'm not sure if that was a compliment or an insult." She slid into the seat and started the engine.

"A compliment." He shut her door and walked around to the passenger seat. "When you want to, you could make my drill sergeant look like a teddy bear."

She put the car into Reverse. "You really think I'm scary?"

"I think you're terrifying," he said. "But in all the right ways."

Millie was quiet for a moment. He hadn't meant to insult her, but she wasn't sure how else she was supposed to take it. Somehow, it didn't seem like the right time to pursue it.

She pointed to the small bag at his feet. "I brought some things to help. Just in case I'm not scary enough."

He bent down and picked it up from the floorboard. He opened the bag and went through the contents. "Ear plugs. Headphones. A stress ball. What's this?"

She looked at the item he was holding up. "It's called a fidget spinner. You hold the middle between your thumb and middle finger and you spin it around."

"Why?" Randon gave the toy an experimental spin.

"In case you need to do something with your hands. There's also a Pop It in there somewhere."

"This?" He stared at the rubber toy covered in raised circles.

"Yes." She grinned and reached across to him to push one of the circles. The toy made a small *pop* sound. "It's almost as fun as popping bubble wrap and, unlike bubble wrap, it's reusable."

He gave her an incredulous stare. "You know I'm not twelve, right?"

"Hey." She glared at him. "Don't make fun of me. Those things got me through nursing school."

"Are they supposed to distract me?"

"Yes. But unless something happens to trigger an episode, which I don't think it will, you shouldn't need them."

He stared at the items on his lap for a moment. "Will there be a lot of things there you think will trigger me?"

She shrugged. "Well, there won't be any fireworks or flashing lights tonight." Millie had even called Tricia to ask. "Also, the music won't be too loud if we stay outside."

The drive into town only took a few minutes. Even though the sun hadn't set yet, the Coronado Community Center was already lit up with orange and yellow lights. Electric lanterns lined the sidewalk and jack-o'-lanterns smiled from the doorway.

She didn't wait for Randon to come around to open the door. She got out and met him in front of the car. "Are you ready?"

His eyes darted around. "Not even close."

Randon had never liked crowded places. He rarely attended school dances or community functions, but Millie had never seen him like this. She could almost feel the anxiety rolling off him.

Coping method number one: distraction. "Doesn't this place look great?"

And it did. The normally drab outdoor space around the community center had been transformed into a sort of mini carnival with food booths and games. Hay bales were scattered around for seating and lights were strung between the booths. Homemade signs directed people to the activities.

Her chest swelled with pride. "We helped set it up, but it looks so much more magical tonight than it did yesterday."

She stopped in front of a roughly drawn map. "The PTO really upped their game this year. They added a hayride, a dunk tank and gunnysack races."

She started up the sidewalk toward the welcome booth and Randon was so close behind her she could hear him breathing. "Just so I know what to look for, exactly what is it about being around people that makes you the most anxious? So many in one place?"

"Not that." His mouth was set in a tight line.

"They ask too many questions. They want to thank me for my service and call me a…"

"Call you what?"

His gaze dropped to the ground. "A hero," he mumbled.

In the past, whenever Randon had been the center of attention, it was usually because he was in trouble. She would have thought he'd enjoy being praised for once, but she wasn't about to say anything.

She sighed as she scanned the crowd already gathering around the community center. "Just don't let anyone talk to you. That should be a piece of cake."

"I don't mind saying hello to people," he grumbled, "but there are some things I don't want to talk about."

"How will I know if you aren't liking the way a conversation is headed?"

"You always seemed to know when something made me uncomfortable before."

Millie didn't respond. What was she supposed to say? Nothing he'd done for the last fifteen years had escaped her attention. She knew him better than he knew himself.

RANDON LOOKED AROUND while Millie stopped to talk to Tricia at the welcome booth. His skin tingled all over. Yesterday, he thought there'd been a lot of people at the community center, but it was nothing compared to now. He didn't know this many people lived in Coronado.

It was the first time he'd been in a crowded area since the ambush in Kuwait. He'd underestimated how difficult it would be.

True to her word, Millie led him around the edge of the property, careful to stay away from the crowds. She glanced over her shoulder at him. "Are you looking for someone?"

"No."

"Then why do you keep looking around like that?"

He took a deep breath and held it for a moment before exhaling. "Force of habit, I guess."

She stopped walking and scanned the area. "So, what are you looking for? Or, I guess I should say, what would you be looking for if you were still in the Army?"

He straightened a little. "I would be watching for people who looked suspicious. Ones that might be hiding a weapon or ones that seemed to be watching people a little too closely."

"I get looking for a hidden weapon, but why ones that are watching closely?"

Her voice sounded sincere. He sensed that she was honestly trying to see the world through his eyes and wasn't just patronizing him.

The tension melted from his shoulders. "They might be a lookout for one of our HVTs, or—"

"What's an HVT?"

"High value target. Someone we're looking for, either for questioning or for capture." He pointed to the buildings across the street. "Snipers could be hiding up top, waiting for a target."

Her gaze followed his. "Is that all you look out for?"

Randon shrugged. "I look for the best escape routes."

"And these are normal things that you and my brother would look for every day?" Millie pressed her lips together. "I never realized how much we take for granted."

He stopped scanning and turned to look at her. His face softened. "Thank you."

"For what?" She cocked her head and looked at him.

"For not telling me I'm crazy."

She looped her arm through his and guided him toward the hay bales at the farthest edge of the property. They walked in silence for a few moments. She closed her eyes and inhaled. "I love the smell of fall."

Randon sniffed. The scents of cinnamon, spiced apples and kettle corn filled his nostrils.

He chuckled. "So does your mom. Your house always smelled like pumpkin spice from September until Thanksgiving."

She frowned. "Weird. She hasn't lit one candle this fall. I hadn't realized it until you said that."

"Millie!" a voice called from the face-painting booth.

"Hi, Khatia." She waved back. In a softer voice, she told Randon, "That's Stacy's oldest daughter. She's five."

A tall, stocky man was standing near the little girl. He saw them and walked over. "Randon Farr?"

"Yes, sir." Randon nodded. He almost didn't recognize Stacy's father. "How are you, Vince?"

Vince Tedford offered his hand to Randon. "Welcome home, son."

"Thank you."

Randon was surprised to see that Vince's eyes were clear and bright. He wasn't sure if he'd ever seen the man sober. Not only did he seem sober but he didn't reek of cigarette smoke for once.

A younger girl ran toward Vince. Her face had been painted like a cat. "Grandpa, look!"

Vince scooped her up. "Who is this? You sound like my little Marina, but you look like a cat."

"Meow," she said before bursting into a fit of giggles.

"And that's Marina, Stacy's other daughter," Millie said. "She's three."

Stacy walked over with Khatia right behind her. "Hi, Randon," she greeted him. "Welcome home."

"Thank you." Randon quickly shifted the attention from him. "Congratulations on your new family."

"Thanks!" Stacy beamed. "Why don't you come out to the campgrounds next week? I'd love for you to meet my husband. He was in the Army also."

His stomach knotted. Civilians always seemed to think all ex-service members were supposed to be best friends. "I'm really busy right now, but if I can manage to get away, I will."

Khatia pulled on Vince's hand. "Grandpa, take us on the hayride!"

Millie watched Vince and the little girls walk away. "He's really good with them."

"I know," Stacy sighed. "He's the best grandpa."

Stacy was only a year ahead of Randon in school, so he knew that there had been a time when Stacy barely spoke to her father. The man's drinking had driven a wedge between them. It was something he had in common with Stacy.

"Where's Caden?" Millie asked.

Stacy gave her a knowing look. "It's Saturday evening."

Millie nodded. "Right. I hope he makes it back soon."

"He'll try, but I'm not holding my breath." Stacy held up her phone. "That's why I'm on camera duty. He doesn't want to miss anything."

With that, Stacy hurried away to catch up with her family.

Randon watched her leave. "Does her husband work on Saturdays?"

"No." Millie shrugged. "Freddy Macias calls him whenever someone's had too much to drink at the Watering Hole and Caden drives them home."

Randon tucked his hands into the front pockets of his jeans. "Kind of like an Uber driver?"

"Sort of, but he doesn't get paid for it. He just watches out for people. Freddy calls him the tavern's guardian angel."

Not many people did something for nothing. "Why does he do that?"

Millie bit her bottom lip. "You'll have to ask Caden."

Something in her tone made him curious. "You don't know?"

"I do," she said. "But it's not my story to tell."

Randon didn't press her for information. She wouldn't tell him if he did. That was something he'd always admired about her. She was trustworthy.

"Randon," a loud voice boomed across the crowd.

He stiffened. A voice that loud could only be one person. Their high school principal. The man had yelled at him often enough.

"Hello, Mr. Simpson." Randon shook his hand.

"We are so proud of you, son." Mr. Simpson clapped Randon on the shoulder. "I'd love for you to come to the school sometime and talk to the kids about your experience. They'll be so excited to meet a real-life hero."

Alarm bells rang in his head and his blood felt like it had frozen in his veins.

Millie stepped in between them. "I doubt if Randon will have time, Mr. Simpson. He's very busy restoring his grandfather's cabin. He'll give you a call if he gets a chance."

"But—"

"I'm sorry, I promised Tricia we'd check on the cake walk for her." She pulled Randon away.

"Breathe," she whispered as they walked away and slipped the stress ball into his hand.

He squeezed the ball and was surprised when it seemed to help. "How did you know I was uncomfortable?"

"Your right eye twitches just a little bit." She held up her hand, her forefinger and thumb close together.

"Huh," he said. He felt it, but he didn't think that anyone else would be able to notice.

Four young boys approached them and Millie moved to stand in front of him. Randon almost laughed at the protective side of her. He touched her arm and shook his head.

"Hi, Eddie. Toby," he greeted two of them. "Are you having fun?"

"Yes," Eddie said. "What are you doing here? Do you have kids?"

Toby's gaze darted between Randon and Millie. "Is that your wife?"

"No to both questions." He glanced at Millie. "She's just a friend."

The other two boys hung back, listening to their conversation.

"Have you been to the haunted house?" Eddie asked.

"Not yet." Randon shook his head. "Is Mr. Avila still in charge of it?"

They nodded.

He leaned in close to them. "Watch out for the barrel in the last room."

"Why?" Toby's eyes were wide.

He glanced over their shoulders at their friends before whispering, "All the stuff sitting on top of it is glued down and when you walk by, the lid comes off and someone jumps out of it."

"Ohhhh, okay. Thanks!"

"See ya," Randon said.

"We told you we knew him," he overheard Eddie say to the others as they disappeared into the crowd.

Millie tsked. "Shame on you, giving away Mr. Avila's secrets. Who were those boys?"

"Not all his secrets. I didn't tell them about the mummy that will grab them right after the barrel," he said, grinning. "I met them when I was walking in the woods by the cabin. I think they live in the trailer park." He didn't want to admit that he'd been hanging out in the tree house.

She nodded, then frowned. "Uh-oh. Here comes trouble."

Randon stiffened and followed her gaze. Two women were making a beeline for them. He didn't know who they were, but Millie obviously did. And from the tone of her voice, she didn't like them. What did they want?

The two women completely ignored Millie and walked right up to him.

"Are you Randon Farr?" The tall blonde was the first to speak.

Randon's gave a slight nod.

Her companion, a petite woman with dark curly hair, held up her phone. "Can we take a picture with you? The girls in our sorority will just die when we tell them we met a real war hero."

"Sorry, ladies." Millie stepped in between them. "Randon's not allowed to pose for pictures." She made a show of looking around before leaning close to them. "It's a matter of national security."

"Oh." Their eyes opened wide.

Randon coughed to cover up a laugh.

The blonde batted her eyes at him and held her hand out. "I'm Courtney Lancaster."

"Lancaster?" Randon ignored her outstretched hand. "Are you related to Cora Lancaster?"

"She's my sister." Courtney stepped close to him. "You know her?"

"I graduated with her." He took a step back.

Millie cleared her throat and crossed her arms.

When the two women looked at her, she raised one eyebrow.

"Let's go, Court." The other woman tugged her friend's arm.

"It was nice meeting you," Courtney called out as the two of them walked away.

Randon watched them disappear into the crowd. "I told you that you were scary," he said.

Millie shrugged one shoulder. "You were doing pretty well on your own. I just hurried them along."

Music drifted from the inside of the community center and Millie's gaze drifted to it.

Randon nodded toward it. "Didn't you say something about checking out the cake walk?"

"I just said that to get you away from Mr. Simpson." Her brow furrowed. "But I'm actually dying to see what kind of cake Abbie brought."

He could tell that she wanted to go inside, but she didn't want to leave him alone. "Let's go check it out."

"Are you sure?"

He held up the stress ball still in his hand. "I've got a secret weapon now."

Every organization in town used the community center. The local churches held bazaars. The city arranged for a farmer's market several times a year. The community held dances once a month. The PTO used it for lots of activities. His high school prom had even been held in the community center. Not that he went.

He couldn't remember the last time he'd been inside the building. As soon as they entered, his anxiety level shot up and he almost told Millie he would wait outside.

"We don't have to do this." Millie's soft voice interrupted his planning an escape route.

He squeezed the ball in his hand. "No. Let's go look at the cakes."

Several tables were pushed against the wall and were filled with desserts of all kinds. Simple sheet cakes with frosting, elaborate cakes decorated in fall colors, cookies and even a few pies. They all looked amazing.

"Which one is Abbie's?" Randon had never met her, but Millie's letters had been full of information about her new friend.

Abbie came to Coronado looking for Stacy, her biological sister. The sisters had been separated as children after their parents died and they were sent to an orphanage in the country of Georgia. Stacy had been adopted by Vince and Melissa Tedford and grew up in Coronado while Abbie had been adopted by a family in New York.

In her letters, Millie had told him that despite the fact that Abbie was a "city girl," she and Noah Sterling had fallen madly in love, and she decided to stay in Coronado. Randon searched the faces in the room for someone who fit Millie's description of Abbie.

When he realized what he was doing, he paused.

It was the first time in a long while that he was looking for a face and not for some unspecified danger.

Someone tapped him and all the tension returned to his body. He spun around, his fist clenching the stress ball as if it were a weapon.

A short balding man grinned at him. "Randon, nice to see you."

"Hello, Pastor Jones." Randon shook his hand, bracing for the inevitable invitation to come to church.

"My wife said she popped in on you this morning and you'd done a lot of work on the cabin."

"Yes, sir. The Ladies' Auxiliary brought some dishes over." That reminded him, he wanted to ask Millie why she hadn't told him she'd been his father's nurse.

Mr. Jones laughed. "They'll keep you well-fed while you're home, that's for sure. I hope to see you at church in the morning."

"I'll try."

After Mr. Jones walked away, several other people stopped to greet him. Every time the conversation turned to his time in the Army, Millie politely steered the topic to something else. His nerves were stretched so tight he felt as if he would snap.

"Are you ready to go?" Millie whispered to him and guided him out of the building.

"More than ready." His chest seemed to get

lighter and lighter with ever step closer to the parking lot.

They stopped only long enough for Millie to buy some kettle corn. When they got inside her car, they sat in silence for few minutes, waiting for her car to warm up.

"What are you thinking about?" She offered him some of the kettle corn.

"I was thinking that that was…different." Randon shook his head.

"What do you mean?"

"I'm used to being avoided. At least in Coronado."

Millie sighed. "I'm sorry you ever felt like that."

He shrugged. "I'm starting to think it was my fault. At least partly."

"Why would you ever think that?"

Randon cracked his knuckles. "One thing I learned in the Army is that people often treat you the way you expect to be treated. I never tried to be Randon Farr. I was too busy feeling sorry for myself because I was Gregory Farr's son."

Millie cocked her head and smiled at him. "That's very mature of you. I always told you that you just needed to give the people here a chance to know the real you."

"They probably wouldn't like the real me, either." He took a handful of kettle corn.

"I don't really feel like going to the dance, do you?"

Relief washed through him as he buckled his seat belt. "I was only going to go because I thought you wanted to."

"I'll let you in on a secret." She backed the car out of the space. "I can't dance."

Randon laughed. "Everyone can dance."

"Not me."

"Then why did you get so upset because no one asked you to the prom that year?" It was the first, and only, time he'd been willing to go to a school function. "I felt so bad for you. I even asked Brian if I could take you."

She cast him a sideways glance. "Mom told me that this afternoon. I never knew about it."

He shrugged. "Brian said no, anyway."

"I'll be having a little talk with him about that, too."

The irritation in her voice pleased him. "So why did you want to go if you don't like to dance?"

They pulled in front of his cabin and she parked the car. She shut the engine off and turned to face him. "I wanted to go because it was your senior year and I knew it would be my last chance to dance with you."

He cocked his head. "But you don't dance."

"I would've danced with you." Her blue eyes pierced his.

He pulled his gaze from hers and opened the car door. "Are you hungry?"

"Even if I wasn't, I'd still come in," she said. "I'm pretty sure Mrs. Jones brought you her famous pulled pork barbeque. I'd fight Big Foot for that stuff."

She followed him up the path to the porch.

"I think you did very well tonight," she said as he opened the door. "How do you feel about it?"

"Better than I thought I would. That stress ball really helped."

"I'm glad." She walked past him and went into the kitchen. "Yes. Mrs. Jones's pulled pork!"

She pulled the dish from the refrigerator and placed it in the microwave. "That little ball got me through a lot of exams in nursing school."

He put a couple of paper plates on the table and waited for the food to heat up. "Mrs. Jones mentioned that you took care of my dad."

"Yeah," she said. "He's the reason I have my job."

Randon raised one eyebrow. "My dad helped you get a job?"

"Well, not on purpose," she laughed. "I was working part-time at the hospital in Springerville and one of the other nurses also worked for the home health company."

"Your dad had just been assigned to her, so she asked me if I knew him. Apparently, he'd ran off every nurse that came to the house."

He nodded. "Sounds like my dad."

"She was scared to go by herself and asked me to go with her," she said. "When we got here, Greg told her to leave but—"

"You told him to knock it off," Randon finished. He shook his head. "I wish I could have seen the day Gregory Farr met his match."

Millie shrugged. "Greg wouldn't let Christy check his vitals or anything, but he let me. Christy was so impressed with how I handled him, she told her boss, who called and offered me a job."

The microwave dinged and she removed the food and carried it to the table. He waited for her to sit down.

He scooped some of the meat onto a plate and handed it to her. "Brian told me it was his drinking and not his cancer that killed him."

Millie's face grew somber. "I tried for a month to get him to go to the hospital, but he refused. One afternoon I walked in and his eyes were so yellow that they almost looked like they were glowing from across the room."

She shuddered and closed her eyes. "I knew then it was probably too late, but I tried anyway. My boss said we couldn't force him to go to the hospital. The next morning, I brought Mom with me, hoping she could talk him into going, but—"

The regret on her face twisted his gut. "It wasn't your fault. He was a stubborn man."

She swallowed. "I know. But I should've stayed with him. No one should die alone like that."

He stood up and moved next to her to pull her into his arms. She wrapped her arms around his waist and leaned her head on chest. He wanted to tell her not to shed any more tears for Gregory Farr. The man wasn't worth it, but he knew it wouldn't make a difference to her. It was part of her nature.

"You always take care of everyone," he said. "Thank you for taking care of my dad. And thanks for running interference for me tonight."

"No problem." She grinned. "I kind of enjoyed chasing Courtney away."

CHAPTER NINE

THE MARKET WAS empty and had been empty for hours, so Millie didn't feel guilty about using her phone while at work. Unlike Kylie, she did her work first. She'd already restocked the deli, checked the inventory and cleaned the bathrooms. And all that had been done within the first hour of her shift.

She hadn't seen or talked to Randon since the festival on Saturday. He hadn't shown up for church yesterday morning, which hadn't surprised her. After being around so many people, he probably needed a break. She didn't want to push him, so she hadn't tried to contact him. Instead, she used her time to research other ways to help him.

The study she was reading pointed out the benefits of using art therapy for people suffering with PTSD. Randon had always been a great artist. He even painted the mural on the outside of the market. Excitement swelled in Millie's chest. Randon started painting as a way to escape the frustrations he felt at home. Could he use it to help him deal with whatever was going on in his head now? She was searching for stores with art supplies in Springerville when the bells on the door chimed.

She put her phone on the counter and smiled at the middle-aged couple that entered. "Good afternoon. Can I help you find anything?"

The man waved his phone. "Do you have any maps of the area? The GPS on our phone doesn't seem to be working."

Millie grabbed several different maps from the shelf behind her. "We have several to choose from. Unfortunately, cell phone service is spotty around here. Is there something in particular you're looking for?"

"You might think this is odd," the man said, "but I'm looking for the grave of an outlaw who is supposed to be buried around here."

"Oscar Shultz." Millie nodded.

"You've heard of him?" The woman placed two bottles of soda on the counter.

"Yes, ma'am." Millie opened one of the maps she'd gotten for the man and circled the spot with a pen. "He's kind of a celebrity in these parts. How did you hear about him?"

The man reached into his wallet and handed her a business card. "I'm a history professor at U of A and I'm writing a book about outlaws of the Old West."

She looked at his business card. "Well, Mr. Randall, I'm afraid Oscar wasn't a very good outlaw. The first man he robbed only had five dollars on him. Oscar was so disgusted with him that he gave the man his money back."

"I read that," Mr. Randall said. "What else can you tell me about him?"

"Not much," Millie said. "But if you walk over to the hardware store next door, Denny Morgan can probably tell you anything you want to know."

"Excellent." He grinned and turned to his wife. "You don't mind, do you? Why don't you pay while I go over?"

"Sure." She smiled sweetly.

Mr. Randall kissed her cheek and rushed out the door.

The woman shook her head at Millie. "It's not like I really have a choice, anyway. He gets so caught up in his research he can't think about anything else."

Millie laughed. "My dad was like that, too."

"I can't complain. I'm the same way with my art. I get so lost in it I could happily paint for hours." She handed Millie some cash for the sodas and map. "Who painted the mural on the side of the building? It's beautiful."

Millie smiled. "Randon Farr. He painted it about eight years ago."

"Is he a local artist?"

She bit her bottom lip. "Not exactly."

Mrs. Randall raised her eyebrows. "Close by? Where is his studio located?"

"No. I mean, he's not exactly an artist."

"What do you mean?" The woman's mouth dropped open. "Surely, that wasn't painted by an amateur."

"He had just graduated high school at the time," Millie said. "It was part of a community service project."

"What does he do now?"

Millie paused, unsure how to answer that. "He just got home from serving in the Army."

She pulled her own business card out of her purse and laid it on the counter in front of Millie. "I work with several art galleries in southern Arizona. If he decides to take up painting again, have him give me a call. I'd love to take a look at his work."

Millie smiled at the woman. "Thank you. I'll make sure he gets it."

As soon as the woman left to join her husband next door, she picked up her phone and sent Stacy a text.

Are you still in Springerville?

Immediately, her phone rang. "Don't worry. Everything is fine," she said as she answered the phone.

"Oh, good," Stacy said, audibly relieved. "Yes, I'm still here. I haven't even left the dentist's office yet. Then I'm going grocery shopping and

Caden needs to pick up some things at the lumberyard. Do you need something?"

Millie tapped her fingers on the counter. She calculated how long it would take Stacy to return home. Probably several hours. She would rather pick out an art set for Randon herself, but she didn't want to risk the store being closed by the time she could get there.

"Could you do me a huge favor?"

"Anything. What do you need?" Stacy's response was quick.

Millie put the phone on speaker so she could talk and scroll on the phone at the same time. "I'm going to send you some links to a few different art kits at the art supplies store."

She looked at some of the kits. "I'll also send you a list of the other stuff I need from there."

Stacy laughed. "The art supplies store? Seriously? You don't have a crafty bone in your body."

Millie wasn't offended by Stacy's remark. It was true. She wasn't the least bit artistic. "It's not for me. It's for Randon."

"Oh! Is he going to start painting again?"

"I hope so," Millie said. "Do you mind picking the stuff up for me?"

"Of course not! If we're not back by the time the store closes, I'll drop it off at your house."

"Thanks so much. I owe you one." Millie ended the call and continued to scroll until she found everything she needed.

Excitement swelled up in her chest. Randon wanted to get better so he could leave Coronado. But what if she could show him there was a future for him here?

RANDON WAS PRYING loose floorboards from the living room when he heard someone pull up in front of the cabin. He froze. Not again.

He eyed the back door. Should he make a run for it? He listened to the noises outside. No talking. Only one set of footsteps. He snuck to the window to peek outside and let out the breath he was holding.

"It's you." He opened the door to Millie.

She gave him a confused look. "Yeah, just me. Were you expecting someone else?"

He stepped back to let her in. "I sure hope not. I thought it was them again."

"Them who?"

"The Ladies' Auxiliary was here again." He nodded toward the kitchen. "I have enough food for any army."

She laughed. "Do you want me to leave?"

"No." He stepped back to let her come inside. "I'm glad you're here. I wanted to talk to you."

"Uh-oh. What did I do?" She walked to the dining area and set the box she was carrying on the table.

Her face was somber when she turned to look at him.

"Thank you," he said and pulled her close to hug her.

"Um…you're welcome." Her voice was muffled against his chest. "For what?"

He peered down at her. She was so tiny that he would have to squat down to look at her eye to eye. "For helping me. For making me feel normal."

She leaned her head back to look up at him. "You don't hate me for dragging you to the festival?"

She smelled like apple pie. He took one more deep breath before stepping away from her.

"Did I have the time of my life? Absolutely not. But dragging me there was the best thing you could have done." He pulled a chair away from the dining table for her to sit on, then sat next to her.

The line between her eyebrows creased. "Explain."

"When I first realized I had PTSD, I took a page out of your book and did all the research I could about it." He rubbed his hands on the denim fabric of his jeans. "Only I got so caught up in what *could happen*, that's all I was able to think about. I wasn't willing to take a chance on becoming a statistic."

She bit her bottom lip. "That's why you reacted badly when the chairs fell. You were more scared of yourself than you were of the actual incident."

He smiled. "Exactly. Then you forced me to look at it from a different point of view."

"And going to the festival helped?"

"Yes," he said. "I hated every minute of it."

She furrowed her brow. "Then how did it help?"

"Because I hated it before I went into the Army, too." He stood up and leaned on the back of the chair. "The military changed a lot of things, but I'm still me."

"What about all that other stuff? Looking for snipers and planning escape routes."

"I don't know one ex-military person who doesn't do that. I think it's a natural thing." He searched for a way to explain it. "Think about when you were little and you walked down the road with your dad," he said. "Where did he walk? On the inside or the outside of the side-walk?"

"On the outside," she responded. "He said it was because he wanted to be between me and any car that might not be paying attention."

He leaned back in the chair and waited.

A second later, her eyes lit up. "I get it. Dad did that because he was protecting me the only way he knew. And you were trained to look for things to protect yourself and the people around you, so now you can't not do it."

"I knew you would get it. I'll probably wrestle with PTSD all my life. But, you're right. I don't have to let it control me."

She grinned. "Maybe I should open a PTSD treatment facility. My tagline could be *you may*

have PTSD but PTSD doesn't need to have you."
She pretended to frame the words on a make-believe sign.

"Don't do that." He rolled his eyes. "The point is, it's all about perspective and you helped me change mine. My fear of PTSD made it worse than it needed to be."

"Do you still think people were only nice to you because of something you did…or didn't do?"

He shrugged. "I still don't want to talk about that. At least not right now."

She nodded. "Whenever you're ready to talk about it, I'm ready to listen."

Her blue eyes held his gaze and he had a sudden urge to kiss her. She was the only person he'd ever known who seemed to get him. She never looked at him with pity or thought he was being stubborn. Sure, she gave him a hard time, but in the end, she always had his back.

Millie set her box on the kitchen table. "Looks like Freddy's wife was here. Her chicken enchiladas are fabulous, by the way. And I see Mrs. Jones brought you her famous lemon bars. This must be Mrs. Brandenburg's German spaetzle. At least you're not going to starve."

"Make it stop," he pleaded.

She opened a small box of cookies. "You've never been very good at accepting gifts."

"Because they weren't gifts."

"I know." She took a bite of the cookie in her

hand. "But this is different. They're trying to show their appreciation for you. It's not because they feel sorry for you."

"I know that." As a child, he'd often been the recipient of charitable organizations that wanted to help needy children. The people in charge would claim he'd won a raffle or been randomly selected, but he knew the truth. And so did everyone else. "But it feels the same."

Millie's blue eyes studied him for a moment. "I'll talk to Mrs. Brandenburg about it."

"Thank you." He reined in his thoughts.

"You're welcome."

He pointed at the box she'd set down. "Don't tell me you brought food, too."

"No. I came here straight from the market. If I had stopped at home, I'm sure Mom would have loaded me down with food for you."

"Why do you still work for Stacy?"

Millie shrugged. "She was always there for me while I was juggling nursing school and work, so I want to help her out as much as I can. She had to take the girls to the dentist today, so I filled in."

Randon walked over to the table. "How often do you do that?"

"Depends on the season. A couple days a week in the summer. As soon as winter's here, I'll only go in once or twice a month."

He picked up the box. It was heavier than he expected. "What is this?"

"Open it."

He handed it to her. "Take it back."

She scowled at him. "You don't even know what it is."

He shrugged. "It doesn't matter. You shouldn't be spending your money on me."

"Fine." She crossed her arms. "Then you can pay me for it. But trust me, you want it."

Curiosity got the best of him and he opened the box.

The box was completely full of art supplies. Tubes of acrylic paint in dozens of colors. A palette for mixing colors, brushes of all sizes and a palette knife. There were even charcoal pencils and a sketch pad.

"This is…" a lump formed in his throat "… great."

"I have some canvases in my car," she said and handed him a small piece of paper.

He eyed it. It wasn't a bill; it was a business card. "Gloretta Randall?"

Millie squealed. "She's an art curator and she's interested in your work."

"What work?" He stared at the card.

"She came into the store today and asked about your mural," Millie explained. "She said if you start painting again, she'd like to see it."

"All because of the mural?"

"Yes," she said. "But even if she hadn't come in, I was still planning to get you art supplies. I was reading that sometimes people who struggle with PTSD need a hobby to help keep their mind off the bad things."

"This is great." His fingers itched to hold the brushes and get started.

Millie waved at the food on the counter. "Has this been sitting out all day?"

He shook his head and took the sketch pad and pencils out of the box and laid them on the table. "They just brought it a little bit ago. Apparently, someone put my name on something called a meal train, so I'm supposed to have dinner delivered every evening."

She laughed. "You're the only person I know who could make a meal train sound like a prison sentence. Go get the easel and canvases from the trunk of my car and I'll heat up some food for us."

"Us?"

"Yes," she said. "I'm starving."

He got halfway to the car when he realized he didn't have the key to open the trunk of her car. Instead of going back in, he decided to check and see if could open the trunk from inside the car. He opened the driver's side door and stuck his head inside.

A bright flyer on the passenger seat caught his eye. He would have ignored it, but he saw PTSD printed on the top. It was a list of kennels in Arizona that trained dogs to assist with symptoms of PTSD. He folded up the flyer and stuck it in his pocket.

By the time he carried all the stuff from her trunk into the cabin, Millie had set the table and heated up the food.

She smiled at him when he walked in. "Hurry. I'm starving."

Randon pulled the flyer out of his pocket and dropped it in front of her as he sat down. "Please don't get me a dog."

Her mouth dropped open. "Why not? They are supposed to do wonders to help keep you calm."

"I'm sure they do," Randon began, "but the whole point of you helping me deal with my issues is so that I can keep my job with Bravos. I can't take a dog with me."

"Why not? Max goes everywhere with Caden."

"Max?" Oh, right. Caden had served in the military also. "Stacy's husband has PTSD, too?"

Millie nodded. "Before he found Max, he couldn't sleep and he definitely couldn't drive a car."

His interest was piqued. Not about the dog—he still didn't want anything tying him down—but about Caden. "Where was his deployment?"

"I don't know. I don't even know if he went overseas."

He frowned. "I never met a soldier who got PTSD stateside. I mean, it's possible, I guess."

Millie swallowed the food in her mouth before

answering. "He didn't get it from the military. At least, that wasn't the primary cause."

"What happened to him?"

She shook her head. "I told you, you'll have to ask him. I only brought him up because I know how much having Max helped him. I think it might be worth a try."

"No."

Her face fell and she set down her fork. Randon could see the wheels spinning in her head as she formulated her argument. As soon as she opened her mouth, he held up his hand to stop her.

"Millie, I appreciate the thought, but I can't take a dog to work with me at Bravos. Most military contractors understand that PTSD goes with the territory, but if they think it'll interfere with me doing my job, then they won't be willing to take a chance on me."

"And having a dog would alert them that you're having trouble dealing with it." Her voice was very matter-of-fact.

"Thanks to you, I'm figuring out how to deal with it." Randon flashed his best teasing smile. "As long as they don't send me someplace with chairs that slide down and crash."

She sucked in her cheeks, then let out her breath in a puff. "I know I've asked you this before, but why would you want to go back? What if going back makes it worse?"

How could he explain it? Even if he could explain, he didn't think she'd understand. The faces of every man in his unit were permanently burned into his memory. So was the face of the teenage boy who gave him the information that led him to the house that night. Had the boy purposely set him up? Or had he been forced? There was no guarantee he'd get any answers by going back, but he wanted to try.

"That's a chance I'm going to have to take."

She shook her head. "Whatever it is that's driving you to do this, is it really worth your well-being?"

"It's a bigger risk to my well-being if I don't go."

"Can't you tell me what it is?"

He swallowed. "Only if you promise not to try to talk me out of it."

Millie tucked a strand of hair behind her ears. "I can't promise that. I can promise not to judge. I can promise not to make assumptions. I can't promise not to try to change your mind. But I'm going to do that whether you tell me or not, so you might as well tell me."

"There was a boy in the village close to where we were based." As soon as he started to talk, images began to dance around the edges of his mind. "His mother was worried because he was getting close to the age where he could be forced into the fighting."

He wiped his palms on the front of his jeans.

"He was the one who told us where to go that night. The night of the ambush."

He waited for the images to come into focus but they didn't. He stared down at his hands. They were steady. Maybe he really was gaining control over his episodes. He almost smiled.

"Did he know about the ambush?" Millie asked. "Did he set you up?"

"That's what I have to find out."

She moved closer to him and cupped his cheek with her hand. "Does it matter?"

"It does to me." He stared at his hands. "I trusted him. We played soccer with him. Every time one of us got a care package, we gave him stuff."

Randon frowned thinking about how much Rashid enjoyed the chocolate bars they'd given him.

The corners of her mouth turned down. "So you want revenge?"

"No," he said. That's not what he wanted, was it? "I want to make sure he's okay. What if he betrayed us because they threatened his family? What if he was forced to join them?"

"Is there any guarantee you'll find him if you go back?" Her voice was skeptical.

"No."

"But you're going to go back, anyway."

He nodded. "He haunts my dreams every night."

She sighed. "I just hope he doesn't turn your dreams into nightmares."

CHAPTER TEN

RANDON WAS UP before dawn the next morning. The closer it got to the beginning of November, the colder the nights were. He didn't have a thermometer, so he wasn't sure if the temperature had dropped below freezing, but judging from the way the floor felt on his feet when he got out of bed, it had. Or at least it would soon.

The sooner he got the fireplace ready, the better. If he got it cleaned out and ready to use, he'd have to chop wood. At least he only needed to chop enough to last him for a couple of weeks and not the entire winter. He wanted to be done by early afternoon so he could get some painting in.

It was hard to believe that he'd only been in Coronado for one week. He felt like a completely different man than the one who got off the bus.

He got dressed and walked into the kitchen to make coffee. While he was waiting for the coffee, he heard a shuffling noise coming from under the sink. He listened. Again, he heard a bump.

Sounded like he was going to need some mouse-traps.

He squatted down and opened up the cabinet. Searching for the telltale sign of mice, he moved a few things to the side. A flash of brown jumped out from behind a box and ran across his arm. The sudden movement caused him to jump back, lose his balance and fall backward. Sitting up, he scrambled away from the sink as the squirrel made its escape.

His heart rate skyrocketed and he couldn't breathe. The room begin to spin and he grabbed the cabinet behind him to try to ground himself. *Not now.* Tremors began to ripple through his body and then he blacked out.

When Randon opened his eyes, the room was filled with light. How long had he been out? He sat up and leaned against the cabinet. He scrubbed his face with his hands. This wasn't supposed to happen anymore.

The blast that destroyed his shoulder also caused a traumatic brain injury. The TBI, combined with his PTSD, had caused it to happen before, but the previous blackouts were all directly related to intense flashback episodes. It was supposed to be his body's way of protecting his mind. But he shouldn't need protection from a squirrel. How was he going to do his job if a squirrel could cause him to faint?

His heart pounded and he forced himself to

breathe slowly. He got his feet under him and started to stand up. His body was still shaky, but his vision wasn't blurry and the room wasn't spinning. That was a good sign.

He made his way back to his bedroom and found the manila envelope he'd been given when he was discharged from the rehabilitation center. Inside the envelope were his release instructions and a folder full of information. Pulling out the folder, he found the page with information about PTSD and traumatic brain injuries.

His body felt drained, so after calling Dr. Harlow's office and leaving a message, Randon lay down on the bed.

WHEN HE WOKE UP, it was after nine. Randon looked at the clock and groaned. So much for getting done early. At least it wasn't quite so cold.

He walked toward the kitchen again. This time the floor stayed where it was supposed to. The coffee in the decanter was cold, and his hands shook as he poured some into a cup. As the microwave heated it up, he gripped the counter, scared that he might black out again. By his second cup of coffee, he was starting to feel normal. He carried his mug to the back porch and sat on the top of the stairs, looking out at the forest.

He took a sip of his coffee. He hadn't blacked out in months. He would feel a lot better if he could figure out why it had happened now. Was there more to it than getting startled by a squirrel? Dr. Harlow said that his concussion was minor and that his brain was mostly recovered, although he may still have headaches occasionally. Maybe he should call Millie. She was a nurse, after all, and might have some answers.

No. It would only make her worry. He'd wait until after he talked to Dr. Harlow's office before he said anything to anyone.

His stomach was in knots as he contemplated what it might mean for him and his future. He needed to stay busy until Dr. Harlow's office called or he would worry about it all day. He went back inside to rinse out his coffee mug before inspecting the fireplace.

Yesterday, he'd cleaned the firebox of the chimney. From the looks of it, it hadn't been cleaned since he left for the Army. If the heavy buildup of creosote inside the flue was half as bad as it had been in the firebox, it was a wonder the entire cabin hadn't burned down last winter. One thing his grandfather had drilled into him was that cleaning the chimney should never be overlooked. It was a lesson his dad must have forgotten.

He opened the sliding back door and stepped onto the back deck. The last time he'd cleaned the chimney, the tools were kept in the storage area under the deck. There was enough room to store tools that were used often and wouldn't deteriorate when the weather got cold or wet.

The wood creaked under Randon's weight as he went down the stairs from the back porch to the ground level. The door to the storage area was warped and Randon had to jerk it hard to get it open. Thankfully, the tools were still there.

He leaned the ladder against the edge of the roof and climbed up to inspect the inside of the chimney. It wasn't as bad as he thought; still, he needed to clean it with the chimney brush to be safe, but he hadn't seen it under the porch with the ladder.

As he started to walk around the house so he could look under the porch one more time, his gaze went to the barn. Well, it was originally a barn. His grandfather had used it as a workshop. His father hadn't done anything with it except park his pickup inside.

Randon glared at the structure. After working at every job he could get as a teen, he'd saved up enough money to buy his own car. A 1972 Chevy Chevelle. The car needed a lot of work, so he and Brian worked on it every day after school. When winter hit, his father refused to move his old pickup truck so that they could work on it inside the barn.

Instead, they stood in the snow and worked until their fingers were too cold to turn a wrench and they couldn't feel their toes. But they kept at it until they got the car running. Randon remembered how proud Brian's dad was of them when he and Brian drove it to the Gibson house. His own father had never said a word about the car or offered to help, even though he'd once been a mechanic.

Randon loved that car. Before he left for basic training, he found a storage place for it and paid the rent for two years. When his lease was up, he was already overseas, so he mailed a check to Darrel and asked him to go pay it for him for another two years. But when Darrel went to the storage unit, Randon's car was gone.

The renewal notice had been mailed to the house and because they had the same first name, Randon's dad had opened it. He went to Springerville and removed the car before Darrel got there. He still didn't know what his dad had done with his beloved car. Probably sold it for alcohol and cigarettes.

He stared at the barn again. If his dad's truck was inside, would it still run? Although he swore not to use anything that belonged to his father, having a vehicle would make things so much easier. He could go to Springerville and get the supplies he needed and not wait for them to be delivered.

He walked across the yard to the weathered building. A hasp lock had been installed on the barn door. Randon frowned at the padlock hanging from it. As long as he could remember, his father had never locked anything.

He went back into the cabin and looked at the keys hanging on the key rack by the back door. There were several sets of keys. One was for the cabin and one held the key to his father's pickup truck. Randon fingered a silver key on the chain. It looked like a padlock key.

His gaze fell on another set of keys on the rack. His heart caught in his throat. They were the keys to his car. Why would his dad keep a set of keys to a car he got rid of? He left them hanging there and walked to the front door.

Millie was getting out of her car when Randon came out of the cabin.

"I wasn't expecting you today."

"I know." She leaned against her car. "I only had one home-health patient this morning, so I'm done for the day."

"So you needed something to do?"

"Not really," she laughed. "I was hoping to talk you into going fishing at Big Lake."

"Sorry," he said, stepping off the porch. "I've got too much to do."

"Like what?" She fell into step beside him.

"I want to clean the chimney and get it going so I don't freeze to death before I can get the rest of the repairs done."

She followed him across the yard and out to the

barn. "I thought all the tools were in the space under the back porch?"

"Just the ones that are used a lot." Randon twisted the key and it opened with a soft click. "The chimney brush isn't under there, so I'm hoping it's out here. I haven't seen my dad's truck, so I wondered if it was in here, too."

"I was out here a lot before he died and I don't remember ever seeing his truck." Millie waited for Randon to take the padlock off the door and slide it open. "I thought he must have sold it."

"There it is," Randon said.

He got into the driver's seat, put the key in the ignition and tried to crank the engine. The truck made a grinding noise, sputtered and then fell silent. "The battery is dead."

He pulled the latch to pop the hood and got out of the vehicle. "There used to be a battery charger on that back counter. Would you look and see if it's there?"

Millie walked to the counter. From where she was standing, she could see around the corner to the back side of the barn. "What's under that tarp?"

Randon propped the hood of the truck open and walked over to where she was.

"I don't know." He walked over and lifted it up.

Millie gasped. "It's your car!"

Randon's heart pounded. "It's my car."

His hands shook as he rolled the tarp all the

way back, revealing the shiny silver car that he'd worked so hard on. He touched the roof as if he were afraid it would disappear.

Millie glanced at him. "Do you think it still runs?"

He tried to swallow. "The battery is probably dead on it, too."

"Do you know where the keys are?"

"Yes," he said. "Be right back."

He sprinted across the yard to the cabin and took the keys from the wall. His hands were still shaking. His dad hadn't sold the car. Not only had he not sold it, he covered it to protect it from the elements.

When Randon got back to the barn, Millie had slid the barn doors open all the way, bathing the interior in light.

He opened the door and slid into the driver's seat. For a moment, he rubbed his hands over the dashboard as the memories of all the time spent working on the car flooded him. All his memories of the car included Brian.

His gaze drifted to Millie, waiting anxiously for him to start the car. "It doesn't seem right to do this without Brian."

"I don't think he'll mind," she said. "He's going to be thrilled that you found it. But just to be sure, I'll record it with my phone and send it to him."

"Wait." Randon handed his phone to her. "Use my phone. I'll send it to him tonight."

MILLIE PUSHED RECORD on his phone and waited for Randon to turn the ignition. The chances of the car starting after sitting in storage for almost two years were pretty slim, but she hoped for Randon's sake that it would. He'd been devastated when he thought his dad had gotten rid of it.

Randon turned the key and the engine whined a moment, then sputtered and finally started. Millie wanted to jump for joy, but the look on Randon's face made her hesitate.

"What's wrong?" She paused the recording and walked over to the still-open driver's door.

His brow furrowed. "I was just thinking about the first time Brian and I got it running."

"I think he was as upset as you were when you told him your dad sold it." Millie put his phone on the dash. "He'll be thrilled to know it's here."

"I know." Randon rubbed the steering wheel again.

"What's wrong?"

Her brother returned from Kuwait three months after Randon. Brian said Randon sometimes avoided his calls. "Did Brian do something wrong?"

He took a deep breath. "No. I just didn't realize how much I missed him until now."

"He misses you, too." She tried to contain her smile. "Will you go to Fort Bliss to see him before you leave?"

If I leave. He glanced at his phone. Why hadn't Dr. Harlow called him back? "Of course, I will."

"What now?" she asked. "Should we go for a spin?"

Randon frowned. "It's been sitting here for a long time. I don't want to go somewhere and have it break down."

Millie could see the longing on his face. "As long as you've got it running, you should drive it to Bear's Garage. Why risk taking a chance on it not starting?"

"Good idea," he said. "Will you follow me in your car?"

She nodded and walked over to her car. She was tempted to call Brian and tell him about finding the car and Randon's promise to send it to him, but she didn't. Whatever had happened between Randon and Brian was between them. Randon said he would text him, so she would wait and give him the chance.

Randon had already backed the car out of the barn by the time she got to her car and turned around. The drive to Bear's Garage took longer than it should've. Why was Randon driving so slow? Maybe something was wrong with the car.

She parked behind him and waited while he went inside to talk to Harry Littlebear, the owner of the garage. Her heart always ached a little when she saw Harry, or Bear, as everyone called him. Harry's only son, Tommy, had been several years ahead of her in school. Tommy joined the Mogollon Rim Hotshots right after he graduated. He jumped out of planes to fight forest fires all over the country with the elite wildland firefighting crew. His wife, Maggie, was a waitress at the local café. Millie babysat their son while Tommy was off fighting forest fires and Maggie was working. She'd just put two-year-old Jacob to bed when she saw on the news that one member of an Arizona hotshot crew had been killed while fighting a fast moving fire in Wyoming. The news anchor hadn't said the firefighter's name, but Millie had had a sinking feeling in her gut. Less than fifteen minutes later, Harry brought Maggie home and Millie's fear was confirmed.

That had been six years ago. The entire community came together to help the Littlebear family. That was one of the things Millie loved about her hometown. Anytime there was a tragedy in the small town, the people of Coronado could always be counted on to support each other. It was too bad Randon hadn't realized that. If he had, he may not have been so anxious to leave Coronado.

Her heart skipped a beat. She probably couldn't convince him not to go back to Kuwait. But if she could show him the advantages of living in Coronado, maybe he would consider coming back sooner. She glanced at the entrance to the garage. There was no sign of Randon. She slid her phone out of the purse on the seat next to her and scrolled through her contacts.

She took a deep breath and hit Call. "Hi, Pastor Jones, this is Millie."

"Hi, Millie," the pastor said. "Is everything all right?"

"Yes." She kept one eye on the door Randon had gone through. "Do you still get firewood donated every fall?"

"More than we can use," Pastor Jones laughed. "Do you know someone who could use it?"

"Yes," she said, "Randon is trying to repair his cabin. You know, his dad wasn't able to keep up with maintenance on the cabin and it's in pretty bad shape."

"I see," Pastor Jones said. "Knowing Randon, he's trying to do all the repairs himself."

"Yes. And to use the fireplace, he'll have to cut a lot of wood, which will take time from everything else he has to do. And with his shoulder injury, I'm not sure how much he can do." Millie knew that Pastor Jones had often bragged about Randon's work ethic. It shouldn't be hard to convince him to help Randon out.

"Do you know what kind of repairs are needed?"

"No, but I can find out." Millie breathed a sigh of relief.

"I'll drop off a load of firewood in the morning," he said. "I'll also start making some phone calls. I bet we have a lot of men at the church who'd love to help him out."

The garage door opened and Randon exited the building.

"Great," Millie said. "I'll find out what I can and call you later."

She'd barely disconnected the call when Randon opened the passenger side door and sat down.

"All set?" she asked him.

He nodded. The lines on his face were tight. Did he get bad news?

Millie started the engine. "Did Bear say how long before he could get to it?"

"A couple of hours," he said.

"Today? Wow. He must not be too busy." She backed out of the parking spot. "Other than the chimney, what else do we need to do today?"

"I hadn't thought past the chimney. That'll probably take me all day. Plus another day to chop wood."

She pressed her lips together to keep from smiling as she turned off the main road and headed through the trailer park toward his cabin. "Are you sure I can't talk you into skipping work and going fishing instead?"

He laughed. "As much as I'd love to, I really can't."

"Fine," she sighed. "I'll drop you off at home, then go change into my chimney cleaning clothes."

"You don't have to do that," he said. "I'm sure you have better things to do."

"No. I don't." She pulled in front of the cabin and stopped. "I'll be back in a few minutes."

"Thanks." He got out of the car. "I'll hook the battery charger up to the truck while I'm waiting. Who knows? Maybe I'll have two running vehicles today."

She nodded as he shut the door and headed home.

"GUESS WHAT," she said as she burst through the front door.

Her parents were sitting at a small card table in the corner of the living room. Every afternoon, they played Scrabble. Her mother had read that brain games were good for Alzheimer's patients, so they played it often.

"What is it?" Darrel asked, not looking up from the board game.

"Randon found his car in the barn." She'd promised not to tell Brian, but there was no reason not to tell her parents.

"He did?" Mom's eyebrows raised. "I thought Greg sold it."

"I did, too." She stopped next to the table to study her dad's game pieces. Her chest tightened when she spotted at least five words he could make.

"Greg needs to stop smoking." Darrel frowned at the board. "Especially in the barn."

Millie's chest tightened more and she cast her

mother a worried look. Mom's lips were set in a straight line.

"You remember Randon's father?" Mom said softly.

He looked up at his wife. "Who's Randon?"

"Randon is Brian's best friend," she responded and nodded at the game board. "It's your turn."

Millie didn't wait to see what word he would spell. It was hard to see the man she once thought knew every word in the dictionary struggling to spell three- and four-letter words. She hurried upstairs to change clothes.

It only took a minute and she was back downstairs. "I'm going to help Randon at the cabin," she told her mother. "Is that okay, or do you need me to stay?"

"We're fine. If your father feels up to it, we might go for a drive later."

Millie twisted her long hair into a messy bun and nodded. "Call me if you need anything."

Instead of driving, she could take the trail. She glanced at the path that cut through the forest and led to Randon's cabin. No, she'd better not. While it was nice outside right now, the temperature dropped quickly in the afternoon and since she had no idea how long she would be at the cabin, she didn't want to turn into an ice cube before she could walk back.

Her phone chimed as she got into her car and she glanced at the message from Pastor Jones.

We have a group of men willing to help.

Millie grinned. One step closer to reminding Randon of all the good things in Coronado. A great support system and a family that loved him. Would it be enough?

CHAPTER ELEVEN

RANDON SAT UP in bed, slowly. Right after he was injured, he would suffer from dizzy spells and sometimes even blackouts first thing in the morning. He waited to see if the symptoms were going to return and he'd have another blackout, like the one he'd had yesterday morning. He stood up and waited. Nothing. As long as he wasn't attacked by angry squirrels, he should be okay.

He reached over to the nightstand and picked up his phone. It had been months since he'd left his phone on overnight. For that matter, it had been months since he'd even turned it on, except to make a quick phone call, usually for a doctor's appointment.

After Millie left to go home last night, he'd texted Brian. His phone rang about three seconds after that. Except for a few text messages, they hadn't really talked since before he arrived in Coronado. It was good to hear Brian's voice and they talked on the phone for over an hour. When Brian had to hang up because his bunkmates wanted to go to sleep, they texted for another hour.

Randon scrolled through the texts and smiled. It felt good to talk to his best friend again. They had been arguing on the night of the accident and Randon had been afraid the argument, combined with his rash decisions that night, had pushed a wedge between them.

Brian had only planned to stay in the Army long enough to earn enough money from the GI Bill to pay for college. When Randon told him he wanted to stay and make the Army a career, Brian tried to talk him out of it. And when Randon told him he was doing it for Millie, Brian got really upset.

After the accident, he'd been so overwhelmed with guilt he was ashamed to face Brian again. Brian, however, was almost as stubborn as Millie when it came to getting what he wanted. When Brian arrived back in the States, he camped outside of Randon's door at the hospital until Randon let him in.

Things were still a little tense occasionally, but last night's conversation was the first time Randon felt like they were really best friends again.

He made his way to the living room. The aroma of coffee drifted down the hall and he followed the smell to kitchen. Thank goodness he'd finally remembered to program it! He poured a cup of coffee and took a long drink of the hot liquid.

A slight chill hung in the air, but it had been late when he and Millie had finished cleaning all the creosote buildup from inside the chimney and he hadn't had time to chop any wood.

Truthfully, he was almost relieved. It took a lot of shoulder movement to swing an axe. He didn't want to try chopping wood in front of Millie and discover he couldn't do it because then she would try to do it for him. That was not going to happen.

Before she left last night, she told him she would be staying home all day with her father today. Her mother was going to Phoenix to see her brother, Jarrod. That gave him all day to test his shoulder and chop wood.

He reviewed the list he was making of everything else that needed to be done while he ate a bowl of cereal. Some of it was cosmetic and could wait, such as painting. Some of it needed to be done as soon as possible. The leaks in the roof and under the sink in the bathroom were at the top of the list.

He needed to go to Springerville to pick up new shingles for the roof, but he wanted to get up there and double-check how many he needed. Before he opened the back door to go outside, someone knocked on the front door.

Not again. He let out a huff of air and walked to the front door. A tall redheaded man stood on his porch. A brown shepherd-mix dog sat next to him.

The man extended his hand to Randon. "I'm Caden Murphy."

Randon stared at the man's outstretched hand for a moment before accepting it. "Randon Farr."

"I just missed you at the festival the other night."

"Oh." Randon nodded. "I thought you looked familiar. You're Stacy's husband."

Caden's brow furrowed. "We've met before?"

"Not officially," he said. "I saw you at church with Stacy just before we shipped out. What can I do for you?"

"Actually, it's what I can do for you." Caden took one step inside and stopped. He nodded toward the dog. "Do you mind if Max comes in, too?"

"That's fine."

Max followed Caden into the living room, his eyes never leaving his master. Millie had suggested that Randon get a dog to help him deal with his PTSD episodes and he wondered how a dog could stop a panic attack.

Caden looked around the cabin. "You don't have any furniture."

"No, sir." Randon nodded toward the dining area. "You're welcome to sit at the table if you like."

"No time for sitting." He motioned around the cabin with his hand. "I heard you were making repairs. It looks like you really have your work cut out for you."

"Yes. I'm afraid my dad wasn't much for keeping up with repairs."

"I'm pretty good with a saw and a hammer," Caden said. "Pastor Jones asked me if I'd be willing to give you a hand."

Randon frowned. He wasn't sure what to say. No one had offered to help him before, so why now? Why did Pastor Jones think he wasn't able to do his own repairs? Had Millie said something to him? He lifted his chin. "I don't need any help."

Caden stood motionless. His face twitched and Randon could tell that he wanted to say something, but was thinking twice about it.

"Pastor Jones wasn't the only one who asked me to come over," Caden admitted.

Randon nodded. "Millie?"

"And my wife." He shook his head. "Millie told her a little about your situation. We do have a lot in common. We both served in the Army. We both saw action overseas. We both have PTSD."

What exactly had Millie told Stacy? Who else did she talk to about him? "Millie thinks I should get a dog. She said Max has helped you a lot."

"Before I found Max, I didn't sleep much." Caden nodded. "When I did sleep, I had nightmares and then—"

"You couldn't go back to sleep," Randon said quietly. He had the same problem. It had been even worse right after he returned to the States. The nightmares were usually accompanied by a headache so intense it made him sick. He shuddered at the memory. Since arriving in Coronado, the nightmares had subsided.

"Max seems to know when I'm about to have a nightmare and he wakes me up before it gets too bad." Caden patted the dog's head.

"Did you have him trained? Where did you get him?" He still didn't want a dog, but he was curious.

"That's the funny thing," Caden said. "I was working at Whispering Pines Campground and he found his way to my cabin. He'd tangled with something a lot bigger than him and he was so torn up I wasn't sure if he'd make it. I slept on the couch so I could hear him if he started whining. Instead, he was the one that woke me up when I started having a nightmare. He's been doing it ever since."

Both men were silent for a moment. Randon really wanted to ask him where his tour of duty was, but he knew how it felt when people tried to get him to talk about his service and he didn't want to do the same thing to Caden.

Caden gave him a serious look. "There are some differences between us. I didn't get my PTSD from my time in the military."

Randon raised his eyebrows in surprise. "Where, then?" The question slipped out before he could stop it. Did it make it easier to talk about if it wasn't incurred from combat? Probably not.

"I'm sorry," Randon said. "It's none of my business."

Caden shrugged. "It's okay. I'm finally at a place where I can talk about it. Mine is from a car accident. It happened a week after I got out of the Army. I probably have some residual PTSD from combat, but the car accident superseded everything else."

"Must have been a bad one," Randon acknowledged.

Caden's gray eyes dropped to the floor. "Millie said you feel guilty because you almost got your best friend killed. Well, I did kill mine."

Randon's heart seemed to stop. If it weren't for the expression on the man's face, he would have thought Caden was joking. His breath caught in his chest. "He was in the car?"

Caden nodded. "We'd been at the bar and I thought I was okay to drive."

Randon's chest felt heavy. The guilt he felt after the ambush had been enough to drive him away from everyone he knew. If Brian, or any of the other members of his squad had been killed, he wasn't sure if he would've been able to survive.

His throat was thick. "How'd you get through it?"

"I almost didn't," Caden said. "My attorney wanted to enter a plea deal. My family begged me to accept it. But I couldn't. I was guilty and

I wanted to accept the responsibility, no matter what."

Randon understood that. He'd begged his commanding officer to file charges on him for dereliction of duty. Anything to make him pay for what he'd done.

"Seven years in prison didn't help the guilt." Caden shrugged. "It wasn't until I met Stacy and learned to forgive myself that the nightmares finally stopped."

"They're gone?" If Caden's nightmares could go away, maybe his flashbacks could, too.

Caden's gaze narrowed. "For the most part. They still sneak in occasionally, especially when I'm overworked and tired. Getting in a car and driving still causes me some anxiety, but Max keeps me calm."

"Millie said that you drive people home from the bar?"

Caden nodded. "I don't want anyone else to ever go through what I went through. If that means I spend my weekends driving people home from the bar, that's what I do."

Randon looked down at Max sitting at Caden's feet. "I'm planning on going back overseas for a while, so I don't think a dog would be a good fit for me right now."

"I'm not here to talk you into getting a dog." Caden held up his hands. "I just wanted to tell you my story and let you know that I'm around if you need to talk about it."

"Thanks. I appreciate that."

Caden let out a big puff of air. "Now that that's over with, let's get to work."

Randon rubbed the back of his neck with his hand. "Truthfully, I appreciate the offer to help, but I'm afraid I can't accept it."

"Why not?"

"Because I'm making repairs so I can sell the place," he said. "And I wouldn't feel right about letting someone else invest time into it, just so I can profit from it."

Caden frowned. "I didn't realize you were planning to sell the cabin."

"I'm going to be moving around a lot, so there's no sense in letting the place sit empty." Randon told him.

"Have you thought about renting it out?" Caden patted one of the columns that rose from the floor to the beamed ceiling. "This place has some amazing features. You could probably make a fortune if you put it on Airbnb."

"I don't know if I want to get into that." The cabin was the only thing tying him to Coronado. Without it, he wouldn't have an excuse to come back. He didn't want to return in a few years and see Millie with a husband and a family of her own. It was better that he make a clean break.

"When do you start your new post?"

Randon's breath caught in his chest. He hadn't heard back from Dr. Harlow about the seizure he'd had yesterday morning. He had no idea what the future might hold. Was it a fluke thing or would it be something he'd have to deal with for the rest of his life? The Army had been plan A for his life. Bravos was plan B. Did he need to start working on plan C?

Regardless, Coronado couldn't be part of the plan.

He was moving forward until something blocked his path. "I report to Bravos headquarters on November fifteenth."

Caden whistled. "You have just under three weeks left to have this place ready to be put on the market?"

Randon nodded and looked around the room. He'd been here for a week and a day and the only thing he'd accomplished was cleaning all the trash, hauling out some furniture and cleaning the chimney. That should have taken a few days at most. He picked up the list he'd made of all the stuff he still wanted to do to the place and handed it to Caden.

Caden studied the list and raised one eyebrow. "Is this everything you want done?"

He nodded. "I won't be able to get to all of it, but the most important stuff is at the top."

"We better get started, then." Caden set the list

on the counter. "I'll start working on the leak in the bathroom."

"You're still willing to help?" A load seemed to lift from his chest. "Thank you."

"No problem." Caden walked out to his truck and returned with his toolbox. When he came back inside, he walked straight to the bathroom. Max lay on the floor in front of the bathroom.

"I'm going to make a trip to Springerville this afternoon to pick up supplies. If you see anything I need, write it on the back of my list."

Caden looked up from where he was sitting on the floor. He'd already removed the P trap from under the sink. He nodded and went back to work.

Randon walked outside to get the ladder and climb on the roof. As irritated as he was with Millie for sending Caden over to talk him out of leaving, he knew she meant well. And Caden gave him hope.

If Caden could overcome everything that he'd gone through and had been able to settle down with a family, maybe he could, too.

"I'M GOING TO call Jarrod and tell him never mind," Millie's mother said.

"No, Mom." Millie opened the door and ushered her to the porch. "Jarrod is only in town for two days and you haven't seen him in three months. You're going."

Mom frowned. "You don't mind staying home with your father all day?"

"He's my dad," Millie said. "I'm sure he had to stay home and take care of me more than once in the past."

"Don't forget to keep the doors locked. He kept trying to go for a walk yesterday." Mom looped her arm in Millie's. "The photo albums are on the coffee table, so if he starts to get confused, sit down and look at those with him."

"I know, Mom." Millie didn't remind her mother that she was the one who'd suggested the photo albums. "Besides, you need a break, too."

"I know," Mom sighed. "I just feel so guilty about leaving him."

"And if you don't go, you'll feel guilty for not seeing Jarrod."

"I don't know what I would do without you." Her mother gave Millie a hug. "I'll be home by noon tomorrow."

"Give Jarrod a hug for me and let me know when you get there." Millie waved as her mother pulled out of the driveway.

Inside the house, her father was watching television. She checked to make sure the front door was locked and went to join him in the living room.

Millie picked up her mother's notebook off the coffee table. Her mother kept detailed notes about everything, from the foods Darrel ate to the medication he was on.

Millie went through the notes. He'd wanted a grilled cheese sandwich for lunch every day for the last two weeks. Before that, he'd wanted spaghetti. She studied the notes, looking to see if there was a pattern in his behavior and if it could be related to his food.

She put the notebook back on the coffee table and stood up. "Do you want to work on your puzzle?"

Her voice must have startled him because he jumped in his chair.

"Who are you?" His eyes were wide. "What do you want?"

Millie stepped away from him. "I'm your daughter, Millie."

His eyes darted around the room. "Where's Laura?"

She could feel the anxiety rolling off him. "Mom went to Phoenix to see Jarrod."

Darrel's eyes narrowed. "Jarrod?"

"Jarrod is your second oldest son." She moved slowly toward the coffee table. "Let's sit on the sofa and we can look at family pictures."

When he nodded and sat on the end of the sofa, she let out a sigh of relief. Sometimes dementia patients reacted violently when they couldn't remember people or places. The thought of her sweet, calm, collected father lashing out at her or anyone else was disturbing.

Most of her home-health patients were older.

Several of them suffered from dementia, so she was accustomed to dealing with erratic behavior. But this was her dad. The man who hugged her when her brothers hurt her feelings, chased monsters out from underneath the bed and taught her to drive. Her throat tightened and she tamped down the anger that always rose up when she thought about his disease.

They were looking at the album when Darrel pointed to a picture of her wearing a pink tutu and an angry expression. "You were so mad about that costume."

"Because I didn't want to be a ballerina."

"Brian gave your Spider-Man costume to Randon," he said. "And even though you were mad at your brother, you didn't want to take it away from Randon, so I took you to the store and that was the only costume left."

Her heart caught in her throat. Most days, he couldn't remember her name; now he remembered something she'd forgotten years ago.

Her fingers touched the photograph. Right after the picture was taken, Randon showed up in the costume, not knowing it had been hers. He told her she made a beautiful ballerina and she twirled and danced for the rest of the night.

After looking at a few more pictures, she put the album away and they worked on his jigsaw puzzle. Millie was pleased with how well her father was doing, both with the puzzle and with remembering things. She watched him as he studied the puzzle piece in his hand.

"It's almost noon," Millie said. "Are you hungry?"

"Grilled cheese." Darrel placed the piece in the correct spot and picked up another one.

She tried not to laugh. "I'll be right back."

Before she started making lunch, she stepped into the laundry room to start a load. She was still sorting clothes when her phone chimed and she checked her message.

A picture of Stacy's girls dressed in their Halloween costumes popped up on the screen. Khatia was dressed as a nurse.

Do you have an old stethoscope Khatia can borrow for her costume? She wants to be a nurse, just like you!

Millie grinned and responded to the text, letting her know that she would bring one over after her mother returned from Phoenix.

She chatted with Stacy via text for a few more minutes while she tossed a load of clothes in the washer and started it.

Her phone chimed again while she was smearing butter on the bread for her dad's sandwich. She glanced at the screen. It was a notification from an online game app, letting her know it was her turn to play. The word scramble app was one of the few games she played on her phone, and that was only because Emily challenged her to play against her.

She set the knife down and picked up her phone. Emily had played a difficult word and pulled ahead of her in points.

One glance at her letters and she thought of a medical term, but she wasn't sure how to spell it. Their rules were that they couldn't use the internet to search for a word, but they were allowed to use "old-school" methods. She didn't have a dictionary, but she did have her medical journals, so she ran upstairs to look up her word. It took a few minutes, but she came up with a word that put her close to Emily's points.

She sent a message to Emily.

Nice try, but I got you!

Emily didn't believe it was really a word, so she had to take a picture of the page and send it to her. After a few more texts, Millie went back downstairs and finished making lunch.

Her phone binged again and she glanced at the text message on her screen. It was from Stacy.

Caden's back.

Millie's heart froze as she read the text. Had it worked? Would Randon be mad at her and accuse her of interfering for sending Caden to talk to him? Of all the people she knew, Caden was the only one who might be able to get through to him. After all, Caden knew more about guilt than anyone she knew. If anyone could help Randon, it was him.

What did he say?

Not much. He said it went well.

Millie groaned.

That's it? That's all he said?

Stacy's response was quick.

He said not to worry.

Millie smiled to herself as she read the last message. She had wanted to introduce Randon to someone who could understand how he was feeling. Someone he could trust. Caden not telling Stacy anything else was proof she'd made the right choice.

Thanks. See you later.

She sat her phone down and put the grilled cheese sandwich on a plate.

"Dad, your sandwich is ready." She put a bag of

chips on the table next to the sandwich and went to the living room.

He wasn't sitting at the card table working on his puzzle.

Her heart rate went up and she checked the front door again. It was still locked. She let out a sigh of relief and walked to her parents' bedroom. The bathroom door was shut.

Satisfied that he was okay, she went back to the kitchen to make herself a grilled cheese sandwich, too.

He still wasn't out of the bathroom by the time her sandwich was done. She went back to the bathroom and knocked on the door. "Dad? You've been in there a while. Are you okay?"

No response.

When he didn't respond to additional knocking, she tested the doorknob. It wasn't locked, so she opened it a little and called for him again.

When he still didn't answer, she pushed the door open and her breath froze in her lungs. He wasn't there.

"Dad!" She ran up the stairs and checked each one of the bedrooms. Nothing.

She went back downstairs and checked the bathroom again. She even opened the shower curtain and checked the closet in his bedroom.

Her pulse pounded in her ears as she checked the front door again. The dead bolt was still engaged, so he hadn't gone out the door. But where was he?

She went back to the kitchen, hoping to see him sitting at the table, eating his sandwich. Two steps into the room and her heart almost stopped. The back door was ajar. It had been locked earlier, she was sure of it.

"Dad!" She opened the door and stepped onto the back porch. "Dad!"

She ran around the outside of the house, yelling for him. There was no sign of him anywhere outside.

Her phone was still inside, so she sprinted to the front door. Locked! She ran to the back door as fast as she could, her insides shaking so badly she could barely hold her phone.

"Please answer," she whispered when the phone began to ring.

"Hello?" Randon picked up the phone.

"I need your help!" Her voice was on the edge of hysteria, but she couldn't help it. "Dad left the house and I can't find him."

"I'll be right there." The call ended.

She scanned the numbers on her phone, looking for Sheriff Tedford's number, but she couldn't find it. She called Stacy and told her what had happened. Stacy assured her she would call her uncle right away. After that, she would call a few other people and they would find her father in no time.

Millie had barely hung up the phone when Randon knocked on the front door. She rushed to open it, only to see him leaning over with his hands on his knees, taking deep breaths.

"What's wrong?" She bent down to him.

"Nothing," he said between breaths. "Ran from the cabin in case he was on the trail between our houses."

"Oh," she said and her stomach knotted. The trail to Randon's house was the first place she'd planned to look, since it was a trail that was familiar to Darrel.

"When was the last time you saw him?"

"He was sitting in the living room, working on his puzzle," she began. "I went to the kitchen to make him lunch."

Her throat tightened as she gasped for breath. This was her fault. She'd been so busy on her phone that she hadn't been paying attention to her father. "He must have slipped out the back door when I went upstairs."

Randon's gaze swept down the street. "Have you called the neighbors to see if he walked over there by accident?"

"No." Just Randon's presence helped her to start being able to focus. "You were the first person I called. Then Stacy. She's calling Sheriff Tedford and some others."

The blast of a siren drew her attention to the SUV pulling into the driveway. The sheriff let the siren run for a few more seconds before shutting it off and getting out of the vehicle. "That oughta get all the neighbors' attention," he said.

Sure enough, within moments people began to emerge from the houses nearby.

Frank gave Randon a nod. "Start rounding up some volunteers while I talk to Millie for a minute."

"Yes, sir." Randon motioned the growing crowd on the sidewalk toward him.

By the time she gave Frank an idea of the timeline, Randon returned.

"I have two people checking all the houses in the neighborhood. Four more are going to start driving up and down the streets, looking for him."

Millie swallowed. She wasn't used to feeling helpless, especially in an emergency situation. "How will we know if they find him?"

"They all have your cell phone number and will call immediately," he said. He nodded at Frank. "Sorry, Sheriff, I should've given them your number, too, but I don't have it."

"That's all right." Frank clapped him on the shoulder. "You did fine."

Millie buried her hands in her hair and tucked her chin to her chest. *They'll find him. They'll find him.*

She was vaguely aware of voices around her, but it was as if a fog surrounded her. A hand touched her shoulder and she jumped.

Randon squeezed her arm. "Are you okay?"

She shook her head, not trusting herself to speak. He pulled her to his chest and wrapped his arms around her. She let herself sink into his embrace, knowing he was the only thing holding her up.

Frank dismissed a group of volunteers and walked over to her. "Where's Laura?"

A fresh wave of panic washed over her. Her mom didn't know. How was she supposed to tell her that she lost her dad?

"She's in Phoenix, visiting Jarrod." She pulled her phone out of her pocket and pressed the button to call her mother.

As soon as she heard her mother's voice, the tears started to flow. "Mom," she sobbed.

Suddenly, the phone left her hand.

"Laura, this is Randon. I don't want you to panic, but we have a bit of a situation. Somehow, Darrel unlocked the back door and wandered away. Sheriff Tedford is here and we've got everyone in the neighborhood looking for him. He couldn't have gotten very far."

Millie leaned against Randon, trying to absorb his calmness. "Thank you," she whispered when he disconnected the call and handed her the phone.

CHAPTER TWELVE

RANDON KEPT MILLIE cocooned in his arms. She wasn't crying, but he hadn't expected her to. Even when they were kids, she'd never been one to show her emotions in front of people. Well, unless you counted anger. That, she was good at expressing.

Frank caught his eye and approached them. "The Mogollon Rim Hotshots are here. They are going to spread out and start searching the woods. He can't have gotten far."

"I'll help." Randon loosened his hold on Millie.

Millie stepped back. Her eyes were red and puffy, but her breath wasn't coming in gasps anymore. "I'm going, too."

"You should stay here." Randon squeezed her shoulders. "When we find him, you may be the only one who can get through to him."

The stubborn tilt of her chin told him she wasn't going to listen. He put one finger under her chin and lifted her face to look at him. "You need to be easy to find."

"That's right," Frank agreed. "We can't be looking all over for you, too."

Randon scanned the area. The entire town seemed to have appeared on Millie's street. "Where do you want me?"

"Get a radio from Shane." Frank pointed toward the truck where the Mogollon Rim Hotshots were organizing volunteers.

He walked over to the man Frank had pointed at. "Frank told me to get a radio from you."

The man handed him one and pointed to the knob on the top of the radio. "Keep it on channel seven, that's the main channel. Check in every fifteen minutes and update your location."

He nodded his understanding. "Where are people looking already?"

Shane motioned him over to a nearby pickup truck. The tailgate had been lowered and a map of the area was spread out. He pointed to locations on the map marked with blue circles. "I have volunteers going here, here and here."

"Those are all well-used hiking trails," Randon said. It made sense that an older man would stay on the easy paths. But Darrel had taken him hiking many times and he knew the man liked to go cross-country. "What about cutting through the forest to Chapman Creek?"

Shane gave him a questioning look. "Why do you think he may go that way?"

Randon shrugged. "Darrel used to take Brian

and me there a couple of times a year. There's an abandoned mine close to the creek and we used to go gold panning."

"Seriously?" Shane raised his eyebrows. "I didn't know people still did that."

"It's still quite popular in Arizona." Randon shrugged. Darrel had been a member of a gold prospectors' club and shared his passion with his boys and their friends.

The man looked at the map and frowned. "That's a rough trail and we are talking about a sixty-five-year-old man. No. He's most likely going to stay on the easy paths."

Randon shook his head. "A sixty-five-year-old man who forgets he's sixty-five. He has Alzheimer's and may not know where he is."

Frank had come up to stand behind them. "You're right, Randon. He may wander that way, strictly out of habit. Don't take any of the volunteers—the path might be too rough for them. Take a couple of hot-shots with you."

"I'll go." Shane marked the area with his pen and turned to Randon. "Let me get my gear from the truck."

As soon as the man walked away, Frank gave Randon a serious look and pointed to the knob on the top of the radio. "Channel seven is for everyone, but if something goes wrong, use channel three. That's for me only."

Randon took in a breath. He knew what the

man was really saying. They didn't want bad news being blasted to the public. "I'll find him."

Frank nodded. "I know you'll do your best, but statistics for these kinds of situations aren't good. Dementia patients often hide from rescuers because they don't know who they are and don't understand that they're trying to help. If we don't find him before dark…"

The thought of Darrel not being found sent waves of panic through him. "I'll find him."

Shane approached with another hotshot crew member. "This is Guillermo. He's coming with us."

Randon shook the man's hand and nodded at their packs. "Do you have climbing gear in those packs?"

Guillermo's eyes narrowed. "You think we'll need it?"

"I hope not, but there are some pretty steep canyons off the trail. Better to be safe than sorry."

Shane nodded. "I'll get the climbing gear."

Fifteen minutes later, Randon took off for the overgrown path with the two firefighters right behind him. A giant weight pressed down on him. His gut told him Darrel had gone toward the creek, but would they find him in time? He could not fail another member of Millie's family.

MILLIE'S BODY FELT numb as she sat on the couch with her face in her hands. Stacy sat next to her on the sofa and wrapped her arm around her shoulders in an attempt to comfort her.

Emily came through the door of the kitchen and offered her a glass of tea. "They'll find him," she said.

"That's right," Stacy agreed. "Don't worry, everything will be all right."

Millie took the glass Emily offered but didn't take a drink. Her throat was too dry and her stomach was in knots. Anything she drank right now was likely to come back up.

"This is all my fault." She ran her hands through her hair.

Emily sat on her other side. "You've said that about a hundred times and you need to stop. It was an accident and could've happened no matter who was with him."

Millie shook her head. "He managed to walk right past me and unlock the door without me noticing because I was so worried about beating you on that game. I'm deleting it. I'm deleting that game and every app on my phone."

"You don't know that it happened while you were playing the game," Stacy said. "For all you know, he could have wandered outside while you were texting with me on the phone about Halloween costumes."

Her chest ached. "I shouldn't have even been on the phone at all. I should have been with my dad."

"Stop being so hard on yourself," Emily said.

"They're going to find him and everything will be fine."

Her phone rang and she jumped. She looked at the screen. It was her mom. Her stomach tensed. "Hello?"

"Any news yet?" Her mother's voice was amazingly calm.

"No. We still haven't heard anything."

"Jarrod and I will be there in thirty minutes. I just wanted to let you know while I still have service."

She put the phone down and looked at her two friends. "Mom and Jarrod will be here soon."

The front door opened and Frank walked in. He removed his hat when Millie jumped up and faced him. Her heart thundered in her chest.

Frank smiled. "Randon found him."

"Is he okay?"

"He's fine. He has a couple of scrapes but other than that, he's fine."

Her chest swelled with air and she felt like it was the first time she had been able to breathe. "Where is he?"

Frank held the door open for her. "They should be here any minute now."

Millie rushed out the door, her eyes scanning the yard. Stacy chased after her with the phone in her hand. "Do you want me to call your mom? Or do you want to?"

She took the phone from Stacy's hand and

pressed the button to call her mom. "They found him. He's okay... No, I haven't seen him yet."

Frank motioned for her to hand him the phone.

"Mom, Sheriff Tedford wants to talk to you." She handed the phone to Frank.

"Laura," Frank said, "Randon and a couple members of the hotshot crew found him and are bringing him back. They said he only has a few scrapes but we have an ambulance waiting here to transport him to Springerville Hospital to have him checked out, just in case."

Millie tried to listen to the conversation, but she never took her eyes off the trees, waiting for the rescue party to emerge from the forest.

"Okay. I'll let Millie know." He disconnected the phone and handed it back to her.

"Let me know what?"

"Your mom says there's no need to take him to the hospital unless you think it's necessary. She's leaving that call up to you."

Millie swallowed the lump in her throat. She couldn't believe her mom still trusted her after what she had done.

Cheers and applause broke out from the crowd on her front lawn. She looked over to see Randon and her father. She ran to meet them and threw her arms around her dad.

"I'm so sorry, Dad."

"Now, now, Millie girl." He patted her back.

"You don't need to make such a fuss. I'm sure we'll find some gold nuggets next time."

"What?" She glanced at Randon.

He gave her a sheepish smile. "We went to Chapman Creek to pan for gold."

"Don't you worry," Darrel said, "we'll find some next time."

She let out a shaky laugh. "Let's go in the house, Dad. I want to put some ointment on those scrapes."

As she led her Dad toward the house, she turned to look at Randon. "Thank you."

He just nodded and walked away.

IT WAS ALMOST dark when Randon finally managed to escape the crowd and get home. After returning to the Gibson house with Darrel, he had been surrounded by people. Everyone was patting him on the back and calling him a hero.

It didn't help that Shane and Guillermo told everyone about how he had rappelled down a steep embankment to rescue Darrel from the ledge he had fallen to.

Shane, Guillermo and the rest of the hotshots wanted to go celebrate at the Watering Hole. They invited him to come, promising to buy him a drink, but he just wanted to be alone. When the crowd finally cleared out, Frank gave him a ride to the cabin.

As he was climbing the porch steps, he noticed a large pile of firewood stacked next to his door.

He had no idea where it had come from, but he suspected it was from Pastor Jones.

Pastor Jones had shown up to help right after Caden left. They were removing broken shutters from the windows when Millie had called. At the same time, Pastor Jones's beeper went off. As a member of the volunteer fire department, he was notified whenever there was an emergency. Randon told him what had happened and left, assuming the emergency call was also about Millie's dad.

He saw Pastor Jones at the Gibson house, but didn't get a chance to talk to him. He would call him tomorrow and thank him for the wood. At least he would be warm tonight.

His body ached and his shoulder was numb from rappelling down the slope. A hot shower should help. He was just about to walk into the bathroom when his phone rang. He glanced at the screen to see that it was the Gibsons' home number.

"Hello?"

"Randon." Laura's frantic voice came across the line.

His adrenaline shot up. Even though Millie had examined her father and declared him to be fine, Randon worried that he could have some internal injuries from falling down the embankment. "Is Darrel okay?"

"He's fine," Laura said. "Is Millie there?"

"No. Is she supposed to be?"

"She's really upset about what happened and blames herself. She went for a walk a little while ago and hasn't come back. I'm starting to get really worried."

"I know where she is," Randon said.

"You do?" Her voice was filled with relief.

There was only one place she would've gone. The tree house. "I'll bring her home."

He disconnected the call and grabbed his jacket. Then he went to his bedroom and picked up an extra sweater and a blanket. He grabbed the flashlight sitting on his table and headed for the tree house.

It didn't take long to get to the meadow where the tree house was. He stood underneath it.

"Millie," he called.

"Go away, Randon." Her voice was muffled. "I want to be alone."

He repeated the words she said to him every time he told her that. "Too bad."

He climbed into the tree house to see her huddled in the corner. Her knees were pulled up to her chest and her arms wrapped around her legs. He moved next to her and draped the blanket over her.

"This is my hiding place," he teased. "What are you doing here?"

She stared out into the meadow. "It's my fault," she said. "Everyone keeps telling me it's not, but it is. I was playing on my phone and not paying attention."

"Maybe," he said honestly. "Maybe it wouldn't have happened if you didn't have your phone. But you don't know that for sure."

She let out a heavy sigh. "So, you think it's my fault, too."

"No. I think that it's natural for you to feel guilty but it's over now. You learn from it and move on."

"How am I supposed to do that? How is my mom ever going to be able to trust me again?"

Her words echoed the same things he'd been feeling for the last six months. Now he was the one on the outside looking in and the perspective was entirely different. "Because she loves you and she knows you would never hurt your dad on purpose."

Even as he spoke those words to her, something inside him shifted. The tight band around his chest loosened.

She leaned against him. "Is this how you felt after Kuwait?"

He wrapped one arm around her and pulled her close. "Yes."

"But you were following orders." Her words were soft. "I don't have anyone to blame but myself."

He swallowed. He wished it were that cut and dry. "It doesn't work that way."

"What do you mean?"

212 HER HOMETOWN SOLDIER'S RETURN

"Our squad didn't have a set route to take or area to patrol. It has to be random or the bad guys would know where to find us and when. The squad leader decides where we patrol."

Millie sat up and studied his face. "You were the squad leader, weren't you?"

He nodded. "So you see, I do know how you feel."

"All I want to do is hide out here and never show my face again." She leaned against his chest. "Brian told us that you wouldn't speak to him after, or to anyone, really. At the time, I couldn't understand why not. I thought Brian must have done something wrong."

"The only thing he ever did wrong was befriend me."

"That's not true," she said. "You're the best friend he could ever have. You may have wandered into the wrong area, but you made up for it by saving his life. And Frank told us how you got Dad off the ledge. You're going to have to get used to being called a hero, whether you like it or not."

Randon stiffened. There was that word again. *Hero.* His throat thickened. She always believed the best in him. "I'm not a hero. I didn't wander into the wrong area. I let my ego override my head and I put my entire squad in danger. On purpose."

"Now I know you're just trying to make me feel

better." Millie snuggled against his chest. "You've never had an ego."

He rubbed her back with the hand that was wrapped around her. "I couldn't have one here. There's always someone in Coronado to remind me that I'm nothing. But in the Army, it was different. I started to believe I could be someone important. And I liked that. I wanted that."

Outside the tree house, it was completely dark and the cold air was beginning to settle in the meadow. Millie pulled the blanket up and covered him, too. "I still don't believe it. How did your ego put you in danger?"

Despite the chill, sweat formed on his forehead. The last thing he wanted to do was tell her just how wrong she was. He wanted to be the kind of man she believed him to be.

He took a deep cleansing breath before telling his story.

"It was my first week as squad leader. If I did a good job, it would pave the way toward eventually becoming a platoon sergeant. We were making rounds in the villages. We tried to build a relationship with some of the people. There was one village that seemed to trust us. We played games with the kids and one of the widows sold us falafel sandwiches. Her son pulled me aside and told me he had seen one of the men we had been looking for."

"The boy you want to go back for?" she asked quietly.

He nodded and forced himself to slow his breathing. "I wanted so badly to be the one who led my team to capture the bad guys. I wanted to be a real hero."

"I took my team around to the back of the village where the boy told me they were. I was so blinded by ambition that I forgot all my training. I ignored all the warning signs."

His face burned with shame. "Even when a couple of my men thought they saw someone following us, I didn't pay much attention. We looked around and didn't see anyone. Normally, I would've looked harder, but I was in too big a hurry to get to my target before he left."

Bits and pieces of that night flashed before his eyes. The buildings, shining white in the moonlight. The smell of Oud wafting out of windows and into the streets. The occasional barking of dogs. The stoic faces of the men in the squad as they walked toward their target.

Millie squeezed his hand. "You don't have to finish."

"Yes, I do." It was the first time he'd allowed himself to talk about it.

It was easier to get his breathing back under control than it had been before. Maybe that meant he needed to do this.

"The most dangerous part is when you enter

an enclosed area. They call it the fatal funnel because we can't see everything until we get inside. The bad guy can pick us off as we go through the door."

The images changed from soft pictures of that night to frantic movements and sounds. He could still smell the gunpowder, see the flashes from gunfire and hear the explosions around them.

"Brian's job was to use a battering ram to knock down the door. Just as he started to ram the door, I saw someone on the roof and knew they were waiting for us. I tried to stop him, but it was too late. He had already broken the door down so I grabbed him by his IBA vest and pulled him back."

Randon inhaled through his nose, held it for a moment and let it out slowly. "The men behind me were paying more attention than I was. They managed to hold the attackers off and drag Brian and me to safety."

Millie clutched his shaking hands in hers. "It's okay," she whispered. "It's over."

He rested his forehead against hers. "I'm not a hero. The heroes were the men who were more alert than I was and saw the danger. They managed to get the rest of us out."

"A hero is someone who shows courage in the face of danger or adversity," she said. "It's not someone who never makes a mistake."

He chuckled. "Who told you that?"

"It was part of the speech my dad gave you and Brian before you got on the plane to leave for basic training." Her voice was thick with emotion.

"I forgot about that."

He'd forgotten about a lot of things while he was gone. Like how much he loved the White Mountains in the fall. Like how much he missed talking to Brian until he fell asleep. Most of all, he forgot how Millie's smile could make him feel like he was floating.

Millie let go of his hands to hold his face. "You're a good man. Don't ever forget that again."

She brushed her lips over his. It was sweet and light and not really a kiss. He knew she wanted to kiss him, but she was holding back. Probably because she knew he was going to leave. It wouldn't be fair to kiss her now.

He pulled her into his arms and kissed her, anyway. He didn't care about fairness.

She melted against him and kissed him back. The world around him was spinning but the tree house was grounded.

"Let's get you home," he whispered against her hair. "Your mother is worried sick."

CHAPTER THIRTEEN

MILLIE TOOK A deep breath at the top of the stairs. Everyone had been asleep when she got home last night, which was fine with her. She pressed a hand against her stomach before walking down the stairs.

As she stepped off the last step and into the foyer, she heard voices in the formal dining room and frowned. Now that all the kids were grown and everyone, except her, had moved out, most of the meals were eaten at the table in the kitchen.

She peeked through the archway that led into the dining room. Her mother, her brother Jarrod and Randon were standing around the table looking at something.

Randon saw her and smiled. "Good morning."

His smile warmed her all the way to her toes. "Morning."

Jarrod looked up. "It's about time you got up, sleepyhead."

Her face flushed. She didn't want to admit that she'd been awake for a long time; she just hadn't been ready to come downstairs yet.

"Are you hungry?" Her mom glanced up. "Breakfast is sitting on the counter."

"I'm okay." She walked over to the table. "What's going on?"

Randon pointed toward the back door. "We know how Darrel got out. The lock is broken. It looks like it's locked, but the minute you pull on it, it gives way."

That made her feel marginally better. "I guess we need new locks."

"Not just any locks," Jarrod said.

He moved over to let her stand between him and Randon. Jarrod's laptop was open in the middle of the table and she looked at the screen. The website was for a childproof lock that was also good for dementia patients.

Mom smiled. "Randon came over first thing this morning to show us this website. These are all easy-to-use and easy-to-install locks that Darrel won't be able to unlock. We just need to decide which ones we want."

"How did you think of this?" It was so simple. Why hadn't they thought of it before?

"I did some research on the internet last night."

"Last night? It was after midnight when you brought me home."

"I couldn't sleep." He shrugged.

She hadn't been able to sleep, either. Between her father wandering off and Randon's kiss, her emotions were too jumbled for her to drift off.

The last time she'd checked the clock, it had been three in the morning.

"What time is it?"

Jarrod gave her a lopsided grin. "It's almost noon."

"You should've woken me up."

Mom squeezed her hand. "I knocked on your door when I got up, but you didn't respond so I let you sleep."

She tucked a stand of hair behind her ear. "How's Dad this morning?"

"He's a little sore." Mom exchanged a look with Jarrod. "He's taking a nap right now."

Millie stiffened. "What's wrong?"

Jarrod's brow furrowed. "I was sitting in the kitchen this morning, drinking coffee, when he walked in. He didn't recognize me and when I tried to tell him who I was, he got upset."

Her heart dropped. "How upset?"

Her brother's gaze dropped to the floor. "He hit at me and tried to run out the door."

"He hit you?" Millie's heart dropped to her stomach.

"No. He didn't *hit* me, like punch me or anything." Jarrod shook his head. "It was more like he slapped at me while trying to get to the door."

No matter how agitated her father had gotten when he couldn't remember something, he'd never been violent.

"It was my fault," Jarrod muttered. "I didn't

realize how bad he'd gotten and I thought he was kidding. I got too close to him too fast and scared him."

"No," Mom said. "It was my fault. I should've warned you how disoriented he can be when he first wakes up. With all the excitement yesterday, I never imagined he would wake up while I was in the shower."

Millie bit her bottom lip. Her brother's crest-fallen face tugged at her heart. She'd never been particularly close to Jarrod, mostly due to the eight-year age gap between them, but she hated to see him so upset.

She wrapped her arms around him and hugged him. He stiffened for a moment before hugging her back.

"I didn't believe it," he said softly. "You and Mom tried to tell me how bad it was, but I didn't believe it."

"We don't want to believe it, either, but we have to accept it."

Jarrod let go and stepped back. He squeezed the top of her arms. "I'm sorry that we all left you here to help Mom alone. That's going to change."

Her stomach knotted. After yesterday's events, he probably didn't think she was capable of helping their mother.

Randon caught her gaze. "Laura was just telling Jarrod how amazing you are and how she couldn't handle this if it weren't for you."

Millie's gaze darted between her mother and brother.

"That's right," Jarrod said. "But we're going to step up and give both of you more help. You have to be exhausted, physically and mentally."

She wasn't sure what to say. It would be nice if her brothers were around more.

Mom pointed to a picture on the table. "I think this is the one we should use. It's simple, but effective."

Randon nodded and picked his phone up from the table. He tapped the screen a few times, scrolled. "Springerville Hardware has it in stock."

Mom frowned. "What about Denny? I'd rather give him the business if I can."

"I'm giving Mr. Morgan plenty of business," Randon said. "Besides, we need to get this installed as soon as possible and it would take him a week to get it in."

"All right." She nodded. "Let's do it."

Jarrod agreed. "I'd also like to set up some security cameras inside the house."

"Oh, Jarrod, no." Mom shook her head. "I don't want to spy on him."

"You wouldn't be spying, Mom. You'd be keeping him safe." He motioned for her to follow him to the kitchen. "Let me show you where I think they should go."

As soon as they left the room, Randon turned

to Millie. "Want to take a ride to Springerville with me?"

"Now?"

He arched one eyebrow at her. "Got something better to do?"

"I was thinking about crawling back into a hole," she said just loud enough for him to hear.

She could feel his warm breath against her neck when he leaned close to her and whispered, "Which is exactly why you need to go with me."

Shivers traveled down her neck and she glanced down at the yoga pants and T-shirt she was wearing. "I'll go change."

She ran back to her bedroom and slipped off her tennis shoes and tossed them in the closet. She traded her yoga pants and T-shirt for a soft pair of worn denim jeans and a navy blue sweater and pulled on her UGG boots.

Her mom was standing at the bottom of the stairs when Millie came back down.

"Dr. Curtis called in a new prescription for your dad," she said. "Will you pick it up while you're in Springerville?"

"Is there anything else we can get while we're there?"

"No, but if I think of anything, I'll text it to Millie."

Millie took her jacket from the coat tree and followed Randon onto the porch. His silver muscle car was parked on the street.

"You picked Cindy up from the shop." She used the pet name he'd given the car years ago.

His grandfather loved John Wayne movies and *Rio Bravo* had been his favorite. Cindy was the name of a song Ricky Nelson sang in the movie and his grandfather was always singing it as he worked.

She hopped off the porch and walked to the car. "Did Bear give her a clean bill of health?"

Randon opened the passenger side door for her. "She's good to go."

Millie slid into the passenger seat and rubbed one hand across the dashboard. "Welcome back, Cindy."

Randon laughed, but she was positive he talked to the car, too.

He started the engine and she put her seat belt on. Butterflies fluttered in her stomach and she stole a quick glance at him. "That was really thoughtful of you to come over and show Mom the locks."

He shrugged. "No trouble. I was coming over this morning, anyway."

"Why?" Her butterflies flapped wildly.

"I wanted to talk to you." His hazel eyes held her gaze for a moment before he turned his attention back to the road.

The butterflies in her stomach rolled into a lead ball. She rubbed the palms of her hands on her jeans and sucked air into her lungs. "Why?"

"I wanted to take you to breakfast."

"Why?" Did he want to let her down on neutral ground?

He laughed. "I'm tired of eating cereal every morning."

She leaned back against the seat. Brian and Randon used to meet at the Bear's Den Diner for breakfast every Saturday morning. Occasionally, she tagged along.

He cast her a sideways glance. "You're not going to ask why?"

Millie's face heated at his teasing smile. "I've seen the way you eat breakfast."

He chuckled and turned onto the highway that led down the mountain toward Springerville.

She readjusted the elastic band holding her messy bun in place. What she really wanted to do was ask him if he regretted their kiss last night.

"You should leave your hair down sometimes."

"I have to put it up while I'm working, so now it's just a habit." Secretly, she was pleased that he even had an opinion on her hair.

She pulled the band from her hair and ran her hand through it. "What made you think about getting locks for the doors?"

"I took out the trash."

"Not sure I see the connection?" She frowned at him.

"When I was about ten, I saw some childproof

cabinet locks at Mr. Morgan's hardware store," he said. "I thought it would be a good idea to install them on the cabinet where my dad kept his vodka."

Millie cocked her head. "It didn't go well?"

"That's an understatement." He kept his eyes on the road as he spoke.

Millie watched his face for any sign of emotion. He was pretty good at masking his emotions anytime he talked about his dad, but his eyes always gave him away. His hazel eyes shifted colors according to how he was feeling. Brown was warm. Calm. When the green flecks in his eyes took over, she knew a storm was coming.

A quiet stillness filled the inside of the car. Millie leaned against the seat and watched the trees zip by. Even though most of the trees were evergreens, patches of orange and gold dotted the landscape.

"I've missed the mountains," Randon said.

Millie's pulse skipped a beat. Was Randon starting to think about staying? She swallowed, trying to keep the conversation light. "So does Brian. When he was overseas, he said the land was so flat and empty it made him claustrophobic." She wrinkled her nose. "It didn't make sense to me. How can open space make you feel closed in?"

"I'm not sure, but it does." Randon shrugged.

"Here, it's easy to tell distances because we can see the mountains and certain peaks, and we always know where we are. Out in the middle of the desert, it's easy to get turned around."

Millie looked out the window. They were now on the long stretch of highway just before entering Springerville. "Is it as flat and empty as this?"

"Worse. This isn't flat," he said. "It's not mountains, but there are rolling hills that break up the landscape. Where Brian and I were, there was nothing. It was desolate."

She bit her bottom lip. "And that's where you want to go back to?"

He was quiet for a moment. Finally, he took a deep breath. "That's where I have to go back to."

"You don't," she said. "You don't have to go back. Finding that boy isn't going to change anything."

"Or it could change everything."

Her stomach rolled with emotion as she tried to think of a way to convince Randon it was pointless to go back overseas. Maybe the truth was that he just didn't want to stay.

"When you find him, will you come back?"

"No." Randon shook his head. "There's nothing for me in Coronado."

Nothing. She was nothing to him. She turned her head to stare out the window so he couldn't see the tears threatening to spill over.

RANDON KNEW MILLIE was upset. What he didn't know was why she wasn't telling him. She'd never had a problem telling anyone what was on her mind.

He glanced across the car to see her staring out the window. Her long hair fell in tight curls over her shoulder.

They entered Springerville and he turned off the main road to park at a small diner.

"I hope you don't mind eating at Doris's." He knew she wouldn't. It was her favorite.

She suppressed a smile. "I haven't eaten here since the day you and Brian left for basic training."

"I've been craving her biscuits and gravy all week."

He got out of the car and walked around to open the door for her. By the time he got there, she'd already gotten out. Yep. She was mad at him.

She started to step up onto the sidewalk, but he moved to block her way. She leaned back and glared at him. "What are you doing? Move."

"Are you going to tell me what you're mad about?"

"Who said I was mad?" Her blue eyes shot daggers at him.

"You don't think I can tell when you're mad at me?" Randon cocked his head. "What is it?"

Millie rolled her eyes and pushed past him.

By the time he caught up with her, she was entering the building. He stood quietly behind her while they waited for the server to seat them at a table.

The server came and led them to a table in the middle of the restaurant. Millie started to sit down, but Randon stopped her.

"Excuse me," he said to the server, "could we have a table closer to the wall? Maybe that one?" He pointed to an empty table close to the back corner.

The woman gave him an odd look. "It's not clean yet."

"I don't mind," Randon said.

"Suit yourself." The woman walked over to the empty table and set down a couple of menus before stacking the dirty dishes that were on the table.

Millie gave him a knowing look as the woman hurried away. "You need your back to the wall?"

He nodded. "I need to be able to see the doors."

As soon as they sat down, Millie picked up the menu and hid her face.

He sighed. He'd seen Millie mad hundreds of times, although he'd never been the object of her anger. Brian, on the other hand, was always doing something to make her mad. Brian usually did something to make her laugh or teased her until she smiled.

It was worth a try. He reached across the table and pushed the menu down so he could see her face. He gave her his best smile. "Did anyone ever tell you that you're cute when you're mad?"

She arched one eyebrow. "Did anyone ever tell you it's condescending to call a grown woman cute?"

He lifted his hands, palms up, and shrugged his shoulders. "What do you want from me?"

"Nothing." She picked the menu up again and held it between them.

Randon took the menu from her and put it on the table in front of him. She leaned back and crossed her arms. He met her stern gaze with his own. "I told you from the beginning that I wasn't going to stay."

Her chin lifted. She leaned on the table with her elbows and rested her chin on her hands. "So what was last night?"

A momentary lapse of judgment. He sighed. "Wishful thinking."

"It doesn't have to be." She reached across the table to touch his hands.

Randon's skin tingled where her fingers stroked the back of his hands. "You see everything in black and white. Sometimes it's not that simple."

For every reason he could think of to stay with her, there were three that said he couldn't. First and foremost was Brian. One of the last things he said to Randon before the ambush that night was, *I told you, Millie is off-limits.*

Before the ambush, he was ready to demand

that Brian tell him why he was against Randon and Millie being together. Then he almost got Brian killed. How could he go against Brian's wishes now?

"I don't want you to go back there," she whispered. "I want you to—"

His phone interrupted her. He glanced at the screen and his heart began to pound. "I'm sorry. I have to take this call."

He walked outside and moved toward the back of the building. "Hello."

"Randon Farr, please," a clipped voice came across the line.

"This is he."

"Please hold for Dr. Harlow."

He inhaled slowly, waiting for his doctor to join the line. So much was riding on this conversation.

"Randon," Dr. Harlow greeted him a moment later. "I'm sorry it took me so long to get back to you. I hear you had an episode. I need you to tell me exactly what happened."

For the next few minutes, he answered a barrage of questions. His doctor wanted to know every detail of his life since he'd arrived in Arizona. What he was eating. How much he was sleeping. The elevation. His diet. The man even wanted details about his bodily functions.

"You sound better," Dr. Harlow said. "I like that you've got an advocate who's helping you with your PTSD."

"Was my blackout related to my traumatic brain injury?"

"I don't know. I doubt it, but I'm going to send orders to the VA Hospital in Phoenix. I want you to have another brain scan. We need to make sure everything is healing and you haven't had a setback."

His stomach dropped. "When? I have a follow-up medical appointment with Bravos on November fifteenth."

"They'll probably be able to get you in by the middle of next week and we'll get your results by the end of the week."

He let out a sigh of relief. "Okay. Thank you."

He disconnected the call and went back inside. Millie must have ordered for him because there were two plates of breakfast food on his side of the table. Eggs, hash browns, sausage, bacon and, best of all, an entire plate of biscuits and gravy.

"For a minute there, I thought you were pulling off a dine-and-dash," Millie said. She picked up her cheeseburger and took a big bite.

"In order to dine-and-dash, don't I have to eat first?" He scanned the room and sat down.

"True." She twirled a french fry in her ketchup. "I hope it's okay that I ordered for you. Is that what you wanted?"

"It's perfect." His mouth was already watering. "You didn't want breakfast?"

"Nope." She shook her head. "I was craving a cheeseburger."

"Excuse me." An older couple stopped next to their table.

They appeared to be in their sixties. The man had a barrel chest and his suspenders looked as if they were about to snap, while the woman was tall and bony. Her makeup was caked on, probably in an effort to cover the wrinkles around her eyes and mouth.

Randon set his fork down and gave them his attention.

Millie nodded at them. "Good morning, Mrs. Porter."

Porter? Randon almost groaned. His old English teacher? He had thought she looked familiar. The woman had done everything she could to fail him. He never understood why she disliked him so much.

The man nodded toward the window at the front of the restaurant. "Is that your Chevelle outside?"

"Yes, sir," he said. "I restored her myself."

"That's a nice car."

He beamed. "Thank you, sir."

The woman peered down a slightly crooked nose at him. "You're Randon Farr, aren't you? Greg Farr's son?"

Warning bells went off in his head. He nodded.

She gave him a smug smile. "I always knew

you'd turn out just like your father. Who did you swindle to get a car like that?"

The venom dripping from the woman's words took him back. "I'm sorry. What?"

"Let's go, Nancy." The man took a few steps but the woman didn't budge.

"Greg claimed that he went bankrupt along with the rest of the people he managed to con into giving him money. I mean, he couldn't even buy you a decent pair of shoes."

He sucked in his breath. He knew from experience that they wouldn't leave until the woman got whatever she wanted to say off her chest. Across the table from him, Millie straightened her shoulders.

"Let's go," the man said again.

The woman jerked her arm away from him. "My father lost everything when he invested in Greg's little scheme. He died almost penniless. But your father must have taught you all his tricks. I mean, classic cars like that don't come cheap."

"Enough, Nancy," her husband growled and pulled her away from the table.

Millie looked at him with wide eyes. "What just happened? Are you okay?"

He shrugged. "It's not the first time people have yelled at me because of what my father did to them."

"Why didn't you set her straight and tell her you bought that car yourself?" Her face was tight.

"It wouldn't do any good. If saying something to me makes them feel better, then let them."

She wiped her mouth with her napkin and stood up. "I'll be right back."

Randon nodded. He felt numb inside and even the biscuits and gravy didn't appeal to him anymore.

He was still sitting in a trance when someone cleared their throat. He almost groaned when he saw the couple standing next to his table again.

The woman pressed her lips together and took a breath. "I want to apologize. I shouldn't have blamed you for your father's mistakes."

The man stepped forward and offered Randon his hand. "I'm sorry about everything."

Randon stood and shook the man's hand. "I understand. My father wasn't a good man."

"But you are. I can see that." The man stepped back. "And thank you for your service." The man tipped his hat and his wife gave Randon the slightest nod before they turned to leave.

He remained standing and watched the couple head for the door. That's when he saw Millie. She leaned against the wall with her arms crossed. When the woman walked by, Millie nodded at her.

After they were gone, Millie came back to the table and sat down.

Randon's gaze darted from the door to her. "You didn't."

"Oh, I did," Millie said very matter-of-factly.

"You don't always have to defend me, you know."

"I'll always defend you. No matter what." She picked up her glass and took a long sip of soda. "Even when you break my heart."

He shook his head. "I never wanted to hurt you."

"I know."

He nodded toward the door. "Now do you see why I can't stay here? There will always be people like Mrs. Porter."

"Don't." She pressed her lips together. "Don't use your dad as an excuse to leave. If you really wanted to stay, it wouldn't matter what anyone thought of your family."

"I wish it were that simple."

"New rule." Millie crossed her arms. "We're not talking about you leaving anymore. I've got a couple more weeks to prove that you belong in Coronado, so we are going to enjoy ourselves. And by November fifteenth, you won't be able to leave."

Randon laughed. "Or you'll want to come with me."

She held her hand across the table. "Care to shake on it?"

He gripped her tiny hand in his. "This will be an interesting few weeks."

CHAPTER FOURTEEN

RANDON COULDN'T BELIEVE it when a group of women knocked on his door soon after he got home from Springerville. All of the women had either helped in the search for Darrel the day before, or had heard about it. The women didn't stay long, but each of them brought a plate of food.

Between that, and all the food that had been delivered before, he had enough food to feed the entire town.

He wasn't sure what was worse. Having people, like his old English teacher at the diner in Springerville, reminding him of his family's shortcomings or people patting him on the back and hailing him as a hero. Either way, he needed to escape from it.

He had the rest of the afternoon to work on the cabin...unless he was bombarded with more people.

After he and Millie left the diner in Springerville, they had stopped in at the hardware store to get the locks for Millie's house and he managed to buy most of what he needed to start repairs on the cabin. If he'd taken his father's pickup truck, he could've gotten even more things, but he would go back another day.

A noise outside caused Randon to stop prying up rotten floorboards in the living room. Not more visitors. He peeked out the window and let out a sigh of relief. It was just Pastor Jones.

"Good afternoon, Pastor." Randon stepped onto the porch. "Was it you who left the firewood on my porch?"

"Yes," he said. "I have a lot more for you in my truck."

Randon's gaze drifted to the pickup and his eyes widened at the sight of the full load of wood. It was enough to last a week, at least. That was enough time for the soreness from Darrel's rescue to wear off. After that, he could chop wood himself. Only now, he could afford to go slowly and not overdo it with his shoulder.

Still, he felt guilty about taking it. "That's very generous of you. Isn't there someone in the church congregation that could use it?"

"We have enough wood to fuel everyone in town," Pastor Jones laughed. "Reed's Lumber Mill donates their leftovers to the church. We give it to anyone in town who can use it. As a matter of fact, we supplied your father with wood last winter."

Randon didn't know that. His stomach twisted.

Even though he'd always been the one to cut wood for heating the cabin, after he left, he'd never given it another thought. Not once had he wondered if his father was sitting in a cold house because he didn't have any wood. That explained how his father kept from freezing to death.

Pastor Jones lowered the tailgate. "We used to have a wood stove in the annex, but last year we upgraded to a furnace, so now we have even more leftovers."

Randon started loading wood in his arms to carry to the porch. He was vaguely aware of the pastor talking, but he was still thinking about his own lack of compassion.

His father was never father-of-the-year material, but apparently he wouldn't win any number-one-son awards, either.

"Are you okay?"

Randon started and saw Pastor Jones looking at him with concern. "I'm fine. It's just been a long couple of days."

"I understand." He placed the last of the wood on the porch. "I better get back. The church is having a trunk-or-treat event tonight in lieu of trick-or-treating."

He'd forgotten that it was Halloween. Hopefully, that would keep people at home and he could get some peace and quiet.

He walked Pastor Jones to his truck and closed

the tailgate for him. "Thanks, I appreciate the firewood."

"No problem. I'll be back tomorrow to start replacing the shutters on the windows."

Randon wanted to tell him not to, but he doubted the man would listen. Instead, he just said his thanks and waited for the truck to disappear down the long drive.

It was only four o'clock, but already the sun was dipping low in the sky and the air was getting colder. The mountains were tinted pink and Randon tipped his head back to see the explosion of colors on the horizon. His chest swelled and he hurried inside to get his art supplies.

It only took him a moment to set an easel up on the back porch. With deft hands, he added a few colors to his palette and mixed until he had what he was looking for.

Randon's anxiety lessened with every stroke of his brush across the canvas. He was so entranced with his work that he didn't hear someone coming up the back porch steps.

"What are you doing, mister?"

He glanced over to see Toby standing on the edge of the porch. "I'm painting." He was surprised to see him. He hadn't seen any of the boys in a few days.

"What are you painting?" Toby moved to get a closer look.

Randon stopped working and studied the boy.

He was dressed in faded jeans that had several holes in the legs. His shirt was at least two sizes too big, but at least it looked warm. "Are you going trick-or-treating tonight?"

Toby shook his head and made an overexaggerated look of disgust. "I'm too old for that."

Randon knew better but wasn't about to call him out on his fib. Instead, he nodded. "I didn't trick-or-treat when I was your age, either. Although, the reason I didn't was because I couldn't afford to buy a costume."

"You couldn't?" Toby moved even closer.

"Nope," Randon said. "And my dad wouldn't buy candy to hand out to people, either. He'd turn off all the lights and pretend no one was home."

"That's what my dad does, too." Toby's voice was clear, but full of regret.

Randon sighed. He and Toby had more in common than he would have liked. "He was always telling me we didn't have money for things, but he always had enough money for his booze."

Toby's face flinched, but he didn't say anything. "How'd you learn to paint like that?"

"Lots of practice." He set his brush on the palette and handed it to Toby. "Hold this. I'll be right back."

He came back out a minute later with a smaller canvas and another palette. He set the canvas up on the table. "Want to try?"

Toby shook his head. "I can't paint."

"Anyone can paint," Randon said. "You don't have to draw a picture—it can be abstract. Just use the colors you want and paint whatever you feel."

The boy hesitated for a minute, then reached for the brush. "What do I do?"

Randon explained how to put the colors on the palette and how to mix them to get the color you want. Using a dry paintbrush, he demonstrated different strokes he could use.

Toby took a deep breath and dipped his brush in the first color.

Twenty minutes later, it was almost completely dark, but they were both still painting. Finally, when Randon couldn't make out the colors anymore, he stopped. "I'm starving. How about you?"

He could see the way Toby's eyes flickered at the mention of food, but Toby shrugged. "I'm okay."

"Are you sure?" Randon pointed toward the kitchen. "People have been bringing me food ever since I got to Coronado and I could really use some help getting rid of it."

"What kind of food?"

"What do you want? I have anything you can think of." Randon walked to the sliding glass door that led into the kitchen. "Don't forget to bring in your brush. The first rule in painting is keeping your brush clean."

He showed Toby how to clean the brushes.

While Toby took care of the brushes, Randon began removing food from the refrigerator.

"You weren't kidding." Toby's mouth dropped open at the sight of so much food.

"Told ya." He handed Toby a paper plate. "Put whatever you want on here and I'll heat it up in the microwave."

Toby laid the paintbrushes on the counter next to the sink. He took the plate and began piling food on it. When he handed the plate to Randon, food was threatening to fall off the edge.

They sat at the table and started eating. Toby was halfway through his second helping when he gave Randon a funny look. "How come you ain't got no furniture?"

"How come I haven't got *any* furniture," Randon corrected Toby's grammar. Whoa. Since when did he become the word police?

"Yeah." Toby didn't seem to get Randon's hint.

"It was all either falling apart or stank so badly of cigarette smoke that I couldn't stand it. So I hauled it all outside."

"Where at? I didn't see it."

"There's a big pit out behind the cabin. My dad didn't want to pay for trash collection, either, so that's where we used to burn all the trash."

"Are you gonna burn it?" Toby's eyes were wide.

"I plan to. Of course, I need to notify the fire department first. That way, they'll be ready if something happens and the fire gets out of control."

"Like the Wallow Fire did?"

"Exactly."

The massive wildfire that ripped through the White Mountains had happened before Toby was even born, but the scars could still be seen all over the landscape.

"Knock-knock," Millie called from the front door.

She walked into the cabin carrying a large paper grocery bag. Randon almost groaned. "Please tell me you didn't bring me more food."

Toby laughed.

"No." She set the bag on the dining table and reached one hand out to Toby. "Hi. I'm Millie."

Toby's face turned red, but he shook her hand. "I'm Toby."

Millie reached inside the bag. "I brought a selection of Halloween-themed movies for us to watch."

Randon laughed. "I'm not sure if you noticed, but I don't have a television. Or a DVD player."

"I got you covered," she said. "I have a television and a DVD player in my car."

Toby's gaze darted around the room and he took a few steps toward the back door.

"What about you?" Millie flashed Toby a big smile. "Want to watch some Halloween movies?"

Randon's heart squeezed. He liked that Millie included Toby.

Toby shrugged and walked around the table to

get a closer look at the movies. "You don't have any scary movies?" He picked up a DVD and shook his head. "*Hocus Pocus*?"

Randon could tell that Toby was trying to sound tough. Before he could say anything, Millie piped up. "Are you kidding?" she said. "Randon can't watch horror movies."

"You can't?" Toby looked at him with disbelief.

Randon shook his head. "If I watched a scary movie, I wouldn't be able to sleep for week." He turned his head and pretended to glare at Millie. "Thanks for throwing me under the bus."

"What?" She gave him an innocent look. "He wouldn't believe it if I said I was the one who was scared."

He crossed his arms. "Why not?"

"I'm a nurse," she said. "I deal with blood and gore all day."

Randon drew in a sharp breath. It was amazing how one word brought such a clear picture to his mind. His stomach quaked and he could see Brian's body underneath him, covered in blood. It wasn't until the men had pulled him away that he realized it wasn't Brian's blood. It was his.

Millie's eyes widened in alarm. "Toby, help me get the TV out of my car."

She directed the boy outside before touching Randon's arm. "I'm sorry. I didn't realize."

"S'okay," he mumbled.

"Go to the bathroom. Sit with your head between your knees for a few minutes. Then wash your face with cold water."

"Bossy." But he headed for the bathroom.

MILLIE'S INSIDES WERE SHAKING. When all the blood seemed to drain from Randon's face, she knew she'd said something wrong. Was it the word *blood*? She wasn't sure, and she certainly wasn't going to ask him. She kept Toby outside with her as long as possible to give Randon a chance to recover.

She and Toby carried in the TV and the DVD player and set them against the wall. Then she sent Toby back to her car to get the blankets and pillows that were in the back seat.

As soon as Toby walked out of the house, she went to the bathroom at the end of the hall and knocked lightly. "Randon. Are you okay?"

"Uh-huh," came the muffled reply.

She pushed the door open. Randon was leaning over the sink, water dripping from his face. His forearm was clammy to her touch, and she stepped closer to him. She rubbed his back with one hand. "Do you want to be alone?"

"No." He stood up straight and took a deep breath. He pulled her into his arms and held her close for a moment. "I'm sorry. It hits me at odd times."

She was pressed against his chest and could

hear his heartbeat. It wasn't too fast. Strong and steady. "You have nothing to apologize for."

"Let's go watch a movie." He took her by the hand and led her to the living room.

Toby glanced up from the DVD player. His gaze dropped to their interlinked hands. "Are you guys a couple?"

Millie held her breath and glanced at Randon.

Randon's brow furrowed for a moment. "No," he said. Lifting the hand holding hers, he pressed a kiss to the back of her hand. "Next to Millie's brother, she's my best friend."

His hazel eyes held her gaze for a moment.

Millie forced a smile, even though her insides were crumbling. "That's right, Toby. We're just good friends."

Toby didn't look convinced but he shrugged and went back to connecting the DVD player to the television.

Millie pulled her hand out of Randon's grasp and picked up a blanket from the pile where Toby had dropped them. She unfolded it and shook it out, spreading it across the floor. Randon picked up another blanket and spread it out on top of hers.

She scanned the emptiness of the room. "When are you going to break down and get some furniture?"

He shook his head. "Why bother?"

"You can't live like this forever." She tossed the

pillows on the blankets. "The dining chairs are comfortable and all, but eventually you'll need a sofa."

"I'll let the new owner pick out the sofa."

She cocked her head. "What are you talking about?"

A guilty look crossed his face. "I thought I told you. I'm putting the cabin up for sale."

"Why?" Her stomach twisted and she felt as if she'd been punched in the gut.

If she had come to terms with the fact that he wanted to go to work with a military contractor, she could. Even the thought of him wanting to go back overseas was something she could accept. Because she knew that sooner or later, he'd be back. This was his home.

"I—"

Toby jumped up from the floor and waved a movie container. "Let's watch *Haunted Mansion*! I bet it has some scary scenes."

Randon looked almost relieved he had been interrupted. "But not too scary, right?"

"No," Toby said. "It's Disney."

"Get comfortable." Randon tossed a pillow at him and sat on the floor, folding his long legs underneath him.

Millie watched Toby sit down and imitate Randon and her heart skipped a beat. The boy was so much like Randon had been at that age. Randon must recognize it, too.

"I'll make some popcorn," she said.

Randon frowned. "I don't have any."

"I brought some."

Toby grinned. "You think of everything."

"She always has," Randon told him. "Millie takes care of everyone. That's what she does."

Millie tucked a lock of hair behind her ear and went to get the popcorn out of her oversized purse. Didn't he know why she was always trying to take care of him? This night was not going the way she'd planned. And it wasn't just because of the extra visitor.

She put the bag of popcorn in the microwave and waited for it to start popping. Her fingers brushed her lips. After the kiss they'd shared, she was sure he felt the same as she did. But selling the cabin? That wasn't something he would do if he wanted to be with her.

She was so deep in thought that she almost let the popcorn burn. Holding the bag by the corner so she didn't burn herself, she carried it to the living room and took her place on the blanket.

Toby went home right after the movie was over. Both she and Randon offered to drive him, but he refused. Millie wondered if he didn't want them to see where he lived.

As soon as he left, she turned to Randon. "Please tell me you were kidding about selling the cabin."

"I'm not." He lifted his chin. "There's no reason for me to hang on to it."

She swallowed. "Your great-grandfather built this cabin. I thought you loved it."

"I love the fact that someone in my family cared enough about something to build it. I love that he had dreams of raising a family and leaving a legacy," he said. "But look around. I can't think of one happy memory I have of this house after Grandpa died."

Her gaze drifted to the kitchen counter that separated the kitchen area from the living room. If she looked close enough, she could probably find bloodstains on the floor from where his father had shoved him into the cabinet hard enough to knock him out.

She would never forget that day. She'd ridden her bike to the market to get an ice-cream cone. While she was waiting for her cone, Greg came into the store. His face was white as a sheet and he was in a panic because he couldn't find the bandages. Millie showed him where they were and asked him why he needed them. He told Millie that Randon had tripped and hit his head on the counter.

That was all Millie heard. She left Greg standing there, jumped on her bike and sped to the cabin.

Her heart almost stopped when she found him lying unconscious, with blood pooling around his head. It was a good thing she always carried a first aid kit on her bicycle. She cleaned the blood off his face and used superglue to close the wound. Then she made him sit on the couch holding an ice pack on his head while she cleaned the blood off the floor.

Greg came into the house shortly after that. It was the only time Millie could remember seeing him look concerned about his son. He asked her if Randon was going to okay or if he needed to go to the emergency room. It was Randon who said he was fine.

Greg only shrugged, got a beer out of the fridge and went outside. She tried to talk Randon into coming home with her, but he refused. Before she left, she told him to be more careful and not to slip and fall anymore. They both knew that she was aware of the truth, but neither of them ever mentioned it.

She couldn't imagine growing up the way he had. Her home had been full of love and laughter. Her parents made sure she never lacked for anything, while his childhood had been full of anger and fear.

Until that day, she thought she wanted to be a veterinarian, but after that, she knew she wanted to be a nurse. Someday, she might even go back to school and become a nurse practitioner.

"Then stay. Finish the legacy your great-grand-father started. Make new memories here. Happy memories." She tried to keep her voice even, but even she could hear the note of desperation.

Randon's face tightened. "You're breaking your own rules. No talking about me leaving, remember?"

She lifted her chin and stomped into the kitchen. She jerked the refrigerator door open and swept one hand across the food containers stacked inside. "If people thought as badly of you as you think they do, why would they do this?"

Randon didn't say anything. He crossed his arms and cocked his head as if waiting for her to finish her rant.

She let out a huff, walked over to the fireplace and picked up a stick of firewood. "What about all the wood on the porch?"

Randon raised one eyebrow. "There are good people in Coronado who want to help others. They even brought my father enough wood to get him through the winter. It has nothing to do with what they think of me."

"How can you say that?" She shook her head. "I had to run interference for you at the festival because people were calling you a hero."

"Right now they think that," he said dryly. "What do you think will happen if I stay? I have no job and no prospects. It wouldn't be long until they started comparing me to my father."

"That won't happen." Her words rushed out. "And why do you have to do anything right now?

You just got home and you're still healing. People understand that you need to take some time for yourself and recuperate."

"How long am I supposed to do that?"

"As long as you need," she said. "You could take your time fixing the cabin. You could paint. It's not like you have to work, anyway. Don't you get money from the Army?"

He recoiled as if she'd slapped him. The muscles in his jaw twitched as he gritted his teeth. "So did my old man and look where it got him."

In her panic at the thought of him leaving, she'd spoken without thinking. "You're nothing like your father."

"But I will be," he said. His hazel eyes flashed with anger. "If I sit around here doing nothing long enough, I will be. Maybe I'll get lucky and the Ladies' Auxiliary will feed me for a year or so before they decide I'm just as worthless as Greg."

She could feel him pulling away from her. "That's not true."

His face softened and he stepped closer to her. He lifted his hand and ran one finger along her jawline. "I know it's not what you want, but I don't belong here."

"You're wrong."

Randon shook his head. "When I joined the Army, I never even considered making a career out of it. I went because Brian was going and I needed to get out of this town. I never imagined

I would find exactly what I needed. The Army didn't care who my father was. They gave me structure. Comradery. A family."

"You have a family." She swallowed.

"No, I don't," he said. "Your parents love me—I don't doubt that. They looked out for me. They helped me when no one else would. But your older brothers barely know me. And while Brian has always been my best friend, even he knows I'm not Gibson-worthy."

"How can you say that? He loves you like a brother."

He chuckled. "Do you know why Brian didn't want me to ask you to the prom?"

She thought about what her mom had said. "Because he was worried that if you and I started dating, he might lose his best friend."

"No." Randon took one hand in his. "It's because he didn't think I was good enough for his sister."

"I'm sure he didn't say that."

"Not in so many words," he said. "But I knew what he meant."

"You're building your entire future on what you think someone meant? What you think people will say?" Millie's temper flared. "You're not being fair."

"Neither are you." Randon walked to the door and opened it. "Good night."

Her gaze narrowed and she pressed her lips together. "You're kicking me out?"

"I'm tired," he said.

A thousand arguments ran through her head, but she bit her tongue. She knew when Randon had been pushed far enough.

CHAPTER FIFTEEN

It took Randon a long time to fall asleep after Millie left. He paced the cabin, his anger building with every step. Did she really think that he could just settle in Coronado and be happy?

Did she think all people were like her? Not everyone tried to see the good in others and give people the benefit of the doubt. She didn't know what it was like to work on a term paper for weeks and get an F because the teacher held a grudge against him. She hadn't been pulled out of class and hauled to the police station whenever someone in the trailer park reported a theft. It didn't matter that he always had an alibi or he wasn't even around. It seemed like anytime something was stolen, someone remembered seeing someone who looked like him hanging around.

Millie had never asked someone out on a date only to be laughed at because their parents would never allow them to go out with a Farr.

He carefully folded up her blankets and stacked the pillows on top. Then he unplugged the television and DVD player and set them next to the blankets. In the morning, he would drop her things off at her house. He would apologize for making her angry. He wouldn't apologize for not wanting to stay in Coronado.

Didn't she know he'd stay if he could? But sooner or later, she'd resent him for not being able to give her the life she deserved. Just like his mother had resented Greg.

His gaze drifted to his father's bedroom. The door was still closed as if keeping it shut would keep memories at bay. He walked to the door and pushed it open. He flipped the light switch on and scanned the space.

With each step he took into the room, his anxiety rose a bit. Not the kind of anxiety he felt when he was on the verge of a PTSD attack, but the anxiety he had as a child sneaking into his father's room.

The light bulb in the closet had burned out, but he didn't need one. The small shoebox he was looking for was in the farthest corner of the closet. Was it still there? He reached up on the top shelf and felt around. His fingers brushed against something hard. He stood up on his tiptoes to grab the box. The last time he took the box down he had needed to stand on a chair.

He carried the box back to the dining room table and set it down. A thick layer of dust coated the lid. Inside was a faded photograph, an envelope full of folded letters and a ring box. He started at the only picture he had of his mother.

Her long blond hair fell over her shoulders and she smiled at the camera. Her name was Tamara. Randon sighed. His father refused to talk about her. What little Randon knew about her was only what his grandfather had told him.

They met when his dad was in the Army. Greg had fallen in love with her right away. Tamara was from a well-to-do family and liked to party. And no one liked to party more than Greg. Before long, Tamara discovered she was pregnant. Greg proposed, expecting to meet her rich father and have it made for the rest of his life.

Only Tamara's father was tired of her partying lifestyle and her sponging off his money. He told her she had to live with her own choices and effectively disowned her. Greg did what he could to make her happy, but a private first class in the Army didn't make much money.

Right after Randon's second birthday, 9-11 happened, and Greg was deployed. As soon as he was gone, Tamara saw her chance to escape. She showed up at the cabin, handed Randon to his grandfather and left a letter for Greg. She walked away and never looked back. Eight months later, his grandfather learned that Tamara had died of a drug overdose. He said Greg never got over her.

Randon dropped the picture into the box and picked up the envelope full of letters. It held all the letters Greg had written to Tamara while he was overseas. Once upon a time, it also held the goodbye note Tamara left with his grandfather.

When he was eight, he found the box and started reading the letter. His father walked in and caught him. Greg ripped the letter from Randon's hands and threw it in the fireplace.

"You don't need to read that letter to know that she didn't want you," Greg told him. "If it wasn't for you, she never would've left me." Then he took the box and put it back in his closet.

At the time, Randon believed him and blamed himself for both his mother's death and her abandonment. He opened the envelope and dumped the rest of the letters on the table. It took him a few moments to arrange them in order by date.

He picked up the first letter from his dad's deployment and began to read. Greg told Tamara how much he missed her. And him. Randon swallowed. His dad had liked him at one time. He kept reading.

His father described life on the military base in the Middle East. The raids they went on. The battles he was in. He talked about friends he lost. Tamara must have written him back occasionally because some of Greg's letters referred to her previous letter. He apologized for her unhappiness. He was also concerned that there was no money in their bank account and wanted to know what she was doing with all the money.

Each letter got a little shorter and a little darker. Even through letters, Randon could see the changes in his father from one month to the next. The toll the war took on him was evident in the tone of his letters to Tamara. Every letter ended with him saying he loved her and Randon.

The last letter was the hardest to read. The wives of some of his Army buddies were reporting to their husbands that Tamara was leaving Randon with them for days at a time while she was out partying. She had been seen with different men and they suspected she was on drugs. Greg pleaded with Tamara to stay home and take care of their son. He promised to make things better when he got home. He forgave her for running around and told her how much he loved her.

Randon looked at the date on the letter. Five days after writing that letter, Greg's Humvee got hit with a bomb. Six months later, his father was discharged from the Army and came home.

Randon's grandfather had already been raising Randon, so Greg seemed content to sit in front of the television all day and drink himself into a stupor. How many times had Grandpa told him that his father wasn't the same as he'd been before the war? Randon never believed him. He glanced at the box of letters. Until now.

It didn't excuse Greg's behavior, but Randon got a better sense of who his father had once been.

It also made him more determined than ever to make sure PTSD didn't ruin his life, too.

HE WOKE UP to the smell of bacon. He rolled out of bed and scrubbed his face with his hands. He must have been dreaming of breakfast. Then he heard noises coming from the kitchen.

Pulling a T-shirt over his head, he walked into the living room.

Millie was standing in his kitchen, flipping pancakes over in a pan. She didn't look at him, but he knew that she knew he was there.

She picked up a plate already piled high with bacon and eggs and placed a pancake on it. She finally looked up at him and handed him the plate. "A peace offering."

His stomach growled and he took the plate. "Thank you. But I'm not the one who was mad."

"I know," she sighed. "I let my feelings cloud my judgment. I'm sorry. I have no right to expect you to want to stay in Coronado just because I want you to."

He carried the plate to the dining room table. "Aren't you going to join me?"

She bit her bottom lip. "I wasn't sure if I was welcome."

"Always," he said.

She fixed herself a plate and sat next to him. "You better fuel up."

"Why?"

"Brian will be here this evening and Mom is making a huge family dinner." Millie poured syrup all over her pancake. "Which, by the way, you're expected to attend."

Randon's stomach twisted at the thought of facing his best friend again. Brian had come to see him at the rehabilitation center in Maryland when he returned to the states, but their reunion had been brief and awkward.

How would things be between them now? While he and Brian had talked and texted a lot since then, seeing each other in person might be different.

After Millie's plate was clean, she stood up and carried it to the sink. "I cooked, so that means you get to clean up."

"Of course," he laughed.

"I have to go to work," she said.

Until then, Randon hadn't noticed she was wearing her scrubs.

"I'll be off before noon, so whatever work you're doing needs to be done by then," she said.

"Why?"

She rolled her eyes. "I know that as soon as Brian gets here, he's going to hog your time, so I want to take advantage of having you all to myself. We're going fishing. No excuses this time."

A moment later, Millie was gone. Randon sat at the table and finished eating. It was nice to wake up to someone else in the house. No. It was nice to wake up and see her.

He sighed. He could do that every day. If he stayed, he had no doubt she would agree to marry him. That's what she wanted, even if she hadn't told him in so many words.

But then what? Would he find small jobs here and there? He might make enough money to pay the electric bill. It certainly wouldn't be enough to support a family.

Right now, he still had enough money in his savings account to live off of. In another few weeks, he'd start getting his medical disability check. He'd already arranged for that money to go into a separate account. His plan was to give that money to charity, because he would never ever be like his father and rely on a disability check to live on. Not working had turned him into a lazy, bitter man.

If he could find work in Coronado, he maybe would have considered staying, but there wasn't a lot to do in the small town. Sooner or later, Millie would resent him. Whether it was because she would have to be the main income earner or because he would inevitably turn out to be just like his father.

MILLIE GOT OFF work a lot earlier than she expected. Mrs. Jennings's feet were worse and Millie convinced her daughter to take Mrs. Jennings to Springerville Hospital. As soon as they left, she went home to change.

The street in front of her home was getting crowded. Her brothers Jarrod and Collin were already home, but there was an additional vehicle on the street that she didn't recognize. Of course, people had been popping in and out of the house a lot since her dad had been found.

She'd made it a point to stay in her room when they had visitors. Somehow, the conversation always turned to her. They would look at her sadly, tsk-tsk and tell her that it wasn't her fault that her dad went missing on her watch. In the next breath, they offered her advice on how not to let it happen again.

Instead of going through the front door, she decided to go around to the kitchen door. It would be much easier to sneak upstairs and avoid visitors that way.

She turned the knob, intending to push the door open quietly, but the door didn't budge. Oh! She forgot that all the doors were always locked now. She reached into her purse to search for her keys.

She was still searching when the door opened.

"I don't know how you can find anything in a purse big enough to swallow you."

"Michael!" She threw her arms around her oldest brother. "When did you get here?"

"About an hour ago." He held the door open for her to come in.

Michael was the only other member of the family blessed with red hair. While hers was a bright, fiery red, his had turned more auburn as he aged. Even though he was eleven years older, they had a close bond. While she was in nursing school, they would video chat and he would drill her on medical terms.

"How did you get away from the hospital?" As happy as she was to see him, she was also concerned. He rarely visited. What little time he got away from work was spent with his wife's family, and Felicity never wanted to come to Coronado. When she did come to Arizona with him, she stayed at a resort in Scottsdale while Michael drove to see his parents.

"Actually, I'm interviewing for a position in Phoenix."

Millie squealed and hugged him again. "That's so exciting! I can't believe you finally talked Felicity into moving out here," she said.

Michael shrugged. "I don't have the job yet, so we'll see what happens."

She cocked her head and studied him for a moment. His smile didn't reach his eyes. She glanced around the kitchen to see if anyone was close by. "She's not coming, is she?"

He shook his head. "We separated two months ago." His voice was little more than a whisper.

Millie knew her brother and his wife had been having problems, but she hadn't realized it was that serious. She squeezed his hand. "Are you okay?"

"Yeah," he said. "Don't say anything to anyone, please. I don't want to give Mom one more thing to worry about."

Millie suspected the possibility of Felicity and Michael getting a divorce would be more of a relief to their mother. It always bothered her that Felicity refused to try to be part of their family. And it bothered her even more that Michael stayed away from them to make his wife happy. She wouldn't tell Michael that, though.

"I won't say a word." She mimed zipping her lips. "I was planning to go fishing with Randon this afternoon, but I can stay here. Unless you want to go fishing with us."

"Thanks, but I think I'll hang out here for a while. You should go, though."

She followed Michael through the kitchen and into the living room.

"Speak of the devil," Jarrod said. "We were just talking about you."

Millie frowned. "Why?"

Jarrod patted the spot next to him on the sofa. "We were talking about your future."

She had a sinking feeling in her stomach as she sat next to him. "I'm not sure why that's any of your business."

"Come on, sis," Collin said. "You can't plan on living with Mom and Dad forever."

She knew where this conversation was going. It seemed like every time they got together, the fact that she was perfectly happy living at home seemed to bother them. "Of course, I won't live with them forever." She decided to try a light approach. "I do plan to outlive them."

"Amen to that," her mother said. She gave Millie an apologetic look.

Michael nudged her. "Don't you want to settle down and start a family of your own?"

She shot him a look that told him she knew Felicity's desire to remain child-free was a major bone of contention between them. "I'm only twenty-four," she reminded them. "I have plenty of time to worry about that."

"Not here," Jarrod said. "I'm pretty sure all the good men in Coronado are already taken. There's a reason the rest of them are still single."

"All right." She stood up. She had had enough of this conversation "I'm going to change out of these scrubs, then I'm going fishing. And I'm naming all the worms after my brothers."

MILLIE KNOCKED ONCE on the cabin door before walking inside. Randon was nowhere to be seen.

"Hello?" She walked through the house.

Her heart began to pound. Where was he?

A pounding noise from overhead echoed through the cabin. She walked out the back door and saw the ladder leaning against the side of the house.

She climbed the ladder to see Randon nailing shingles in place. "Hey," she said.

"Hmm," he mumbled. That was about all he could say. He was holding a dozen nails between his lips.

She finished climbing the rest of the way to the roof and sat next to him. He took one nail from his mouth and pounded it into the roof. He'd barely stopped hammering when he took another nail and did the same thing.

She waited patiently for him to finish. "Are you ready?"

Randon laughed. "I can't go fishing, Millie. I have way too much to do."

"Sorry," she said. "That answer is not acceptable. I need to go work out some frustration by stabbing worms with hooks. Besides, I heard Jarrod telling my mother that once Brian gets here, all my brothers are coming over to help."

He frowned. "I can't let them do that."

"Sorry," she laughed. "That answer is not acceptable. Now let's go."

She inched over to the edge of the roof. Her heart pounded as she moved one foot to the ladder.

Suddenly, Randon was there. "Still scared of heights, I see."

He moved her away from the ladder and took a few steps onto it. Then he offered her one hand and guided her as she made her way off the roof.

With his chest at her back, she relaxed and together, they moved down the ladder.

He put the ladder and toolbox away and then walked to the barn to get his fishing gear.

She strode toward her car when a sharp whistle stopped her. She turned to see Randon standing outside of the barn.

"Let's take the truck," he said.

She popped the trunk of her car and grabbed two fishing poles and a small tackle box. She put them in the bed of the truck and hopped into the passenger seat.

Randon started the engine. "Big Lake?"

Millie shook her head. "Let's try the east fork of the Black River."

He nodded and put the truck into gear. "Why are you frustrated?"

"My brothers." She rolled her eyes. "Every time I see them, they find it necessary to tell me how to live my life."

"It's not a bad thing to have people care about you," he said.

"No. But they have to accept the fact that I'm grown and I make my own decisions."

Randon raised one eyebrow, but didn't say anything. She rolled down the window of the truck and let fresh air fill the cab.

They drove through town and he turned on a wide well-maintained gravel road. Dozens of smaller forest service roads branched off the main one. Many of them wound through the forest, often crossing other forest service roads, before rejoining the main road. Some of the roads were barely usable without a four-wheel drive vehicle.

Usually, it was only hunters and those people who preferred self-contained camping who ventured away from the main roads. The main road to Black River was smooth enough that even her car could make it easily. Randon chose to take some of the smaller, rougher roads to get to the river.

The roar of the engine kept talking to a minimum, so she sat back in the seat and enjoyed the drive. The White Mountains were always beautiful in the fall. The aspen trees exploded with color and the bright green pine trees balanced out the red and gold.

A familiar landmark was just off the road, not far ahead. "Stop there." She pointed toward the gravesite of Oscar Shultz.

Randon pulled off the main road and parked near the site. "Why do you want to visit Oscar?"

Millie pulled a quarter out of her purse. "Remember the lady who asked about your art? Her husband was asking about Oscar and it made me realize I haven't visited in a while."

She got out of the truck and walked over to the tombstone. A fence surrounded the lone grave. Her quarter joined dozens of others that spread out over the rocks that were heaped on top of Oscar's final resting place.

"I wonder who started tossing quarters on his grave." Randon joined her at the fence.

"I don't know," she said. "He decided to rob a bank to help out his mother, so maybe people felt sorry for him and wanted to help."

Randon laughed. "Do you think people come out here and take them?"

"They wouldn't dare." Millie shook her head. "Bye, Oscar."

Randon opened the door for her. "Our usual fees? One dollar to the person who catches the first, the biggest and the most fish?"

Millie nodded, pleased that he remembered. "I hope you've got three dollars on you. I don't take credit."

"I'm not scared of you," he laughed and slid into the driver's seat. "I've always been a better fisherman."

"No. You just get lucky."

Once the truck was back in motion, she stole glances at him while he was driving. His shoulders were relaxed, his face void of tight worry lines, it almost felt like old times. There were small changes, so insignificant that people who didn't know him might not notice. Like the way he slowed down at every corner instead of speeding into the curve like he always loved to do. Or how his eyes constantly scanned the roadside while he drove.

Small camping areas were situated between the

road and the stream. Most of the camping spots were empty this time of year, so it was easy to find a place to park. Millie tossed her line in the water and sat cross-legged on the grass.

"So, what's really bothering you?" Randon sat down next to her.

She sighed. "I know why my mother asked all my brothers to come home."

"Why?"

"A few months ago, my mom showed me a box of letters that my dad wrote to each of us right after he was diagnosed." Her throat was thick and she swallowed. "He wanted to talk to each of us about his last wishes while he still could."

Randon wrapped one arm around her shoulder. "That was good thinking on his part. What did your letter say?"

"Mom wouldn't let me read it. She said when the time was right she would give all of us our letter." Her chest ached every time she thought about it. She leaned on him. "I have a feeling I know what it's going to say."

"He wants to go to a home, doesn't he?"

Millie blinked away tears. "How did you know?"

"Because I know Darrel," he said. "He would never want to be a burden to his family."

"But he's not," she cried. "I can take care of him better than anyone. It's part of the reason I became a nurse."

"Maybe he doesn't want you to have to take care of him." A small tug on his line caused him to move his arm from around her shoulder and pick up his fishing pole.

He gently pinched the fishing line between his thumb and his middle finger, just above the reel.

She let out a huff of air and shook her head. "That's ridiculous. Mom would never put him in a home. Besides, my brothers and I would never allow it."

"You're getting a bite." Randon nodded at her pole. "Your mom will do what's best for Darrel, even if you and your brothers disagree."

She glared at him and picked up her pole. "So you think he should go into a home, too?"

He moved the end of his pole slightly. "No. But you've always put everyone else's needs before your own wants. Maybe your dad is doing the same thing."

"Millie!" a high-pitched voice called from behind them.

She turned to see a woman waving from a car on the road. The car pulled into the camp spot and the woman jumped out.

Millie jumped up. "Jessica! What are you doing here? I thought you moved to Tucson."

"I did." Millie's old classmate grinned. "But Barry has never been trout fishing and I wanted him to see where I grew up. So we took a few days off and rented a cabin at Whispering Pines."

"Barry?" Millie glanced at the man who had just gotten out of the car. He definitely didn't appear to be the outdoor type.

Jessica held her left hand out and wiggled her fingers to show off the shiny diamond ring.

"You're engaged! Congratulations!" Millie gave her a hug.

"Barry—" Jessica motioned to the man by the car to come over "—this is the woman who took my favorite fishing spot. Millie, meet my fiancé, Barry Martin."

"Nice to meet you." She shook his hand. She nodded toward Randon, who was standing back at a distance. "This is Randon Farr."

Randon stepped forward and shook Barry's hand. Barry asked him how the fishing was and the two men chatted for a moment while Jessica pulled Millie away from them.

"Millie," she whispered, "are you going out with Randon?"

She shook her head. "No. We're just friends."

"Thank goodness." Jessica darted a glance at Randon. "I know he and Brian were friends, but aren't you scared of him?"

"Why would I be?" She knew that some people were intimidated by Randon's size, but he'd never even gotten into fights in high school.

"He was so mean," Jessica whispered. "He threatened my brother a couple of times. And he followed Dane Kirby into the locker room and shoved him into a locker. And there were other things, too."

"Your brother was a bully," Millie said. "And the rest is just rumors. He doesn't have a mean bone in his body."

Jessica glanced toward Randon. "Just be careful. What if there's a side to him you don't know about?"

"There's not." Millie lifted her chin and leveled a stare at her. "Randon is one of the best men I know."

Jessica's face turned red. "I hope you're right."

"Jessica, are you ready?" Barry called.

"Coming." Jessica waved one hand toward her fiancé. "Since you already got the best fishing spot, I guess we'll head up to Big Lake."

"Have fun," Millie told her. "Maybe I'll see you around before you leave."

Jessica gave Millie one more hug and jumped back in the car.

Millie glanced at Randon. He'd gone back to pick up the fishing pole off the ground. Had he heard Jessica's comments?

Her neck felt hot. Maybe Randon was right. Maybe he'd never get a fair shot in Coronado.

She walked to her pole and sat back down. "I better check my bait."

Randon nodded. "The crawdads are bad here, so I'm sure it's gone."

She reeled her line in and reached for the small

tub of worms. While she baited her hook, she stole a sideways glance at Randon. Jessica was wrong. There wasn't another side to him. She knew Randon better than almost anyone, and she knew he was good through and through.

CHAPTER SIXTEEN

MILLIE CHECKED THE mail when she got home from fishing. She sucked in a breath when she saw a letter from Bravos. She opened it up and her stomach turned. Randon had used her as a reference. There was a list of questions for her to answer, as well as space to write any additional information that she might want to provide.

She scanned the questions. Some of them were easy. *Does the applicant demonstrate a strong moral and ethical character? Has the applicant ever committed a crime?*

Others weren't so simple. *Does the applicant suffer from PTSD? Have you ever witnessed the applicant experience a flashback, seizure or other PTSD-related episode?*

If she answered any of the questions wrong, would it ruin Randon's chances of getting the job? And if he didn't get the job, would he blame her?

"What do you have there?"

Millie looked up to see Collin holding the front door open for her. "A reference request for Randon."

"He's looking for work?" Collin looked surprised.

"Yes." She cocked her head. "Why wouldn't he?"

He shrugged. "I don't know. Most people in his position wouldn't worry about it."

"What position is that?" She wasn't sure she liked the tone of Collin's voice.

"He gets a monthly check from the government for disability, right?" He closed and locked the door behind Millie.

She drew in a sharp breath. "Actually, he was medically retired, so technically, it's not a disability check."

Collin raised his hands in surrender. "I didn't mean anything by it. I just know that's how he was raised. His dad never worked, either. I'm glad he isn't that way."

"You make it sound like being a lazy bum is inherited."

Collin chuckled. "For a lot of people, it seems to be. At least the ones I work with."

Millie folded the letter up and took it to her room.

Collin was a public defender, so most of his clients were people who couldn't afford to pay for a lawyer.

She placed the envelope on top of her dresser and sat on the edge of her bed. She wanted to be angry with Collin for suggesting Randon would not want to work. But hadn't she basically said the same thing to Randon?

She flopped back on her bed and covered her eyes with her arm. It felt like the universe was conspiring against her. Every time she turned around, it seemed like something or someone was pointing out what Randon had been saying all along: no one expected him to succeed in Coronado.

She had been so determined to show Randon that he belonged in Coronado because that's what she wanted. She never understood why it wasn't what he wanted, too. If he stayed, what would he do? There weren't a lot of jobs in town. After nursing school, she had to drive to Springerville several times a week to work at the hospital there. It was purely by accident she discovered a home-health agency that needed nurses to service the Coronado area. And there were weeks she didn't have one patient.

Most of the businesses were family-owned and -run. The largest employer in the area was the school district and the forest service. Maybe her brothers could help her think of something.

She got off the bed and started to walk toward her door. The sun reflected off a windshield and into her bedroom window, almost blinding her. She peered out the window.

"He's home!" Millie yelled and rushed down the stairs and flew to the door to greet her brother.

While she loved all her brothers, she was the

closest to Brian. Probably because he was nearest her age.

"Brian!" She jumped into his arms, hugging him tight.

He whirled her around. "Hey, squirt!"

Soon, they were surrounded by the rest of the boys and she had to step back to keep from getting jostled anymore.

"Out of the way, boys," Mom scolded them.

The boys all stepped back so that their mother could get to her son.

"Mom." Brian pulled her close. "How is he?"

"You'll see soon enough. Now let me look at you. You haven't been eating enough." Mom frowned. "You've lost weight."

He winked at her. "I'm sorry. The chow hall can't compete with your home cooking."

"I'll see what I can do about fattening you up while you're here." Mom wrapped her arm around his waist and led him inside.

Millie stood on the porch for a moment and watched her family file in. Her chest expanded with happiness. She couldn't remember the last time the entire family had been together. For every holiday, at least one person seemed to be missing. For the last six years, it was usually Brian. But he was home now. She followed everyone inside.

Darrel sat in his recliner in the living room and frowned at all the noise in the foyer. Mom still had Brian's arm looped with hers and guided him into the room.

"Look, Darrel. Brian's home."

Darrel stood up and gave his wife a confused look.

"Hi, Dad." Brian's voice was cautious.

"Brian?" Darrel's brow furrowed.

Mom moved closer to his side. "Yes. Brian's our youngest son."

"Oh!" His face lit up. "Brian. Where've you been? You were supposed to walk Millie home from school today."

Brian's eyes widened and he looked at his mother. Mom just pressed her lips together and shook her head slightly.

Michael took the lead. "Dad, let's look at the photo album for pictures with Brian to help you remember."

Michael, Collin and Jarrod led Darrel to the sofa. Mom shooed Brian to follow. A few minutes later, they were all looking at the large album on the coffee table.

Millie glanced at her mother, who watched the scene with tear-filled eyes. "You okay?" she whispered.

"It's just happening so fast." Mom let out a huff of air. "Help me get dinner on the table."

Before long, the usually empty dining room table was bursting with food.

"Where is Randon?" Mom asked. "You did tell him to come, didn't you?"

"Of course, I did, Mom," she said. "He'll be here."

"You've been spending a lot of time with him," she commented. "How are things going?"

She shrugged. "Fine. He's come a long way in understanding his PTSD symptoms. He shouldn't have any trouble going to work for a military contractor."

Mom gave her a pointed look. "How do you feel about that?"

"I hate it," Millie answered honestly. "But there's nothing I can do about it. He doesn't think he'll ever overcome his father's reputation here and I'm starting to think that maybe he's right."

"You love him, don't you?"

She bit her bottom lip. "I shouldn't. But I do."

"And how does he feel about you? Does he feel the same way?"

"I think so." She thought about the kiss they'd shared at the tree house. "At least I know he doesn't think of me as a sister."

"Has he asked you to go with him?"

"Once. Before he was deployed." Millie folded a napkin and placed it next to the plate on the table.

"And now?"

"He knows better."

"What is that supposed to mean? If you love each other, then you should want to be together." Mom placed another plate on the table.

"He knows I'll never leave Coronado," she said. "And he doesn't want to stay here. So, that's it."

Admitting that there was no chance for a future between them sent sharp pains through her heart.

"Oh, honey. Please don't make your decisions based on me and your father. We'll be fine. I'll be fine. There's no reason for you to stay in Coronado."

Millie dropped the pile of napkins she was holding on the table and skirted the edge to hug her mother. "I know you will be, but I won't be fine leaving you."

When her mother walked away, she pulled out her phone.

Where are you? Brian is already here.

Be there soon. Toby brought some friends over for an art lesson.

She grinned. It seemed like the boys were spending a lot of time with Randon lately. It was good for all of them.

Twenty minutes later, there was a knock at the front door and Brian ran to open it. "Randon!"

"Brian."

The two embraced, slapping each other on the back.

"I have your stuff from the old barracks," Brian told him.

Randon glanced into the kitchen and gave Millie a quick smile before following Brian out to his SUV.

Mom called everyone to the dining room and the other boys escorted their dad to the table just as Brian and Randon came in from outside. Each of the Gibson men stopped to shake hands with Randon.

Millie's heart ached. He fit in so well with her family. Would they ever have a chance?

Mom asked Jarrod to say the blessing before they all sat down to eat. Her dad seemed to blossom under all the attention he was getting. He passed the plates around, talked and joked, and for a few minutes, things seemed just like they used to be.

More than once, she saw Brian's eyes darting around the room. He glanced toward the door every few seconds. When her mother stood up to get more napkins from the kitchen, her chair made a loud scraping sound and he jumped.

She glanced at Randon, who was also watching Brian. He seemed to sense her staring at him and turned slightly to look at her. She darted her eyes at Brian and then back to him. Randon nodded. He saw it, too. Was Brian getting help for his PTSD? Would he talk to her about it if she asked?

"Can you pass me the rolls?" her father interrupted her thoughts. He crinkled his forehead. "I'm sorry. I can't remember your name."

"I'm Millie," she said and handed him the basket. Even when things were good, they weren't the same. And they never would be again.

She glanced across the table at Randon, who gave her an encouraging smile.

After dinner, the men retired to the living room to find a football game on the television. She was helping her mom with the dishes when Brian came up behind her.

"Is something going on with you and Randon?"

"Why?" She didn't like the tone in his voice.

"I saw the two of you looking at each other a lot," Brian said.

"So?" Millie turned and leaned against the kitchen counter. "It's not really any of your business."

Brian shrugged and walked out of the room.

Mom watched him walk away as well. "He doesn't seem himself."

"You mean the way he's constantly looking around the room? How he made Collin trade chairs with him so he could face the door? The way he startled at every sound?"

Her mother's brow furrowed. "You noticed more than I did, but yes."

Millie pressed her lips together. "I'm afraid Brian might have PTSD, too."

"So, what do we do?"

She sighed. "I'll talk to him later. Alone."

If her brother was suffering from some of the same issues as Randon, she doubted he'd want to talk about it in front of everyone, especially their mother.

Randon poked his head into the kitchen. "Thank you for dinner."

"Are you leaving?" Mom placed her dish towel down and walked over to him.

"Yes, ma'am," he said. "Brian and I are taking a ride in my car."

His gaze locked with Millie's and he winked at her before turning to leave.

Millie watched Brian and Randon walk out the front door before turning back to the dishes.

Mom smiled. "There is definitely something going on between the two of you."

RANDON'S SHOULDERS WERE tight as tension built with every step he took toward his car. He knew Brian was walking behind him, even though he didn't hear a sound.

He stopped and waited for Brian to open the passenger door.

"I can't believe you found her." Brian patted the top of the car.

"Me, either." Randon got in and started the engine. "I took her to Bear's Garage to get looked at. Harry told me that my dad brought her in and had the fluid changed just a few months before he died. He said he wanted the car to be ready for me when I got home."

Brian's eyes widened. "Your dad? The same

one who refused to move his car so we wouldn't have to stand in the snow to work on it?"

"Yep, that dad," Randon said.

They drove in silence for a few minutes. Randon's mind buzzed with questions. What kind of action had Brian seen after he left? It hadn't escaped his attention that Brian was even jumpier than he was.

He had to ask. "You okay, man?"

"I'm fine. I should be asking you. How's your shoulder?" Brian blew his question off.

"Sore sometimes." Randon tried to think of the best way to approach it. "I also get spooked easy and sometimes my mind goes places I don't want it to go. Does that ever happen to you?"

"No." Brian shook his head. He gave Randon a playful punch. "Maybe you're just weak-minded."

Randon frowned. He couldn't force Brian to admit that he also had PTSD. It would take time. "How are you liking Fort Bliss?"

"It's not the same without you. It's nice that I'm closer to home now," Brian said. "I had no idea how bad my dad had gotten."

"It shocked me, too, the first time I saw him."

"Thanks, by the way," Brian said. "I heard you were the one who found him when he wandered off."

Randon nodded. "Glad I was there."

"Millie will have to keep a better eye on him," Brian said.

Randon tensed. "It wasn't Millie's fault. And she feels bad enough about it already."

"Whoa." Brian held up his hands. "I have to ask—is something going on between you and my sister?"

"No."

"That's what she said, too. I hope it's the truth."

Randon stiffened. "Why? Would it be so horrible for the two of us to date?"

"Well…yeah." Brian leaned forward to fiddle with the radio. "You're my best friend. She's my little sister. That would just be weird."

He relaxed slightly. At least Brian hadn't said he wasn't good enough.

"What are your plans now? Are you just going to enjoy living in the lap of luxury now that you don't have to work?"

He knew Brian was referring to the money he was supposed to get from the military. "No. I'm going to work for Bravos."

"Why? If I were in your position, I'd enjoy life. Go fishing every day." Brian winked at him.

"I think that's what a lot of people expect me to do."

"Yeah." Brian shrugged. "I guess they expect you to turn out like your old man."

"Exactly. Which is why I won't do it." His stomach tied itself into a knot.

Randon pulled the car over to the side of the road. "Anywhere you want to go?"

"Let's go to the Watering Hole and have a few drinks."

"I can't." The last thing Randon needed was alcohol. Brian, either.

Brian scoffed. "Since when?"

"I have a doctor's appointment next week and I can't have any alcohol in my system." He wasn't sure when his appointment would be, but it was the best excuse he could come up with.

"Sucks for you," Brian laughed. "Why don't you drop me off there, then? I'm not ready to go back to the house, yet. It's depressing to see my dad like that."

"I don't think that's a good idea," Randon said.

Brian frowned. "I didn't ask for your permission."

Randon bit his bottom lip, but turned in the direction of the tavern. When he pulled in front of the bar, he reached out and put his hand on Brian's arm before he got out of the car. "Call me when you're ready to go home."

"Sure." Brian jumped out and slammed the door.

Randon waited until Brian entered the building before pulling out his phone and texting Millie.

Just dropped Brian off at the Watering Hole. I couldn't talk him out of it. I told him to call me when he was ready to go home.

He stared at the screen, waiting for a reply. Instead, his phone rang.

Millie didn't wait for him to say hello before she started talking. "He's not okay, is he?"

"I don't think so." His voice was quiet.

"Did you talk to him about it?" Concern filled her voice.

Randon sighed. "I tried. He's not ready to hear it yet."

"What are you doing right now?"

He paused. "I'm going home."

Millie said exactly what he thought she would say. "I'm coming over."

"No," Randon told her. Brian's voice ran through his mind.

"Why not?"

"I want to be alone for a while," he told her. That was mostly true. He didn't want to do anything that might upset Brian.

"Okay. Will I see you tomorrow?"

"Sure."

He ended the call and put his phone on the seat next to him, then drove back to the cabin. By the time he got inside, his body was tight with tension. It was too late and too cold to go jogging. Instead, he paced around inside the living room.

His eyes fell on the art set sitting on the table. Earlier that day, Toby and Eddie had come over for an art lesson and brought two friends with them. In exchange, the boys helped him do some of the smaller jobs around the cabin. They worked for a while, then painted for a while. Toby even commented that it was a great way to get rid of bad emotions. What did he call it? Bad mojo?

It was worth a try. He grabbed a blank canvas, set it up and began painting. He didn't paint with anything in mind—he just painted. Before long, he was lost in what he was doing.

A little after midnight, his phone rang. He set down the paintbrush and looked at the screen. He didn't recognize the number. "Hello?"

"Randon," a male voice said. "This is Caden."

"Hey. What's up?"

"Can you come to the Watering Hole and pick up your friend? He refused to let me take him home and he's already started two fights."

"I'll be right there." Randon put the brushes away and grabbed his car keys. He was going to have to have a long talk with Brian, whether he wanted to listen or not.

CHAPTER SEVENTEEN

THE NEXT MORNING, Randon was up before the sun. He trudged into the kitchen to pour himself a cup of coffee. He glanced into his father's bedroom. Brian was snoring on the bed. Apparently, he'd been too drunk for the cigarette smoke–infused mattress to bother him.

Despite the freezing temperatures outside, he went for a quick jog around the loop that circled the trailer park. When he got back, Brian was sitting at the table, drinking a cup of coffee.

"How are you feeling?" Randon asked him.

"Fine." Brian's focus wasn't on Randon. He was staring at some of the paintings Randon had finished, lined up on the floor against the wall.

A couple were of Millie. Randon tried to distract him. "Want some breakfast?"

Brian set the coffee cup down. "Sure."

He opened the refrigerator. "I have so much food. What do you want? Biscuits and gravy? Doughnuts? I can cook some eggs."

"Yeah. Scrambled, please." Brian kept looking at the paintings.

All through breakfast, Randon watched Brian carefully for more signs that his mental state was not good. Brian talked about old times, high school friends and his new base, but every time Randon asked about other members of their squad, Brian avoided the question, just like Randon had evaded all talk of his time overseas when he first returned.

They had just finished eating when his phone rang. He frowned at the screen. He didn't want Brian to get upset because Millie was calling him. But he didn't want Millie to worry, either.

"Hello?"

A few moments later, he disconnected the call. "Your brothers are on their way."

He avoided mentioning that the call was from Millie.

"Oh, yeah." Brian nodded. "I was supposed to tell you they all wanted to come over and help you with repairs."

Randon wanted to call Millie back and tell them not to come. But the truth was he was running out of time and he appreciated the help.

Everyone took a different part of the property and the sound of hammers and saws rang through the forest. At lunchtime, Randon opened up the refrigerator and the Gibson brothers were quick to tackle the leftovers.

"Man, I love Mrs. Macias's chicken enchiladas." Collin patted his stomach.

Michael laughed. "Right now, I would even take Millie's Mexican food. Seattle doesn't even know what it is!"

The boys groaned at the mention of Millie's cooking.

Throughout the day, Randon watched Brian closely. There were times he seemed almost like his old self. But he knew all it would take would be one thing that could set him off.

By late afternoon, the cabin looked almost brand-new. The shutters were hanging in their proper place. The steps on the front porch and the back deck had been replaced. All it needed was a new coat of paint.

Everyone walked outside to admire their work. Randon's chest swelled with gratitude. "Thank you. I'd never have gotten this done without you."

"It's the least we could do." Michael slapped Randon on the arm. "You saved our brother and our dad."

Randon cringed. "Brian saved me long before that."

"We'd better get back. Mom is probably ready to start that family meeting she was talking about," Collin reminded them. The others groaned but they all headed for the SUV they had come in.

"Thanks again for all your help," Randon said, shaking each of the Gibson brothers' hands. When he got to Brian, he pulled him in for a hug and gave him a slap on the back. "I've missed you, man."

Brian nodded. "I've missed you, too. Like I said, it's not the same without you there at the base."

Randon waited for them all to drive off before he walked back into the cabin. Looking around, he couldn't believe how much work had gotten done. This was a cabin he would be proud for someone to see.

His phone buzzed, indicating that he had a voicemail. That was weird; he hadn't heard his phone ring. He put in his passcode and listened to the message. It was Dr. Harlow's office. They had set up an appointment at the VA Hospital in Phoenix for Monday morning.

Wow. That was fast. He wasn't sure if that was a good thing or a bad thing.

He went back inside the cabin to put the few leftovers that hadn't been eaten back in the fridge. As he closed the fridge door, he saw a business card had been stuck on the front with a magnet. He pulled the card off and looked at it.

Meghan Simpson, Realtor.

He needed to call her and put the cabin on the market. Still, he hesitated to do it before his appointment. What if the tests showed it was his traumatic brain injury that had caused his blackout? Bravos wouldn't hire him, then. He didn't want to be homeless and jobless.

A knock on the door took him away from staring at the card. He put the card back on the refrigerator and walked into the living room. It was probably Toby and Eddie. He was tired and it was a little late for their daily art lesson, but he couldn't deny them.

Truthfully, he thought they enjoyed talking more than they did painting. He tried to listen to the boys' concerns without offering too much parental advice. He never wanted them to feel like he was judging them. Still, when Toby expressed a desire to get even with a boy in his school, Randon told him it wasn't a good idea. Instead, he gave him a few ways to deal with the boy without resorting to violence.

Both boys were required to bring their homework and either finish it before they could start painting, or show him that they were already finished. He thought that idea was rather brilliant. His dad never cared if he did his homework or not.

He opened the door and saw Millie standing on the other side. "It's you."

"Expecting someone else?" She stepped inside the cabin.

"I thought maybe it was Toby and Eddie."

"They've been over here a lot," she said. "You must really be making an impression on them."

He shrugged. "It's weird. I never thought I would be able to relate to kids like that. I wish I had had someone who could relate to me when I was that age. What are you doing here?"

"I wanted to stop by and see how things went with Brian today."

Randon could tell by the look on her face that there was more to it than that. "Why are you really here?"

She swallowed. "We had our family meeting today." The word *meeting* was emphasized with air quotes. "You were right. Dad's letter said he wanted to be put into a home once he hit the final stage of Alzheimer's."

"I thought he might have said that." Randon pulled her into his arms. "How does everyone else feel?"

"Everyone voted to accept Dad's wishes and put him in a home when things get too rough."

"Everyone except you."

"He's my dad. No one else needs to take care of him but me."

"Did you tell your brothers that?" Randon knew she had. She never held back when it came to letting people know how she felt.

"Yes." She rolled her eyes. "They're all more worried about me building a life of my own. And Dad's letter to me said the same thing. He said I'd never have a family if all I did was take care of him."

"He's right, you know." He knew that someday

Millie would want a family and he was glad he wouldn't be around to see it.

Millie's phone buzzed and she checked her text messages. "I have to go. Mom thinks Brian went back down to the bar and she wants me to go look."

"Want me to go with you?"

"You better not. He's a little sensitive about seeing us together."

"Okay. Text me when you find him."

He opened the door and walked Millie to her car. As she drove away, he realized he forgot to tell her he would be gone for a few days next week. Oh, well. He would talk to her later.

Without repairs to do, he was able to spend the next couple of hours painting. He painted the cabin tucked inside the trees with a sunset dropping behind the mountains.

A loud knock on the door interrupted him. He could tell by the knock that it was Brian. He wasn't surprised to see the glassy look in Brian's eyes when he opened the door.

"How'd you get here?" He looked outside for a vehicle.

"Walked," Brian slurred. "Not that far. We run farther than this in PT every morning. But you don't have to do that anymore."

"Actually, I run five miles every morning. I'm trying to get in shape for Bravos."

Brian wrinkled his nose. "I don't get it, man… Why?"

Randon walked into the kitchen. "Do you want some coffee?"

Brian followed him. "You didn't answer the question. You got a get-out-of-jail-free card. Why are you throwing it away?"

Randon turned on the coffeepot. He'd have to reset it for in the morning, but Brian needed it more than he did right now.

"What else am I going to do, Brian? When you get out of the Army, you're going to college."

"You were already taking college classes," Brian reminded him. "Go to college with me. It'll be great."

"I was taking classes so I could stay in the Army. But I'm not going to college just to go." He was twenty-six years old and still had no idea what he wanted to do with his life.

"Do you hate me?" Brian flopped onto the dining room chair.

"Of course not. Why would you think that?" He poured Brian a cup of coffee.

"'Cause I made you go into the Army with me and then you got hurt."

"That's not your fault," Randon told him. "Besides, I almost got us all killed."

Brian yawned. "'S not your fault. You told me not to go until you double-checked it. I decided to go in, anyway. Didn't know it was a trap."

Randon scratched the back of his head. He didn't remember doing that. But there were several things about that night he didn't remember.

"When I get into Bravos, I'm going back there to find Rashid." Randon sat in the chair next to him. "I think he was forced to take us there. I want to make sure he's okay."

Brian folded his arms on the table and laid his head on them. "Don't bother. Rashid's gone."

His heart skipped a beat. "Gone? What do you mean?"

Brian yawned again. "Gone," he mumbled before passing out.

Randon texted Millie to let her know Brian was there and he'd bring him home in a little while. He paced around the cabin, thinking about the boy whom he'd befriended. What did he mean by *gone*? Had he been moved? Killed?

He walked into his father's bedroom and pulled the covers down for Brian.

"Okay, buddy," he said as he moved back into the dining room, "let's get you to bed."

He put his hand on Brian's shoulder and shook him.

Brian flew out of the chair, twisted around and drove his shoulder into Randon's middle.

Caught off guard, Randon stumbled backward. "Brian, it's just me."

Brian's eyes had a wild look as his gaze darted around the room.

Randon held up his hands and took a step toward him.

A strange, guttural scream came from Brian and he attacked Randon.

Randon dodged his fists and tried to move away. Brian was in a rage and moved faster.

After a few minutes of dodging Brian's blows, he realized the only way to stop Brian was to subdue him. He rushed at Brian, caught him around the waist and body-slammed him to the ground. He managed to roll Brian onto his stomach, pin his arm behind him and sit on him.

"What are you doing?" Millie's voice screamed from the door of the cabin.

"Stay back, Millie," Randon warned her.

She froze, not moving from her spot.

Randon had Brian pinned so he couldn't move much. After a few moments, he stopped struggling. Randon loosened his hold and moved away.

Brian rolled over and sat up. He glanced at Randon in confusion. "What happened?"

"I tried to wake you up."

"Oh." Brian's face fell.

Randon took a deep breath. "This has happened before?"

Brian nodded. "That's why I keep coming over here at night. I didn't want anyone else to find out."

"You can stay here as long as you need to." He glanced at Millie. "I'll bring him home in the morning."

Brian stood up and rubbed his arm. He looked at Millie. "Don't tell Mom. Please."

Millie nodded. "But tomorrow we're going to talk about getting you help."

"I'm going to bed." Brian turned and walked toward Greg's old room.

Millie stared after her brother. "Wow." She turned to Randon. "I've read about those kinds of episodes, but I've never seen one."

"Want some coffee? I just made a pot."

She nodded. "Brian always had a temper. I wonder if that makes him more susceptible to rages like that."

"I don't know," Randon said. "I have a temper, too, and I have never reacted like that."

"You do not." Millie shook her head.

He laughed. "You've just never seen it."

She frowned. "Who has?"

He handed her a cup of coffee. "Let's see. Dane Kirby got a taste of it once. Jessica's brother, Kole, and I had words on more than one occasion. That kid Aaron who used to tease you on the playground. Daniel Uriah, Terry Gordan. Want me to go on?"

Millie's face paled. "So there is a side to you I don't know about."

He shrugged. "I guess you could say that."

All the people he named had one thing in common: at one time, they had either said something about Millie or bothered her in some way. When it came to people who might hurt her, he definitely had a temper.

"And you still want to go back?"

His thoughts drifted to the thirteen-year-old kid who may or may not have betrayed him. He nodded. "I have to."

She set her coffee cup on the table. "I can't do this. I haven't tried to help you recover just so you can go back and make it worse. I'm not going to worry about you every day, wondering if you're okay over there. And then walk on eggshells when you get back because I'm afraid of setting you off."

Where was this coming from? "I didn't ask you to."

"I know." She took a deep breath. "That's the problem. You didn't ask me to do anything. I did everything I could to get you to choose me. But that's not enough, is it? I'm not enough."

"You've always been enough." He stepped closer to her. "I'm the one who wasn't good enough for you."

She let out a choked laugh. "Then why weren't you willing to come back to me three years ago? You wanted to stay in the Army and I asked you to come home. You said no."

"Why does everything have to be on your terms?" Randon felt his own anger bubbling to the surface. "You can love me and be with me, but only as long as it's where you want. Only as long as you have your way."

Millie lifted her chin. "Well, it looks like you win this time. I'm done."

She turned and stalked out the door. Randon walked to the doorway and watched her as she drove off. A knot formed in his stomach. This time, he was certain he'd lost her for good.

MILLIE TAPPED HER fingers on the coffee cup in her hands. Between worrying about Brian and her argument with Randon, she'd hardly slept at all last night.

Mom walked into the kitchen. "How many cups of coffee are you going to drink today?"

"Enough to get me through all my patients," she joked.

She glanced at her watch. Her first patient was in fifteen minutes. She'd hoped to talk to Brian before she left, but he still wasn't home.

She rinsed her coffee cup and put it in the sink. "I'm going, Mom."

"Have a good day." Mom walked to the front door with her. "Will you be done this afternoon? We were going to take a tour of the nursing home Stacy recommended."

Millie stared at her mother. "I thought Dad wanted that one in Phoenix."

"I can't be that far away from him," Mom said. "Even if he doesn't remember me."

Her heart raced. Stacy's mother had Huntington's disease and spent the last few years of her life in a nursing home close to the county line. If she could get hired at the nursing home, she would be able to see to his care.

"I'll try, but today is going to be a long day. I have patients in Luna, Hannigan Meadow and Springerville."

"Okay." Mom nodded. "Be careful."

"I will. And please, text me when Brian gets home."

CHAPTER EIGHTEEN

RANDON WANTED TO get to the VA Hospital in Phoenix as early as possible. It was a four-hour drive, so he left before Brian had woken up. He left him a note, letting him know where he was.

The evaluations Dr. Harlow requested took most of the day. There was also a lot of time in between tests. Time spent worrying about Millie. Worrying about Brian. Wondering what had happened to Rashid.

What did Millie want from him? Did she really think he could just settle down in Coronado with no job and no future and be happy?

He was in the waiting room, once again, waiting to meet with the doctor one last time and get his results. His knee bounced fast enough to cause a small earthquake, but he couldn't help it. His entire future hung in the balance.

Finally, a nurse called his name. He was ushered back to the same patient room he'd been in earlier that day.

A few minutes later, Dr. Patel came in. "Hello again."

"Hi." Randon didn't want to beat around the bush. "Do you have my results?"

"Yes and no," he said. "We have them, but we're waiting to hear back from Dr. Harlow. I want you to come back in the morning, after he's had a chance to go over everything."

"Morning?" Randon's stomach dropped. He must have found something wrong if he wanted that much time to review the results. "I guess I don't have much choice, do I?"

Dr. Patel just nodded. "Stop by the receptionist and make an appointment for tomorrow morning."

As soon as he got out of the building, he turned his phone on. Several pings came through and he scrolled through his text messages, hoping to see one from Millie.

Most of the messages were from Brian. Nothing from Millie.

He got into his car, but didn't start the engine. He called Brian's number.

"Hey," Brian answered on the first ring. "Are you still in Phoenix?"

"Yeah. I have to stay one more night." He was relieved that Brian's voice sounded a lot better. "Are you okay?"

"I will be," Brian said. "Millie stopped by in between patients to load me up with brochures and information about dealing with PTSD."

"Let me guess. She wants you to get a dog."

"How'd you know?" Brian laughed. "Seriously, man, when are you coming back? I have to leave tomorrow."

"My appointment is at nine thirty. I'll head home as soon as I'm done."

"I'll probably be gone before you get home, then."

Randon wasn't sure if Brian remembered anything about their conversation the night before, but he had to ask. "Last night, when you said Rashid was gone, what did you mean?"

"They moved him out. Him and his mother," Brian said. "He went to the commander right after you were flown out. Apparently, they were threatening to kill his mother if he didn't help them. He felt so bad after you got hurt that he snuck onto the base and talked to the commander. Thanks to him, we got our man. In exchange, they moved Rashid and his mother to a refugee camp."

All the tension left Randon's body and the weight lifted from his shoulders. "Are you sure?"

"Absolutely." Brian paused. "Wait. That wasn't the only reason why you wanted to join Bravos, is it?"

"Kind of," Randon admitted.

"What did you do to Millie, by the way?" Brian asked. "She wouldn't even talk about you today."

"She wanted me to do something I couldn't do." His mind was still reeling from the news that Rashid was safe.

"Well, you better hurry up and make up with her or she's going to make everyone miserable."

"Make up? Aren't you the one who keeps telling me to stay away from your sister?"

"Yeah," Brian sighed. "That was before I realized how perfect you two are for each other."

His heart skipped a beat. "So you wouldn't mind if Millie and I were together?"

"No. But she needs to know that you're my best friend first."

He laughed, but there was no mirth in it. "It doesn't matter, anyway. She's done with me."

"Don't be so sure about that," Brian said. "I gotta go. We're going to visit a nursing home and Mom is waiting for me."

"Okay. Talk to you later."

He disconnected the call and started the car. He stopped at the first cheap motel he found and got a room. It was a good thing he packed a suitcase, just in case.

Now that he didn't need to find Rashid, did he still want to join Bravos? He had loved the military lifestyle and that was part of what drew him to the military contractor. He wanted to feel that sense of brotherhood again. But did he still need to go back to Kuwait? No.

If he didn't join Bravos, what would he do? He could stay in Coronado like Millie wanted. But where would he work? How could he hold his head up in the community if he didn't have a job? He wanted to contribute to the town, not sit at home and draw a monthly check.

Once he'd checked into the motel, he pulled the paperwork from Bravos out of his suitcase and flipped through it. They had lots of things he could do without being deployed.

It would make Millie happy to know that he wasn't going back overseas. But she'd made it clear that unless he was willing to stay in Coronado, they didn't have a future.

He opened his wallet and found the business card he had taken from the refrigerator. He stared at it for a few minutes before picking up his phone and dialing the number.

"Hi, Meghan Simpson? This is Randon Farr. I'd like to talk to you about putting my cabin up for sale."

"Randon," Meghan said brightly. "I heard that you were repairing the cabin. I haven't been out there in a long time but I'd love to go look around. When can we meet?"

"I'm in Phoenix for a few days. How about Wednesday afternoon?"

"Of course. Will two o'clock work?"

"That's fine," Randon said.

"Great. I can't wait to see you. I'll talk to you then."

Randon disconnected the call. He was doing the right thing. If tomorrow the doctor told him he had issues with his brain and he had no chance of working for Bravos, he would still leave. He would find something to do, even if he had to rent an apartment in Phoenix and live off his monthly check until he found a good job, he would. If he couldn't have Millie, he definitely didn't want to be in Coronado. They were both better off.

He stared at his phone for a minute. Finally, he typed out a text to Millie.

I'm not going to Kuwait.

He waited for a response. It never came.

ALL EVENING, Millie stared at the text message. He wasn't going. Those words made her happy, but they weren't the right words. What she wanted him to say was that he was staying.

"Are you still moody?" Brian walked into the kitchen and caught her looking at her phone.

"I'm not moody," she snapped.

He shook his head. "Just call Randon and apologize already."

"I thought you didn't approve of Randon and me going out."

"Can't fight love." He winked at her. "Besides, you're perfect together."

She bit her lip. "Have you ever seen Randon have a temper?"

Brian got a soda out of the fridge and walked over to the kitchen table. He sat down across from her. "A few times. He always had a good reason, though."

"Jessica said he had a mean side that I don't know about."

He choked on his drink. "She's been listening to her brother."

"Even Randon told me that a few people have seen his temper."

"Like I said, not without good reason. He threatened Jessica's brother because he was trying to bully me. Dane was stalking you after you wouldn't go out with him. Come to think about it, just about everyone he threatened or fought was someone you had an issue with."

Millie's eyes widened. Her brother had just confirmed what she'd been thinking.

She felt guilty for not trusting Randon. "Do you know he's not going to Kuwait, after all?"

Brian nodded. "He doesn't need to. I told him Rashid is safe."

"Oh." She had hoped that he changed his mind for her.

"Why wouldn't you go with him when he asked you to?" Brian asked. "Why did you pick Coronado over him?"

"I didn't pick Coronado over him," she said. "The rest of you all left. I couldn't leave Mom here to take care of Dad alone."

Is that what Randon thought, too? That she

picked Coronado over him? She frowned. "What will he do now if he's not going to Kuwait?"

"I don't know." Brian shrugged. "Bravos has lots of domestic jobs available. He could go almost anywhere in the country."

She stood up. "I need to go see him."

"He's not home," Brian told her. "He probably won't be back for a couple of days."

Millie stared at the text message still on her phone and she almost called him. No. She wanted to talk to him in person.

CHAPTER NINETEEN

It was almost noon when Randon was finally called into the doctor's office. With every minute he waited, he got more and more anxious. It couldn't possibly be good news if they needed this much time to review his results.

When the door opened and the nurse called him, he thought his heart was going to explode right out of his chest. He followed her down the hall and into one of the rooms. He sat down and waited some more.

"Good morning, Randon," Dr. Patel said, flipping through some papers in his chart.

"Afternoon," Randon corrected him.

"Oh." Dr. Patel checked his wristwatch. "Yes. Anyway, I've been going over your chart with Dr. Harlow."

"Yes?" Randon could barely breathe.

"Good news. I don't see any sign of the traumatic brain injury you suffered as a result of the explosion. As a matter of fact, everything seems to look good."

Relief flooded through him. "Really? But what about my blackout?"

"Yes." The doctor wrinkled his forehead. "You said a squirrel ran out from underneath the sink and scared you?"

"I opened the cabinet underneath the sink because I thought I heard a mouse. When I moved things around, he ran up my arm and it startled me."

"And you say the symptoms you had after that were the same as the blackouts you had before?"

"Yes." Randon nodded. "Shortness of breath. Dizziness."

The doctor smiled. "Well, it has nothing to do with your brain injury. It could be related to your PTSD, but from the other tests we ran yesterday and your conversation with our psychiatrist, you seem to be handling it all fairly well. I don't see any reason that you can't go on and live a completely normal life."

Randon wanted to jump for joy. "Thank you." He stood up and pumped the man's hand enthusiastically.

"THIS CABIN IS FABULOUS." Meghan walked quickly from one room to the other, taking notes. "Are you sure you want to sell this? You know you could put it on Vrbo and make a fortune? I would be happy to manage it for you."

"No." Randon shook his head. He didn't want

any more ties to Coronado. "I just want to sell it and be done."

"All right." She wrote a number on the paper and handed it to him. "I think this is where you should start."

The number was way higher than anything Randon possibly could have imagined. "Are you sure? I don't want to gouge people. I just want to get a fair price for it."

"Trust me," she said. "That's a fair price. It probably won't last more than a couple of days on the market."

"Okay. Let's do it."

"Great. I'll have the papers drawn up and ready for you to sign by the end of the day."

He looked around the cabin again. He wanted to make sure the cabin went to a good family. Someone who would love it like his grandfather had loved it. "I do have one stipulation," he said.

"What's that?"

"Whenever you show the house to someone, I want Millie Gibson to accompany them. If Millie doesn't approve of the sale, it doesn't happen."

"Millie?" Meghan gave him an odd look. "Why Millie?"

"I'm leaving in a few days, so I won't be around. But Millie will be able to tell who belongs in this house and who doesn't."

"It might be hard to work around her schedule. I'd hate to see you lose out on a good sale because of that."

"If that's all it takes to lose a sale, then it wasn't meant to be," he said.

As Meghan was driving away, another car came up the driveway. A man in a suit got out.

"Excuse me," he said. "I'm looking for Randon Farr."

"That's me." Randon took the steps down to meet him at the car.

"My name is Philip Johnson. I'm the principal at Coronado Middle School. I understand you've been spending a lot of time with Toby and Eddie."

Randon took in a sharp breath. "Yes, sir. Is there a problem?"

"Not really," he laughed. "At least not anymore, thanks to you."

"I'm not sure I know what you mean."

"Did you know that Toby has been suspended five times in the last three years for fighting?"

"No," Randon said. "But I had the feeling he'd been into some trouble."

"In the last few weeks, we've seen a major change in him. And in art class, he painted a picture that just knocked our socks off. He said he's been taking lessons from you. Is that right?"

"Yes, sir. He's been painting with me some."

"More than painting from what Eddie tells me," Mr. Johnson continued. "Today, a boy tried to start a fight with Toby and Toby walked away. That's never happened before."

"I'm glad that some of the things I said to him got through."

"You painted the mural on the side of the Coronado Market, too?"

"Yes, sir, I did." Where was he going with this? Randon shoved his hands in the front pockets of his jeans.

"And you just got out of the military?"

Randon nodded. "Yes, I just got out. What's going on? Am I in some kind of trouble? Did I break some kind of rule about working with kids?"

"Not at all." Mr. Johnson pulled a brochure from his suit pocket. "Have you ever heard of a program called Troops to Teachers?"

"No, I'm afraid I haven't."

"It's a program designed to help men and women who just got out of the military become educators. They pay for your schooling, your books, everything. And at the end of the program, you're a fully certified teacher. Does that sound like something you're interested in?"

Randon shook his head. "I never thought about doing something like that, but I have enjoyed working with the boys."

"Do you have any college credits at all?"

"Some."

"Our art teacher is leaving after the Christmas break. If you're interested, I'd really like to have you apply for the job. I'd offer it to you outright but it has to go through the school board. I'm sure they won't have a problem with it."

"I wouldn't count on that," Randon laughed. "A lot of the school board members might remember me from when I was in school. And even if I was interested, I'm pretty sure I couldn't finish the program by Christmas."

"The school board usually goes with whoever I recommend. And as long as you have some college credits, we can get you an emergency teacher certification so that you can go ahead and start teaching before your degree is even finished."

"Thank you, but I'm afraid I've already got a job. I'm leaving at the end of the week."

"That's too bad," he said. "I was going to suggest that in addition to teaching art, once you get your degree, you might consider becoming a school counselor. Goodness knows our students need someone like you."

Randon wasn't sure what to say. He'd never even considered teaching as a career. He was surprised how much the idea appealed to him. "I'll think about it."

The man handed him the Troops to Teachers brochure and his business card. "Give me a call if you change your mind."

Randon watched the man drive away before going into the house. If he took the job and stayed, it would make Millie happy—that is, if she was even still interested in having a relationship. But would she be with him because she really and truly loved him? Or because he was familiar and it was convenient?

CHAPTER TWENTY

SATURDAY MORNING MILLIE dragged herself out of bed. Randon had been gone for an entire week. She'd texted him several times throughout the week, but he never responded. Last night, she'd broken down and called. He didn't answer, of course. She left a message on his phone.

"Randon, I'm sorry. I love you. If you'll still have me, I'll go anywhere in the country you want me to go."

She thought for sure he'd return her call.

"Millie," her mother called from downstairs. "You've got a phone call."

A phone call? She rushed down the stairs. Maybe it was Randon. She had no idea why he would call the house landline and not her cell phone. "Hello?"

"Hi, Millie. This is Meghan Simpson."

Millie frowned. "The realtor?"

"Yes. I was wondering if you were free this morning. I have someone who wants to look at the Farr cabin."

"Why do you need me?"

"When Randon listed his cabin with me, he insisted that you have to attend all of the showings. He said he wouldn't sell it to anyone you didn't approve of."

Her breath caught in her throat. Despite the fact that he was selling the cabin, she knew he loved it and wanted it to go to someone who would love it, too. And he'd trusted her with it.

"What time do you want me there?"

"How about ten o'clock?"

"I'll see you then." Millie hung up the phone. "Mom, I have to go out to Randon's cabin," she said.

"Right now?"

"As soon as I shower and change." She wanted to spend some time at the cabin alone.

THIRTY MINUTES LATER, she walked into the cabin and looked around. On the table was a stack of paintings and an envelope with her name on it. With shaking hands, she opened the envelope.

Dear Millie,
I know you're probably wondering why I put this task up to you, but I know that no one else would understand the cabin like you do. All these paintings are yours. I can't very well drag them across the country with me.

Keep them or give them to the art lady. It doesn't matter to me. I will always love you.

Sincerely,
Randon

She sucked in her breath. If she ever saw him again, she would give him a piece of her mind. She picked up the paintings and looked at them one by one. Each one pulled at her heartstrings a little bit. There was a picture of a redheaded girl sitting on the side of the lake, fishing. Pictures of sunsets. A picture of the Coronado Forest.

She looked around the cabin. It looked so good. like it was waiting for a family. She hung the paintings around the cabin because that was the only place they belonged. After she hung up each picture, she took a snapshot of it with her phone. She would send the photos to the art gallery and see if the lady was interested or not.

She had just hung the last painting when two cars pulled up in front of the cabin.

"Millie," Meghan greeted her. "You made it." She introduced the couple who followed her onto the porch.

"You're planning to move to Coronado?" she asked the couple.

"Oh, heavens, no," the older woman replied. "There's not nearly enough shopping here for me.

It will be an occasional vacation spot for when my husband feels like he has to go fishing."

The man chuckled. "Yes. And in between, we'll probably rent it out with Vrbo or something similar."

Millie frowned. "You're not going to stay here full-time?"

Again, they told her their plans and she walked around outside as Meghan showed them inside the cabin. She knew in her heart that Randon didn't want the cabin to be a vacation home for someone. He wanted it to go to a family who would live in it full-time.

Meghan and the couple spent over a half hour walking around the cabin, examining everything from the wooden beams to the porch deck. As they walked out, they seemed excited and told Meghan they would be ready to make an offer by the following day. They had some changes they wanted to make to the cabin, so it would affect the price they offered.

"What kind of changes?" Millie interrupted.

"I would want to enlarge and update the kitchen," the woman said. "And the loft is way too small. It needs to be expanded. We might even knock out the back wall and extend the cabin a little bit farther."

"I'm sorry," Millie told them. "The cabin is no longer for sale."

"What?" Meghan looked flustered. "Do you know something I don't?"

Millie gave her a level stare. "I'll meet you in your office in an hour and we can settle this."

After they left, she walked back through the cabin. She stood in each one of the rooms and a sense of peace settled over her.

This was *her* cabin. Even if Randon never came back to Coronado, this was hers. Her family wanted her to have a life of her own. They kept telling her she couldn't live with her parents forever.

This was the best solution. She still didn't want to leave Coronado. She wanted to be close by to help her mother. After New Year's, her father was going into the nursing home. She'd already applied for a job there. Now she could have her own house. And something to always remember Randon by.

RANDON STEPPED UP to the counter at the phone store.

"Can I help you?" the young woman behind the counter asked.

He stared at her bright purple hair. The girl reminded him of the Reed twins. Their hair was always some bright, unnatural color. "Yes. I need a new phone."

He held up what was left of his.

Right after he left Coronado, he'd stopped to

eat, and on his way back out to the car, he pulled his phone out of his pocket. He had been, and still was, holding on to the hope that he would hear from Millie. A man walking the other direction had bumped into him and his phone went sliding across the parking lot. Right in front of a large semitruck.

The girl's eyes widened. "That is one smashed phone."

It took over an hour, but he walked out of the store with a phone in his hand. The saleswoman assured him any calls or text messages that had been sent after his phone was destroyed would appear.

He got in his car and held his breath as he waited for the messages to appear. A dozen from Brian. Each one a little more alarmed. His heart raced. Several from Millie.

I'm sorry.

I miss you.

Please respond.

He started to text her when the next message said he had voicemails. Three from Brian. A couple from Meghan checking in. Then he heard the message from Millie and his heart soared.

She loved him! She wanted to be with him.

He listened to the very last message.

"Hi, Randon. Good news. I have a Millie-approved buyer for the house. Give me a call and let me know where to send the paperwork. Most of it can be done electronically, so you don't have to worry about being here in person."

Someone wanted to put an offer in on his cabin. He swallowed. Could he really sell it? First, he'd talk to Millie. If she wanted to keep it so they had some place to stay when they came home to visit, wherever they landed, then he wouldn't sell it.

He opened his wallet to put the receipt for the new phone inside and Mr. Johnson's business card fell out. He picked up the card and stared at it. Imagine, him teaching middle school art. He took a deep breath. Teaching art at a middle school. In Coronado. Nothing had ever sounded so perfect.

CHAPTER TWENTY-ONE

FRIDAY MORNING, Randon turned onto the road that led to his cabin. He had driven all night long and his entire body ached.

He saw a boy walking down the road, toward the path that led to the tree house. He stopped and got out.

"Hey, Toby. Why aren't you at school?"

Toby kicked a rock with his shoe and looked down. "I got suspended again."

"Why?" Randon shook his head. "We talked about this. I even talked to your principal last week. He said you were doing better."

"Yeah. What do you care?" Toby said. "You left just like everybody else. Just like my mom. Nobody cares if I get in trouble at school."

Randon's heart ached. "Your mom left? That's rough. I'm sorry I was gone when that happened. But people do care. I care."

"Right." Toby snorted and turned to walk away.

Randon couldn't believe how badly he had missed working with the boys. "You're not going to get away with much in my class. I just want you to know that."

Toby stopped and turned around. "What are you talking about?"

"I hear the art teacher is leaving after Christmas."

"Yeah. She's getting married and moving away."

Randon leaned against the car. "Do you know who the new art teacher will be yet?"

"No," Toby said. "My homeroom teacher said we probably wouldn't have art anymore. Nobody wants to move to a town this small."

Randon nodded. "What if I did it? Would you like that?"

Toby's face lit up. "Are you serious? I thought you were moving away. I thought you had a new job."

"I did," Randon answered. "But for some reason, I feel like this might be where I belong."

Even as he said the words, excitement coursed through him. *Belong.* As a kid, he never felt like he belonged anywhere.

Toby threw his arms around Randon's waist and hugged him. "I can't wait to tell Eddie."

"Here's the deal," Randon said sternly. "If you get into one more fight, if you get suspended one more time, you will not be in my art class. Understand?"

"Yes, sir." Toby gave him a mock salute before turning and running down the road.

He walked into the cabin. His paintings were hung on every wall and he couldn't help but smile. Even Millie knew they belonged here. Just like him.

He glanced at his watch. He was supposed to meet Meghan right after lunch. That gave him time to take a nap, shower and get there in time. This was one meeting he couldn't wait for.

MILLIE PULLED UP to the real-estate office and checked her watch. Right on time. Her heart hummed with excitement. She couldn't believe Meghan had gotten the paperwork back from Randon so quickly. He must be really anxious to sell the cabin.

But not talk to her. At least he'd finally texted her. He'd said he was sorry he left the way he had. He also said his phone broke and he just got a new one. He was on the road, but he would call her when he got where he was going and they would have a long talk.

He didn't tell her where he was going. Nor did he say anything about the voicemail she'd left him. She'd offered to leave everything behind and go with him and he hadn't even taken the time to respond. She swallowed the lump in her throat.

She would not dwell on that right now. Today was a day for new beginnings. Today was the day she was going to sign papers for the cabin and become a homeowner. It was time for her to stop waiting on Randon. He certainly wasn't waiting on her.

She got out of the car and went inside.

Meghan greeted her as soon as she came in. "Let's go back to my office. Are you excited?"

"Yes," she said. "I'm just ready for this to be done."

They walked into Meghan's office and she sat down across from the desk. Meghan pulled out a stack of folders.

"I feel it's only fair to warn you that there are a few non-negotiables that come with the cabin."

Millie frowned. "Okay. What are they?"

Meghan opened one of the folders and looked at the papers inside. "First, you have to be willing to let the local boys cut through the property on their way to the tree house."

"Not a problem," Millie said.

"And—" Meghan stood up "—there's one more thing that comes with the property."

Millie waited. "Okay? What is it?"

"Me."

Her stomach quivered and she turned to look at the voice behind her. Randon stood in the doorway, his hazel eyes locked on her.

"What?" she breathed.

Randon stepped into the office as Meghan slipped out and shut the door.

"You can only have the cabin if you take me, too."

"But—" she couldn't catch her breath "—you left. You're going to work for Bravos. You didn't call me back."

He knelt down next to her chair. "I'm not working for Bravos. I'm staying in Coronado."

Her pulse roared in her ears. "Why?"

"Because I love you. I don't want to be without you."

"I thought you didn't want to stay? There's nothing for you here."

He shook his head and took her hand. "I shouldn't have let my pride get in the way. A couple of days ago, I had two job offers. One that paid a lot of money and would allow me to go anywhere in the country. And one that hardly pays anything, but it's doing something I love and puts me close to someone I love."

She pressed one hand to her chest. "What's that?"

"The middle school principal offered me a job as an art teacher."

"In Coronado?" She couldn't believe it. "Can you do that? You don't have a degree."

"Yes." He nodded. "I'll explain later. Right now, I want to hear you say you love me." He pulled a ring from his pocket. "Millie Gibson, I love you. I don't want to be without you. Will you please let this soldier return home, where he belongs?"

"Yes." The tears began to well up in her eyes

as she wrapped her arms around his neck and kissed him.

When the kiss ended, she touched his face and grinned. "I hate to tell you, but it looks like I got my way again. Are you okay with that?"

Randon wrapped his arms around her. "I'll spend the rest of my life making sure you get your way."

"Then kiss me, soldier, because you're all I ever wanted."

"Yes, ma'am." He lowered his head and kissed her again.

* * * * *

Don't miss the next book in LeAnne Bristow's
Coronado, Arizona miniseries,
coming July 2025
from Harlequin Heartwarming